or not to be

or not to be

laura lanni

LMNOPress

Published by LMNO Press, P.O. Box 544, Chapin, SC 29036

Library of Congress Control Number: 2014917181

ISBN 978-0-9907757-0-6 (pbk.)

Cover design and image by Kate Lanni

For every soul,
Living or dead,
Separated from loved ones,
Forever listening.

I would be delighted if there were a life after death, especially if it permitted me to continue to learn about this world and others, if it gave me a chance to discover how history turns out.

Carl Sagan

Anna

1

November 11, Morning

AT THE BEGINNING of the last day of my marriage, I didn't notice anything different. There were no signs or warnings, no flashing lights. The day began as bad and sad as the five dozen before it. I'd learned to live under that crushing dread in the same way the receptors in my nose disregarded the persnickety molecules of a bad smell. Gradually the daily battles that colored my marriage wore me down and I became numb, almost oblivious.

When I walked into the kitchen on that morning, my final November eleventh, I went straight to my five-year-old, Joey, and smacked a kiss onto his fluffy head. The boy needed a bath. I took the cup of coffee that my husband and ex-best friend, Eddie, was offering. He looked guilty. Nothing new there. Avoiding eye contact was the man's newest form of torturing me.

I'd just swallowed my first daily hit of caffeine when Joey looked up at me and revealed the chocolate crumbs around his mouth. Then he surprised me with this stunt. "Ooh, Mommy. I don't feel too good today. I need to stay home. Bellyache. Ooh." My boy who loved going to school leaned to me for a hug. I let him wrap his dirty hands around the silk sleeve of my blouse. I tried to catch Eddie's eye, but his gaze crept between the cereal bowls and onto the floor.

A gush of tears and snot rose up and threatened to dissolve my crystalline wall of defense. Crying was ineffective in our current battles. It wouldn't get me the hug I needed. He'd just shake his head and walk away, leaving me in my own entropic mess. If I could hold it all in, I'd earn ten good minutes of crying alone in the car after I dropped Joey at kindergarten.

I wrapped one arm around Joey's bony shoulders and got a firm grip on his chin with my free hand. We were nose to nose when I said, "Show me those teeth."

My sweet boy giggled, threw his head back, and revealed Oreo chunks between his baby teeth.

"Joey, come on, now. How'd you get chocolate for breakfast?"

My little boy's green eyes grew huge when he realized he was in trouble. He looked to his father for support, but Eddie turned away from him. I resisted the urge to hurl my coffee at the back of my husband's head for abandoning our son.

"Joe. We all know why you have a bellyache. You can't stay home from school today."

I jabbed my finger at Eddie, the true perpetrator of this breakfast fiasco, demanding he meet my eyes and acknowledge me. "You gave him cookies for breakfast?" I flung these words at him like knives, and when he finally looked up his guilty eyes gave him away. He didn't even defend himself.

At 7:30 we all left the house to start our days. I helped Joey with his seat belt. It was hard with gloves on and tears in my eyes, but crying was so common for me that I lived in a blurry haze. I tossed my heavy school bag into the front seat and realized with the saddest heart that I was relieved to be leaving my own house.

Sunglasses on. Key in ignition. Escape.

"Honey?"

This was Eddie. He was leaning his head in the passenger window of my car, closer to me than he'd been since August.

"Anna, how about a day off today? You and me and Joey. Let's all play hooky."

Was he kidding me? After so many weeks of treating me to

the grim profile of his face, grunting answers to my questions, walking away—now he wanted to spend a day together. My mind and heart were firing on all cylinders, blocking whatever the hell he was saying. When he shut up, I said, "You're calling me *honey* now? Where'd that come from?"

I pulled on my seat belt, put the car in gear, checked my mirrors, and turned back to him. "I'm going to work." Glad the sunglasses blocked my wet eyes yet fully aware that this man knew my crying face by my crumpled chin, I blew out a giant sigh and said, "See you tonight, *honey*," and I backed out of our garage.

2

Flashback: Asked Out by My Teacher

IF I'D STAYED home this morning, Eddie and I would still be together. Maybe. But every day of your life you can play that game, and it's always futile—that hindsight crap. You do what you do. Make choices in the moment and live, or die, with them. One chance, one choice, and everything flows from that point. The other paths don't even count. They are only imaginary.

If I'd stayed home, if I'd made myself talk to Eddie and hash out our problems, actually meet them head on, we might still have split up. It was coming, I'm sure of that, but I'm not sure it would have been any more pleasant than death. So many ifs. If I hadn't taken that crippling elective Particle Physics course twenty years ago when Eddie was the teaching assistant for my class, if I hadn't been such a math geek, if I'd tried out for cheerleading, if I had a normal mother, I'd never have met Eddie in the first place. See what I mean? Live with your choices.

Here are my facts, the products of these choices: I love my small family fiercely—my husband, sister, and two kids. I'm an accomplished and proud geek. My marriage disintegrated, unraveled so quickly that I couldn't distinguish the loose thread from the knotted weave, because my husband mysteriously became unreachable, untouchable, and alien to me. He left me helpless, weak.

I remember also feeling helpless when Eddie and I met half a lifetime ago, but that flavor of helplessness was delicious. He crashed, uninvited, into my orbit and showed me that my life wasn't only mine to live but was under the influence of forces beyond my control. I was twenty-two and finishing my master's degree in engineering at my half-life. I remember that self-assured, arrogant girl and still marvel that she, a fresher version of me, managed to win over a guy on the order of Eddie Wixim.

He asked me out at the end of a killer week. I was a wee bit delirious. I'd taken three exams and written two long lab reports that, on top of typing through two long nights, required a dozen extra hours in the lab. My strategy for survival had worked. I'd traded sleep time for study time and abandoned all personal hygiene time in favor of an extra twenty minutes of sleep in the stupid mornings.

In the hug of the long-anticipated Saturday, I hadn't intended to leave my bed, but I got hungry so I was making myself a batch of blueberry muffins. Mentally and physically exhausted, I couldn't remember the last time I'd touched soap or even toothpaste. I got my toothbrush from the bathroom and, to be efficient, brushed my teeth while I stirred the muffin batter. That's when the doorbell rang. Great. I threw down the wooden spoon, spat in the kitchen sink, and yanked open the door.

And there he stood. Mr. Wixim, in the flesh. The only good-looking instructor on campus. The guy that all the idiot girls talked about. At my door. I tossed my toothbrush onto the couch, out of his sight.

Smooth, Anna.

All the undergrad girls were after Mr. Wixim. I didn't quite understand all of the hoopla. Sure, he had good hair, thick and dark. Sure, he had some massive shoulders, but he always hid them under ragged flannel shirts. He was so serious all the time, but I had seen him smile once, laughing silently, shoulders shaking, at his own dark joke during recitation, and I did think he was cute. I did. But I'd never admit that. Especially to the girly girls with their eyeliner and nail polish and hair that they brushed every single day whether it needed brushing or not.

The guy stood on my porch with his lower lip hanging down, his bottom teeth exposed. Not too impressive. He looked a little stupid today. The prince turned back into a toad. In my presence. Figures.

I asked if he'd maybe misplaced my assignment, and he said no.

He told me to call him Ed instead of Mr. Wixim. Really? What the hell was going on?

The alarm dinged on my oven to announce that the ancient thing was hot enough to bake my muffins. My stomach growled and reminded me of my urgent need for sugar molecules. I was fairly sure I'd eaten since my last shower but couldn't remember exactly what—maybe a box of Pop-Tarts—or when. Extraneous details were a blur that week. I had to get rid of this guy so I could address my many issues.

His mouth opened and a stream of words blew past me. He made no sense. "Anna, listen. I've been watching you in class . . ."

How creepy.

". . . and I like the way you help explain things, even to the guys who hate girls telling them anything. You are a very take-charge person."

Was he going to offer me a job? Did they need more teaching assistants? I didn't have a spare minute to consider something like that.

I realized I was way off base when he said, "I wondered if you had time on Friday to celebrate the end of the week with me. That is, if I actually survive."

Survive what? Holy shit. Did my teacher, the hot guy, just ask me out?

"You're asking me out? Can you do that? I mean, you're my teacher."

He was talking again. I really had to pay attention and focus on his words. But he was talking so damn fast and saying such ridiculous things; I could not keep up so I focused on his mouth. His teeth were nice. White and straight.

"I'm not really your teacher. I'm just the teaching assistant. Professor Hornsby is the teacher of record. He establishes grades and writes the tests. Do you see the difference?" He tossed his hair out of his eyes and stared at me. He looked a bit pathetic.

From the depths of my murky mind I suddenly realized how funny this was. I barked a laugh, the one that usually scared guys away, and said, "That's not the only difference! He's old and bald and fat, and I would never go out with him."

And, somehow, in the next three minutes, through no fault of my own, we made a date. Eddie was grinning like an idiot. I was shocked. He left. I went back to my muffins and ate half the raw dough with a spoon while I baked the other half.

So, yeah, though we had a rocky start, Eddie pursued me, and I, so confused by the entire charade, let him catch me, ignorant of the future we'd have, the pain that would ooze from our entwined thread of choices. Our beginning was sweet. Our ending was not. This man, who changed my life twenty-two years ago, left me as he found me—helpless.

3

November 11, Evening

THE LIGHTS ARE DIMMED at the elementary school where I dropped off my son this morning. I would've picked him up hours ago; his dad is late.

Buried under his puffy coat and backpack, Joey's left knee jiggles—bent, straight, bent—as he blows frost clouds on the glass door. He draws a sad face on the cold pane, writes his name under it, and then glances at his teacher, Miss Abby, who ignores him and stares over his head. She's annoyed that she drew the short straw and had to stay late, and too self-absorbed to notice that her student can sense her anger. The dent of Joey's eyebrows and the straight line of his mouth, lips closed tight, are familiar components of his worried face. My son shouldn't know how to worry. I hope he didn't hear his teachers gossiping about me, those busybodies. He shouldn't find out like that.

I whisper in his ear, "Don't worry, Joey. Daddy's on the way." But he doesn't hear me. When the bright headlights pull in the parking lot with his dad's car behind them, Joey is sweating a little. As soon as the blinding lights blink off, Miss Abby yanks his hat down over his ears, and she pushes him out the door.

Eddie leans his forehead on the steering wheel. "Anna, how am I going to do this?"

"Come on, Eddie, he's been waiting for hours," I insist in the nagging voice that annoys my husband. This is the tone I save especially for him whenever there's no other choice and

I'm required to speak to him. He's got that annoyed look right now as he raises his eyes to the door, focuses on Joey, and doesn't answer me. My husband rushes past me without a glance and scoops our boy up in a big hug. He tells Miss Abby he's sorry, and she says she's sorry, and he says it again. He ducks his head and won't meet her eyes. Interesting. The man looks guilty even when he's not alone with me.

Eddie carries Joey to the car. He tosses Joey's backpack into the passenger seat and helps him get his seat belt buckled. It's hard with gloves on. Harder with tears blurring his eyes. He turns his head so Joey won't see him cry.

Joey's mittened hands pat his dad's thinning hair, and he asks the question, "Dad, where's Mommy?"

"I'm right here, Joe," I say. He ignores me.

Eddie meets our son's eyes. Great. He's going to tell Joey in the damn car.

"Don't you mess this up, Eddie." I can hear the blame in my own voice.

Stalling, Eddie wipes his nose with the back of his glove. "Joey," he begins and stops. He takes a ragged breath. Come on, Eddie, get on with it if you're going to do it in the school parking lot. He squats down beside the open car door in a slushy puddle and rests his hands on Joey's knees. His eyes leak. Joey's eyes are wide and dry, unblinking, locked on his dad.

I watch my husband raise his hand to our son's shoulder and say, "Mommy died."

I'm not surprised because death isn't something that sneaks up on you. When you're dead, the universe makes sure you feel it.

Joey considers this news. He studies his father's wet eyes and then asks, "Where is she?"

Eddie leans in to kiss the top of Joey's capped head and says, "At the hospital."

I'm not at the hospital, you fool. I'm right here.

He gives his head a hard shake and angrily wipes his eyes. I'm certain Joey has never seen his dad cry before. In two decades, I've never seen it. "Let's go home and call your sister, okay?" Joey nods, but he doesn't look convinced.

Joey's sister, Bethany, is a freshman in college, one hundred long miles away. I hope her bumbling father improves his death announcement skills on his second try. I don't approve of his parking lot approach.

When Eddie starts the car, Joey asks, "Can we go see Mommy? Will she come home tonight?"

"No, Joey. Mom isn't coming home." Eddie repeats the impossible words. "Mommy died." His eyes plead with Joey. *Understand this, kid. Don't make me keep saying it.*

Anna?

"Did she die like Grammy?"

Anna! Where the hell are you?

Even Eddie doesn't know I'm here.

"Yes, Joe. She's with Grammy now."

Eddie continues to leak tears while he drives toward the house where we live. Well, where they live. I no longer live. Anywhere.

"Don't cry, Daddy. We can go to the hospital and get Mommy on the way home."

Damn it, Eddie, quit your blubbering and explain this to him. He's a smart kid. He can understand if you spell it out.

Eddie stops the car at a red light and gives his face a rough rub before he turns all the way around in his seat and meets Joey's eyes. "She's gone, honey. Mom can't come home."

He considers how much truth to tell our little boy and weighs the value of a compassionate lie. "When somebody dies, they don't come home anymore."

There's a loud beep. Eddie is sobbing again. Joey says, "Light's green, Dad."

At home, Eddie gives Joey a peanut butter sandwich for

dinner while he calls my two women: our daughter, Bethany, and my sister, Michelle. Every time he says I'm dead, it smacks me all over again. After he tucks Joey in bed, he sits in the blue chair and stares at the black night out the window. Joey watches him from the stairs for a long time.

| | | |

THE SUN PEEKS UNDER THE CURTAINS the next morning and warms a patch of rug beside Joey's bed. The room smells like Oreos. The only sound is snoring, and it comes from under the bed. Of course, he's under there. Whenever he was sad or scared, I told Joey to go there, and I promised to always find him and protect him. I can't even hug him from my fresh post on the dead side.

I never had time during my life—between work and cooking and laundry—to do this, so I snuggle down beside him and watch my boy snooze until he stirs and rubs his sleepy eyes. After a gigantic yawn he shoves his fingers up his nose and commences what must be his daily ritual of digging. I remember the day, after years of harassing him about this disgusting male habit, when my son took a stand. Rather than issuing his blatant daily fib of promising to never pick his nose again, he said, "But Mommy, if I'm not supposed to pick out the boogies, why does my finger fit so good?" At five years of age, the kid had used evolution and his father's tone, spot on, to shut down his mother's nagging.

Now, with those boogie-covered fingers, Joey reaches into the cookie wrapper and pops one into his mouth. He's as stubborn as I ever was. He won't cry. He'll wait for me under that bed indefinitely.

Or until the cookies run out.

He doesn't know I'm here. I don't know how I got here. I'm just dead and wandering, and, somehow, I can hear my little boy's thoughts.

Yesterday morning Mommy got mad at Daddy. She never came home last night. She must be really mad about the Oreos.

But I'm not mad at you, Joey.

Me and Daddy almost tricked Mom. But she always figures stuff out, and we got caught.

Joey sneaks his hand out from under the bed and rubs the soft spot of rug warmed by the morning sun. After spending the whole night under the bed, he has no plans to emerge today. His stash of Oreos and Ritz crackers makes him thirsty, and he has to pee. But he waits. He hears a car on the gravel driveway.

Maybe it's Mommy.

Bethany fumbles at the back door. Our daughter, as always, is carrying too much—her giant purse, some groceries, and our cat, Stink.

I watched her drive home from college last night. Once Joey was settled in his nest of blankets, I sought Bethany and immediately, by some inexplicable scramble of space and time, I was riding with her, right beside her in her car, for two hours on the deserted highway. One hundred and twenty minutes of watching my daughter hold her breath, clench the wheel. Seventy-two hundred seconds during which I could not hug her and make her feel better. Just like so many times during my life, I couldn't ease my daughter's pain. Eddie shouldn't have let her drive home. He should've gone to get her. He shouldn't have told Joey about me in the car. So many should'ves. None of them matter. Toss the should'ves in with the ifs and let them rot.

Bethany tiptoed into our house after midnight. She covered her dad with an old quilt, slid a flashlight and a half pack of Oreos under the bed with Joey, and sat awake almost all night. I stayed beside her the best I could, given my lack of a body. Like everyone else, she didn't know I was there. When the sun woke her up this morning, she snuck out of the house and went to the grocery store. The living need to eat.

Bethany drops the cat in his favorite chair by the window, and, as she dumps the grocery bag on the table, I can suddenly hear her.

How many times will this happen? I can distract myself and push down the ache, but then it hits me all over again. Fresh. Like a train I forgot I was trying to outrun. The engine carries the news: your mother is dead. I forget to leap off the tracks. Slam. Pierces me like flying glass.

My mother is dead.

Oh, honey. I'm right here.

A groan from the lump in the blue chair pulls Bethany back out of her head. She kisses her dad's cheek and crawls into his lap like she did when she was small. He wraps his arms around her, and he sobs. Bethany lets him cry into her hair. Her eyes are dry. Her mind is closed. It provides no further glimpse of her thoughts, no more inkling of her pain.

The ring of the phone pierces our silent home. Joey charges out of his room and yells, "Is it *Mommy*?" Bethany climbs off Eddie's lap to answer it. She shakes her head at Joey. When she hangs up, she crumples to the cold tile floor in the foyer and pulls my lost boy into a hug. Joey remains rigid, but his sister isn't lacking in the stubborn gene. She won't let him go.

Finally, Joey puts his head on her shoulder. Her hair smells like mine. He turns his face into her neck and cries.

Mommy! Mommy!

My children are calling for me, and I am helpless, stuck. Though I know I'm the dead one, I feel as though my entire family has died. Maybe it doesn't matter who dies—the separation and pain are the same. I'm separated from my family by a force beyond my control. I'm right here beside them, but without my body I'm light years away.

I am not fond of death so far.

4
Falling Apart

THE LIGHT of the bright fall afternoon shines through the windows at the back of our house and glances off Bethany's glasses as she peels apples, slowly, each in one long coil. She mixes butter with flour, not gently. Clouds of the white dust waft around my kitchen. Eventually, each speck succumbs to gravity, settling upon any horizontal surface that will stop its fall and convert kinetic back to potential energy.

My daughter is the only functioning body in the place. The cat sleeps on the heating vent with his long, bushy tail shielding the day from his eyes. Joey must be under his bed again. Eddie hasn't moved from the blue chair yet. The stubble on his chin is graying. I imagine his breath is deadly. He is pathetic. I should feel sympathy for him because he looks like he could use a hug. But I don't. I can't yet because I don't understand his reaction to my death. I wish I could have hugged him and made him smile more while I was alive, but we squandered our time together. Regrets overwhelm me.

I watch my Eddie frown when he smells the apples and cinnamon from the kitchen. I know he's thinking about me, about us. I try to stay away, but he pulls me into his thoughts with the same magnetic intensity as when he pulled me into his arms thousands of times, still never enough, when I lived.

Anna?

Cinnamon reminds me of you. I can't go into the kitchen. With both of his large hands, he rubs his face hard and blows out his breath. *You were so sexy in there.*

Shut up, Eddie.

I mean I was nuts about you when you cooked things I loved, just for me. Just for me, Anna.

The man is still a jerk. He throws around the L-word for food. So nonchalant.

That's when I knew you loved me back.

Eddie's the one who said we didn't need the L-word. We didn't need to say it. Could he give me a sign he loved me back?

Feeding me was how you showed me, for sure, that you were still mine.

Still yours? You didn't even want me around.

I was so shook up when your cooking ability began leaking out. Remember? That's what you called it—leaking.

I remember that day last spring when I made those apple squares, and I burned them to a crisp. I had the oven set too hot and forgot to set the timer. I got distracted.

I found you sitting on the kitchen counter dripping salty tears. The whole house smelled like scorched caramel, but the cinnamon still smelled incredible.

Cinnamon has a high thermal stability. Sugar decomposes first. Eddie came in covered in mud from digging a drainage ditch in the rain. He had that little-boy grin and that expectant look in his eye, the one that says he's hunting cookies.

There wasn't much I could do except eat all the nasty, charred things and keep telling you they were great—that I liked them better that way.

What a rotten liar. But he made me laugh.

I couldn't tell you the real reason you were leaking because I wasn't even supposed to know.

What did you know?

That's when you told me you thought you had Alzheimer's. It became our standard joke to explain away your absentmindedness.

He told me if I had it, I would be the last, not the first, to know. Always so logical.

You came over for a hug, so I danced you around the kitchen and you cried some more.

He teased me to make me smile. He said, "If your cooking skills are going, there's only one thing left for us to do."

We had one of our cryptic conversations about sex. Anna, you were always a trooper. You snorted and laughed through your tears when I said I hoped you didn't forget how to do everything *I liked.*

He asked how much longer his favorite thing was going to last. The man could be funny when he gave it some effort.

You wiped your wet face on the front of my shirt and grinned and said, "Eh, maybe a year. Fifteen months, tops. Then you'll have to find someone else." Sarcasm is my friend. She used to be my wife.

I used to be his wife.

No. I'm done here. This hurts too much. I don't have the strength to wallow in Eddie's thoughts. I can't let him pull me back in, the bastard. He's sad and misses me now, but he was an unforgivable ass the last months of my life.

Just run away. That always worked for me in life. Don't look at Eddie crying. Let me out of his head. I couldn't face our problems while I was alive, and I still don't want to because it hurts too much. My life unraveled at the end, and I couldn't find my way back to the good times. I couldn't find the source of the problem, so I blamed myself and hated my best friend, wondering how we got stuck so far apart, taunted by memories of how good we used to be.

| | | |

ON A LATE SUMMER MORNING just three months before I died, I awoke without a care in my head because my life was quite sweet before it started to rot. It was our anniversary, and Eddie's forehead rested against the middle of my back right between my shoulder blades. He snored like a bear, unaware that we were touching and that in his sleep he'd crossed the imaginary line down the center of our bed that marked territory. My pillows, soft and deep, lay beside his firm, unyielding foam ones. The stiff sheet, which I always hated, was crumpled at the foot of the bed under the comforter on my side. It wasn't yet dawn. My coffee pot would soon gurgle to life. I fought down my brain's insistent to-do list and tried to slide back into sleep. That's when Eddie's breath shifted perceptibly, and then he lazily stifled a yawn.

I scooted back into his lap, and his arm came around me; his hand rested on my chest, his fingers brushed my throat. Under the comforting weight of his arm, I synced my breathing to his and fell back to sleep. An hour later the coffee pot did its morning spit-spit. The sound woke me just before the molecules delighted my nose.

Eddie's sleepy voice asked, "Want a cup in bed?" His head still rested against my back.

"Yeah, thanks." I rolled into the puddle of his sleep spot and purred when he vacated the bed. I stretched and grinned while I watched Eddie try to tiptoe as he limped on his sore runner's ankles into the kitchen. Smug. That's how I felt at the start of that day. Twenty-two years together. Two elevens. We were still together. Still strong.

Eddie came back with steaming mugs and the newspaper. "This is all I got you for our anniversary. Read quick. The boy will be up soon." That's how we did anniversaries—we blew past them. Even Valentine's Day was ignored. On February fifteenth every year we went to the pharmacy together and brought home the orphaned, half-priced chocolates.

"I know. God, I miss Bethany." Our daughter had started college a week before, and our house was eerily still without the tremors of her mood swings. I dug through the paper to find the crossword. I could read later, but if our kindergartener woke too soon and heard the newspaper crackle, he'd want to help, and he just didn't understand that the letters had to spell actual and very specific words. "Joey can get his own cereal now, you know."

"Really? I bet he spills all over the kitchen." Eddie crawled under the covers and nudged me back to the middle of the bed. "I miss Bethany, too, but it sure is more peaceful without all her drama."

"Don't make me feel guilty, Ed." I folded the paper into a precise rectangle of blank crossword, leaned back against him, and tapped the pen on my chin. "Joey got his own breakfast by himself last week. I found a bowl when I cleaned under his bed fort. It still had a skim of milk in it. Ready?"

I felt his chin bump my shoulder when he nodded. "Yep. Go."

"One across: Phil of Genesis."

"How many letters?"

"Seven."

"Collins." He rubbed the back of my neck. "How does he pour the milk?"

"I put it in a cup for him before I go to bed and leave it on the bottom shelf in the fridge. Two down, four letters: cookie, starts with O."

"Uh oh. Anna, I drank that milk last night. Oreo. Are you sure Joey's having cereal and not cookies?" he asked with a snort.

"Very funny, Eddie. He wouldn't dare."

Eddie kissed the side of my neck between slurps of coffee, leaving a trail of sticky. "Yeah, he would. One down is clap because eight across is Aesop, and four down is loo." He kissed me some more, slowly yet greedily, on my shoulder and between my shoulder blades. He breathed in my ear like he used to on the rose path back when he had broad shoulders and forearms muscled like Popeye. And hair. I smiled.

"Thanks." I wrote these in without even bothering to read the clues. "Let me get some, will you, Ed?" I took a long swallow of my sweet coffee and turned the paper away from his view.

"I'll let you get some." He unbuttoned my nightgown and

whispered, "I bet your boy is in the cookies right now. Let's risk it, though. It'll give us a few more minutes." His husky voice in my ear said, "Alone."

"To finish the puzzle?" I asked. I met his eyes and felt our link through all of the fibers and cells, nerves, and capillaries of my body. For two decades, my life was balanced and anchored by this man. He was my friend, partner, and essential other half. He got me now, just like he had on our first date, when he knew our future before I even knew I liked him enough for a second date.

He laughed at me and said, "Yeah. Of course. The puzzle. Three across is . . ."

"Shut up, will you?" I whacked him with the paper as he tackled me.

Later, I told him I was relieved that Joey was starting to do things on his own.

"School starts in a few weeks. Then, you know how the fall always is—crazy busy. It'll be good for him *and* me if he becomes more independent and less reliant on me for everything. I won't be around forever and for everything. He needs to learn that."

And in that little instant, Eddie looked stricken. What did I say? Why did Joey growing up bother him so?

His affectionate playfulness evaporated. Eddie pulled away from me, and I didn't live long enough for him to come back this time. His funk slammed back in on our anniversary, knocking me flat, and it sealed my best friend in an untouchable gloom. It lanced my heart to have him so close and lose him to the vacuum while I waited in limbo, leaving him all the power to choose us again.

Eddie left me alone, lonely and sad, and wondering when the hell he'd make his way back. Was this my fault? Could I have prevented the crack from widening? The same worries that kept me awake, sweating, eye twitching, and desperate at the end of my life have tagged along to the dead side.

That's enough. I will not waste any more energy worrying about Eddie. He's not my problem anymore.

| | | |

ENTICED BY THE GOOD SMELLS from the kitchen, Joey creeps down the stairs and climbs up on the step stool. He leans to Bethany for a hug. She starts to cry when she hugs him back. She sits him in a pile of flour on the counter. Joey is alarmed by her tears; now that his sister has started to cry, she can't seem to stop. She wipes her face on the belly of his shirt and gives him an apple slice slathered in sugar and cinnamon.

He takes in the mess of flour and butter she's concocting and asks shyly, "Apple squares?" He pops the chunk of apple into his mouth.

Bethany nods as she wipes her nose on her sleeve and eats a slice, too. Joey thinks he can help her stop crying. He says with a full mouth, "Hey, Bethy, hold your tongue and say apple." He shines his wicked grin on her.

Bethany sticks out her tongue and holds it and says, "Athole," and Joey loses himself in giggles. Eddie hears the sound from the other room, and we both think at the same instant: *My children are laughing?*

Now, I have left them all. It was not my intention, and I am infinitely pissed. Given a second chance at that choice, now I would have stayed home on Friday, November eleventh. I would've tried harder to stay on the same team as Eddie to keep us from falling apart.

As I watch my children, I feel like they are holding my heart.

Death really hurts.

5
Advice and Kissing Lessons

ON THE DEAD SIDE, once again I have lost all control of my position in both space and time. I feel a twinge of the guilty relief that colored the end of my life. This much has not changed—it is still too painful for me to be in my own home. I'm grateful for another flashback.

I watch younger me, again, back in my old college apartment. I had no idea I was so cute in my good old days, even when sleep-deprived, unshowered, and free of makeup. Back on that rainy Saturday morning, more than two decades ago, my life was fresh when Eddie first stepped into my path. It was the time of the beginning of us.

After Mr. Wixim, I mean Ed, left my apartment, consumption of too much raw blueberry muffin batter had turned out to be a bad idea. I took a giant slug of Pepto straight from the bottle, and fell into a coma on my couch under the flannel blanket to sleep away the afternoon. I awoke hours later with my toothbrush wedged into the back of my thigh and in severe need of coffee to clear the fuzz lining the inside of my forehead. I shivered and then hopped barefoot on the kitchen tile and watched each drip of my coffee as it gushed into the pot until my frozen feet demanded action. I pulled the pot away and shoved a cup under the drip. Snuggled back under my blanket, my feet thawed as I sipped from the warm mug and ate a muffin from the top down.

The caffeine in my bloodstream crashed into my fogged head, and I remembered my visitor. After about four lucid seconds, I leaped off the couch in panic, sloshing brown liquid and blue crumbs onto the floor. I couldn't go on a date with Ed Wixim. I'd never been on a real date before. I didn't attract men; I scared them off. There were many I liked who were cute or smart or both, but they were always petrified of me, and I did not find that deer-in-the-headlights look particularly attractive.

But this Wixim guy was brave. He came to my door. *Unarmed.* What nerve. What spine. I called my sister at her college three states away to agonize.

"Michelle, I need help," I said, instead of hello.

"Yeah. I've been telling you that for years, girl." My sister always had my back.

"Shut up, jerk, and listen. A guy asked me out."

"What?" She nearly blew my ear off.

"Don't sound so surprised. I'm not that ugly."

"No, Anna, you're not that ugly. You're scary like a grizzly bear. I might be the only human on the planet not afraid of you."

"Huh. You *are* afraid of me."

"A little," she admitted. "So, what's he look like?"

"Gorgeous. Tall. Older."

"How much?"

"Two or three years, I think. He's finishing his Ph.D. this spring."

"Good. Good. Mom will love him 'cause he's smart. That'll help her not hate him so much 'cause he's cute."

"Do not tell Mom."

"I know. Don't worry. You said you needed help?"

"I guess just tell me what to do. What to wear? How to act?"

Michelle snorted. "What's the goal here? Do you want to marry this guy or just use him to learn how to kiss? I need to see the prize."

"Those are my only choices?" She stumped me. I didn't have a goal beyond remembering to breathe during the date. I'd only been on two dates before, both set up by friends, both awkward as hell. I'd never been asked out directly by the guy before. "What was your goal with Danny?"

A grunt. My sister made many noises. Soon she'd probably start whistling. She finally answered, "Honestly? I just didn't want to get pregnant."

She was light years ahead of me. My sister could handle men. "Well, I don't think I'll have that concern. It's just one date. But what should I wear?"

"Do you like him?"

"I don't know. I'm a little nervous."

"Good. That means you do. So then it matters how you look. You should shower, Anna. And wear mascara and blush. And earrings. Then just concentrate on the kissing lessons. If he doesn't kiss you, you fail, and don't come crying to me."

"Slow down, will you?" I demanded.

"Are you writing this down?"

"Of course. Okay, keep going."

Michelle sighed before continuing. "Wear a cute skirt or dress. Sandals or heels. Shave those legs! And do something with that hair, will you?"

"Okay, okay, I'll work on it."

"First dates suck, Anna, but I'm sure you'll be fine. Call me when it's over."

"I wish you were here with me."

"Yeah, me too. Maybe we'll live next door someday when we both have real jobs."

"I wish."

"Love you, Anna." And she whistled a line from "The Rose" as she hung up.

FRIDAY, the day I agreed to go on a date with Ed Wixim, came way too fast. I tried to do everything Michelle said. I even remembered to shave my legs, and I got my hair cut and permed for the first time in my life. But I was nervous when Eddie knocked on my door, right on time. The only thing I felt confident about was my new look. My haircut made me look so much older and mature. I loved it. Something unexpected happened to me during that week. I admitted to myself that I wanted this guy to like me. I would do my best to make him the second person in the world not afraid of me.

I opened the door and tried a new tactic. I smiled at him instead of emitting my normal growl. It didn't work. His face fell, and he said, "Your hair."

That reminded me that I at least looked pretty. I touched my hair and said, "What?" in that impish tone, just like those goofy girls who wait for compliments from guys. I hated myself for a minute. Until Eddie spoke. Then I hated him instead.

He said, "I liked it better the other way."

The hell with him. I changed my mind. I wanted him to fear me. I slammed the door and stomped in circles in my tiny apartment like a caged bull. I puffed like Ursula with indignation as I imagined the pain I could crash down upon this idiot man who had the nerve to knock on my door and insult me.

But Eddie didn't leave. He kept knocking on my door and asking me to come out. He even suggested a sweater in case I got cold, which popped my Ursula shield and made me like him again. Drats. I didn't know the social protocol for this—being insulted and yet still being expected to go on the date. My stomach, the bottomless pit, answered for me when he mentioned being late to the steakhouse. I grabbed a sweater, kicked myself in the head, and went on the damn date.

And it wasn't that bad. He was more nervous than I was, which made me think that maybe he liked me. This hot guy liked me. That'd never happened before. And he wasn't just gorgeous—he was funny and not very much afraid of me. I thought I might use that to my advantage for a while. This could get interesting. Maybe Michelle was right. I might use this guy to try out the kissing thing.

The date lasted forever, and, hours later, Eddie somehow got me pinned under his giant arm and trapped on a bench in the rose garden. From this captive position, I considered my situation.

The cold stone of the bench met the hot backs of my thighs and did what every cold object does when it encounters a warmer one—kinetic energy was neatly transferred by elastic collisions between the frenetic particles to their sedater neighbors. The smell of the flowers, produced by vaporous bulky molecules colliding with receptors in my nose, made the air literally heavy on my cool skin. Those smelly molecules were an order of magnitude heavier than the nitrogen and oxygen in the cool air.

The light from a lamppost illuminated only half of Eddie's face, leaving the other half hidden in black shadows. Though I knew the missing half of his face wasn't actually gone, I entertained myself with imagining "what isn't seen does not exist," a fun mind game I almost mentioned out loud and would have if only my brain could have made my lips function. But Eddie's large hand on my waist had somehow alerted a colony of my eager neurons to start a chain reaction that made me lightheaded. And then, by a series of moves not under my control, perhaps only understood by males of the species, Eddie managed to get his lips close to my paralyzed ones.

Really close. Closer than any lips had ever been to the molecules of me. His molecules exerted an inexplicable force that mine found irresistible.

For a full minute, I held my breath. For sixty seconds, maybe more, I existed in an idiotic state of self-denial from completely free, available, and fresh oxygen. I like oxygen. It's one of my favorite elements. Its absence was not helping with my lightheaded situation.

And then he did it. Eddie Wixim, my *teacher*, touched his lips to mine, and for the first time in my life I wasn't thinking with my brain.

| | | |

IN JUNE, mere months after our first kiss, he went and did it: Eddie proposed in the drive-thru line at McDonald's on a Tuesday in June. He paid for our Big Macs, and while we waited, he sucked hard on the straw of his chocolate shake and asked me to get a cassette tape out of the glove box. I opened the box and saw nothing like a cassette tape. A top layer of papers and wrappers and newspapers peeled away to reveal a baseball, a wad of napkins, one red and one green tube sock, a comb, a dozen pencils, and even more entropy below.

"Eddie? What the heck? It's a disaster in here."

"Just dig in there. I know the Doobie Brothers are in the back somewhere."

I dug my hand in because I trusted him, this competent, sweet, intelligent man who liked me in spite of me, or maybe because of me. I never understood that part. My hand felt around for the sharp corners of a cassette case and just came up with more sticky wrappers, which I tossed in handfuls over my shoulder into his back seat. The McDonald's chick handed Eddie a huge greasy, salt-encrusted bag. He dragged out french fries, two at a time, and shoved them the long way down his throat. I don't even think he chewed

"Hey," I said, "don't eat mine." He always ate my fries.

"I won't," he lied.

I was still up to my elbows in male disorganization. It was making me twitch. "There's no cassette in here, Eddie."

"Anna, come on. This is easy. Just reach in the back."

That's when my fingers landed on the square velvet box. I pulled it out and was about to toss it over my shoulder with the other crap when Eddie's hand caught my wrist. He said, "Oh, yeah, I forgot about that. It's for you. See if you like it." So nonchalantly, the man ate a few more of my fries.

I looked down at the blue box and suddenly understood that there was a ring inside. Holy shit.

Unable to breathe, I choked out, "What are you thinking?"

"That I want you to come with me," he managed to say around a mouthful.

"Why?" It came out in a whisper. I couldn't pull in a full breath.

"Because I don't want to go without you. I can't go without you." I'd been dreading the time when he would leave me when he started medical school. I'd never even considered going with him. I was headed to frigid upstate New York for my own doctoral program in the fall.

Eddie put the bag of fries on the dashboard and turned to me. He took the little box from my clenched claw and popped it open. He looked from the box to my eyes and said, "Oh, look Anna. It's pretty. Just like you." He pulled the ring out and wiggled it in the midday sun to make it catch the light.

I was mesmerized by the sparkle of the tiny diamond. Graduate students are poor. It's a requirement.

I could barely breathe, but I heard myself ask, "You want me to come with you? Wait. You mean you want me to *marry* you?"

"Yes, Anna, I do." He leaned to me and touched my lips with his salty ones.

And that's how Eddie Wixim, my hot teacher, asked me to marry him without ever saying the words. Without actually asking. Just the same way he loved me during our marriage— without actually saying the words. That man got away with a lot of crap because I was so crazy about him. After the tiniest feather of a kiss, he slipped the ring on my finger without my verbal consent, but I let him because my answer to the unasked question was clear when I kissed him back. And why bother answering a question that was never asked? Logic prevailed. The car behind us beeped loudly. Just like that, I was engaged to marry the best guy I'd ever known—my favorite person on the planet—and all of my future plans succumbed to an entropic scramble.

| | | |

OUR WEDDING DAY ARRIVED seven weeks later. My vintage dress didn't fit me. It was too big in the boobs and three inches too long. I wore heels and held my shoulders back. Mom, who sniffled behind me, helped me get into the dress.

"Mom," I asked, unable to see her face in the big mirror, "are you crying?" I think it's genetic: my mother doesn't like to cry in front of anyone.

"No, of course not, Anna." But she was. She'd made it clear all summer and even the night before the wedding that she didn't want me to go through with this. I couldn't convince her and was tired of arguing, so I just stayed silent and let her stew. But I didn't want her crying.

"I'll come visit, Mom. You know that, right?"

"No, you won't. You can't afford it. And in a year or two you'll have my grandchild and you'll never finish your education."

I didn't argue. I didn't want to fight with her on my wedding day. But in the end, as always, my mother was right.

Daddy walked me down the aisle, which was just a path of grass between two blocks of twenty chairs. Eddie waited for me in front of everyone, beaming like he was the luckiest man alive. I was dizzy and relieved when Daddy transferred my hand from his arm directly to Eddie's so there wasn't an instant during which I had to support my own weight. This was good because during most of the ceremony I was certain I would pass out.

A giant oak provided shade, yet I sweated through my heavy silk dress. Eddie wiggled his eyebrows at me and nodded to my left shoulder as my too large dress began to slip off. I hunched it back up and grinned right back at him.

The professor who married us had little to do during the ceremony except to welcome everyone, ask that ridiculous question of the spectators about whether anyone wanted to object to our union—as though that would have had any impact on our decision to marry each other—and pronounce us man and wife at the end. He did his part to start us off. I held my breath and waited for my mother to object, and when she did not—Daddy must have gagged her—I took my first full gulp of oxygen in almost twenty-four hours. Then we took over.

Eddie went first.

He looked alternately from my eyes to his wrist, where he had scribbled some notes, and began, "Anna, since our first date, I have been unable to think of anything, anyone, but you."

I smiled. My mother sobbed. Eddie's stomach rumbled.

He winked at me and continued, "You, my Anna, are my other half. Your amazing mind, your sense of humor, and your feistiness make you the missing piece that makes me whole. Though I worried I might scare you away, it didn't take me long to realize that you fear nothing, and to know you are the one I need beside me for the rest of my life."

He reached into his pocket and took out the tiny gold ring, looked back into my eyes, and asked, "Anna, will you take me as your husband, to have, hold, love, and support; do you promise to bake cookies for me, rub my back, kiss my lips, and cherish me and us together until death parts us?"

One renegade tear dripped down my cheek. Eddie caught it on his thumb as I said, "Until death parts us, I do." He slipped the ring on my finger, and I sniffled.

Then it was my turn.

I took a tiny note card from my poufy sleeve and said, "Eddie, on our first date, I was certain that we would never speak again, let alone date and end up married. But you, my friend, did grow on me."

I heard my dad laugh.

I glanced at my notes and continued, "It wasn't your green eyes, your broad shoulders, or your smile that won me. It was your humility, your intelligence, and your effortless way of caring for me. You chased me down. You made me realize I was lonely when I'd never noticed before. I want you beside me for the rest of my life."

I took his ring from the cleavage of my gown, and he wiggled those eyebrows at me again, which made me laugh as I asked, "Eddie, will you take me as your wife, to have, hold, love, and support; do you promise to change my oil, take out the trash, rub my neck every day, and cherish me and us together until death parts us?"

He squeezed my hand, gave a sharp nod, and shouted, "Until death parts us, I do!"

I put the ring on his finger, and when I looked up, his face was in my space, stealing my air, and he caught me breathless in a kiss. Everyone cheered.

The professor announced, "I now pronounce you husband and wife. You may continue to kiss your bride."

He did. Eddie kissed me and kissed me some more. Our wedding photo album is full of pictures of that kiss. When we came back down to Earth, the guitar dude had finished his recessional song, and the guests were on their second drink.

| | | |

AND THERE YOU HAVE IT. Losing Eddie's affection felt like dying before I died. I couldn't have lived my life without him anymore than I could have lived without water or oxygen. I would've continued to suffer right alongside him for the rest of my life. Though dying relieved me of having to face our problems, the pain of our separation stings.

6
Wandering and Guidance After Death

WHEN I DIED, I surrendered everything—my family, my life, and all control. Now it seems I am being tossed around randomly, riding on the whim of an unsympathetic universe, back and forth in time, only able to wallow in sadness and regret.

It's hard to get a grip on my perspective from the dead side. From here, as I watch my family, I feel their agony, but not in my heart as I always thought I did when emotional things hit me in life. In death, I feel their pain everywhere, within me and without me.

I have no arms or legs or organs, no ears, eyes, or skin, and yet I can still sense everything. The materials of me—my proteins and DNA—were stolen away by death. My well-used carbon, nitrogen, and oxygen allowed me to exist on Earth and live my life and take care of my family, but were merely a minor part of me. Without my molecules, my family thinks I'm gone from them. But I keep coming back, remembering the past, and somehow I'm maintaining a level of voyeuristic interaction with them.

This is a remarkable surprise. When I considered in life what death might be like, I never imagined that I would lose only the use of my atoms. My power to think and love has survived my death.

The daunting notion that I may ponder and observe for all of eternity is also glorious. Infinite time to contemplate these mysteries should provide comfort to a soul like me who finds pleasure in thinking. Now I sound like Eddie. He could always play devil's advocate and help me see the good side of a bad situation. He would always say I should try to relax and appreciate the wonders around me.

"I think you're preparing to depart, Anna."

"Excuse me?" Where did that voice come from?

"Departure is a choice that all newly dead must make at their own pace. You appear to be ready," says the voice.

How did a voice reach me out here in nowhere? I'm all alone. It should be silent.

My hard-earned equilibrium is shattered.

"Did you call me 'newly dead'?" I demand. "It seems to me that I've been dead for a very long time. I've been watching my family and having flashbacks, and I do miss my body."

"You don't need your body anymore, Anna. You have your soul."

"Soul? Is that all I am now?"

"Soul is our human term for it. And it's not all you are *now*; it's all you have *ever been*."

All I have ever been, my ass. I was a mom and wife and teacher. I had a life, and I'm useless here and dead. I need my damn molecules *to be*. When I'm greeted on the dead side, they tell me my soul is all I have ever been? Preparing to depart? Damn it, I don't want to depart. I'm not ready!

"Calm down. There's no hurry."

"How are you hearing my thoughts? Stay the hell out of my head! Who are you anyway?"

"Are we having a full-blown mood swing here?" she answers with a question. She seems calm, cool, and collected, but I know that tone. There's an edge to her voice that says, "Watch yourself, missy."

I'm afraid to respond.

Finally, she says, "It's me, Anna. It's Mom. Latch on and let me drive for a while."

Instantly, my resistance fades, and I'm drawn to her like a magnet and willing to follow her anywhere. For the first time since I crossed to the dead side, I'm not alone.

7
Bethany's Birth

EIGHTEEN YEARS AGO, at four in the morning, I listened to the sound of Eddie's sleeping breath. Just short of a snore yet much deeper than his awake breathing, I let the rhythm of his effortless intake of oxygen lull me back to sleep for a few more precious minutes.

My water hadn't yet broken, but with each contraction I wanted to wake Eddie and share my exhausted excitement. The baby had been quiet all night. He didn't move or kick, hiccup or roll. Now I knew why. He was getting ready to be born. I missed his kicks. I'd become accustomed to our daily routines together. He, the passenger. Me, the vessel of life. Now, the core of this vessel was squeezing the breath out of me and the kick out of our baby.

I rolled like a whale from my back to my side, and my belly bumped Eddie. He grunted in his sleep. I knew that grunt like I knew our baby's kicks. It was his sleepy hello. He wasn't fully awake but was aware of me. I stroked his stubbly cheek and grunted back. He rubbed my belly. I stayed still while the next contraction wrapped me up, thinking I'd ride out a few more in my warm bed with my best friend by my side. The cold October wind whipped rain against our windows. It would've been a good morning to stay in bed and sleep late. Mom had warned me. Our four years of sleeping late on weekend mornings would soon end. We'd be at the service of an infant.

I burrowed into my pillow and relished the quiet. I'd been in labor for hours. What began as cramps in my back had developed into a periodic rubber band wrap, each wave ebbing soon after it started. Now, with Eddie's warm hand on our baby, the next contraction was more intense. He felt it. His eyes opened wide and met mine. He raised his eyebrows. I could see them in the dark. Those eyebrows and the sleepy eyes under them asked me all the questions. I smiled back in response. He was fully awake by the end of the contraction and felt it leave me. For the first time all night, the baby kicked and bumped the hand of his daddy, the doctor, the anchor of our lives. The doctor, my friend, nuzzled my neck and pressed his face into my swollen breasts. He chuckled.

"Gonna have to share these soon, eh?" His hands caressed me territorially.

"'Fraid so, Doc." I pushed up against his face as another contraction hit. This one was different, another order of magnitude on my Richter scale. I breathed like I'd been trained to in those ridiculous Lamaze classes. Eddie matched me breath for breath. I let my fingers linger in his thick hair while my mind wandered away from the pain and visited my normal early morning pregnant obsession: I wanted food. Maybe the breathing worked. A little.

When the contraction released me, I asked, "Can I eat, do you think?"

"Yeah. Let's get me coffee and you and the wee one some eggs and juice." Eddie swung his legs over the edge of the bed and his feet into his slippers, and then he came around to help me up. I was, lately, like a turtle on my back and required being levered out of bed.

"And bacon, please." Eddie took my water-puffy hands in his strong ones and pulled me up into his arms. Still a perfect fit. My head on his chest. His arms around my weeble body. That's when my water broke in a flood, all over the hardwood floor and Eddie's favorite slippers.

Three hours later we checked into the hospital. I don't

remember much about that part. The labor pains lived up to their name after the great flood. I went into my head. Eddie took care of everything else.

My labor lasted all day long, but the delivery was quick. I pushed for less than an hour once they let me.

"Eddie, Eddie!" I gasped his name whenever I came up for air between the vice-grip contractions. He was right beside me. We were in constant contact. His hands were on me, holding me, supporting me, helping me bring our baby into the world. I had a vague memory of swearing at him and throwing a cup of ice at his head. No. Impossible. That couldn't have happened. He was the center of my world.

"What? What do you need, Anna?" he whispered in my ear.

"Just don't let go, okay?"

"I gotcha, girl. You know I do."

And I was pulled again over the cliff, in the pain, in my head, all alone but gripping this strong hand that let me squeeze the blood out of it. The song in my head was a verse from Simon and Garfunkel's "I Am a Rock." Eddie sang along, off-key, in my ear. My baby tried to be born.

I tried to push him out. The doctor was doing something down there, stretching me, telling me to push.

NOW.

I did. I ripped in half with the pain of that push. Eddie stopped singing and said, "Open your eyes, Anna. Don't miss it." I opened my eyes and saw our baby's head, bald and bloody, squished nose in profile.

The doctor said, "One or two more good pushes, Anna, and we'll see if you have a son or daughter."

Good idea, I thought. Let's get this party started.

I pushed.

I pushed.

I pushed with all of the clenched muscles of my entire body. And it worked.

laura lanni

Our baby slipped out, and Eddie's voice proclaimed to the world, "He's a *girl*!"

"He *is*?" I looked for confirmation and saw it was true. We had a daughter. A tiny, six-pound wiggly girl whom we'd called "him" for nine months. We named her Bethany in homage to Eddie's favorite grandmother Elizabeth.

It was love at first sight for both of us, but our sweet baby girl disrupted the equilibrium of the force field of our relationship. Instead of circling each other, Eddie and I orbited our daughter like planets around the sun.

8
My Sister

ON A QUIET COUNTRY ROAD, I was deep inside my own thoughts. A Sarah McLachlan song was playing on repeat in my mind to the thudding rhythm of my sneakers pounding the road. Half a year before I died, I was healthy and strong, happy and running my long loop. The cell phone Eddie made me carry was thudding against my hip and ringing in the hand-stitched pocket of my shorts.

"Anna! You all right? You've been gone a long time." Eddie's nagging, worried voice in my ear shattered my running zone. The man had a ridiculous fear for my safety. He carried all of our worry. I feared nothing.

"Eddie, *huff*, I'm fine—*huff, huff*—be home in twenty minutes." Without breaking my stride, I squeezed the phone back into the tiny pocket.

It rang again.

"Eddie! I'm fine!" I yelled into it.

"Hi, Annabella!" Not Eddie this time. It was my sister.

"'Chelle—*huff*—I'll call you later. Can't talk now—*huff*—I'm running."

"I'm running late, too. God, the traffic is horrible. I just got out of a stupid faculty meeting. You would not *believe* the things these teachers do! One guy wants help removing a picture of himself that a student posted online. Of course, they don't tell us the whole story. After half an hour of complaining and whining, it finally comes out—from his principal—that he's been working on retrieving the picture for more than a week and has failed. The teacher wants to take legal action."

Huff. "Michelle?"

"Anyway, turns out the picture was taken at Field Day. To make a long story short, it was ninety-five degrees and humid as hell. This teacher is one giant man. He was dripping and sweated right through his clothes and underwear. And when he tried to change into a dry shirt and was bent over the trunk of his car, some smartass kid took his picture—plumber's crack at full moon!" She takes a break to cackle.

Huff. "Michelle? I can't hold my arm up while I'm running." *Huff.*

"Yeah, I gotta run, too. There's a cop. Can't be on a cell phone while I'm driving and all that crap. Love you. 'Bye." And she clicked off.

| | | |

MOM'S VOICE INTERRUPTS MY THOUGHTS and somehow magically redirects me from the past to the present. "Now your sister is on her way to your house. Look at her. She's a mess."

We watch together. Michelle is driving alone from Virginia, clothes and a pile of shampoo, shoes, and Pop-Tarts tossed into the backseat in her rush to leave. Wadded tissues form a heap on the passenger seat. My little sister is not looking good.

Gotta hurry. Gotta get there fast. Get to those kids.

Damn it, Anna. Why'd you go and die, girl? What will we do without you? Who can I call every other minute?

"Mom, are you still here? How can I hear Michelle and everyone when they're thinking?"

"The same way you hear me thinking. You are linked. You can listen to the people you love."

"Why don't they hear me?"

"They don't know they can."

A Michelle snort. *There's a copper, hiding. Idiot thinks we can't see the big butt of his car.* She thumbs her nose at him as she hits her brakes. *I'm not on my cell phone, copper.* She starts to sob. *I would be if I had a sister to call.*

Damn it, Anna.

She grabs a wad of used tissues and blows her nose with a loud honk. She wipes her eyes and tosses the wet blob over her shoulder.

Something was up with them. Anna hasn't been happy lately. Wouldn't return my calls. Hadn't told her funny Eddie stories that always hurt a little. Torturing her single sister with all her lovey-husband stories— you'd think a girl as smart as Anna would have a clue about anyone but herself.

The hell with the cop. She hits the gas. *I'm speeding. I'm passing every car on this effing road. I need to hug Bethy and crawl under the bed with my Joey. Those poor kids. Eddie sounded bad. Probably nothing I can do for him, though.*

| | | |

JOEY HIDES UNDER HIS BED again with his stuffed black bear, as old as he is and wearing thin. I've been dead twenty-four hours, and my house is still and hollow without me. The sound of the ignored television echoes up from downstairs.

"How'd we get here, Mom?" I ask.

"You did it this time," she says.

"Not intentionally. That's how it's been for me so far. I just jump around."

"Don't worry. You'll develop better control. Just focus on your son. If you brought us here, you need to be with him."

Joey's eyes are closed, but he's not napping. His scrunched eyebrows give him away. His mouth is pulled firmly into a scowl. He is definitely thinking, and I can hear him.

I helped Daddy make a good list before he went to the store. I asked for Fruity Pebbles. Mommy always makes me eat Wheaties or Cheerios or a bagel, but Daddy might let me have good cereal for breakfast. He just nodded and wrote it on the list. I don't know why Daddy even went to the store. Amy and Miss Evelyn and all the ladies from church, and even mean old Mrs. Smithers, all brought over pies and smelly casseroles today.

Daddy wanted Bethany to go with him. I'm the only one who knows where all the stuff is, and he didn't even ask me to come. Daddy might get lost in that big store all alone.

Good thing Bethy didn't go—her face is all red and blotchy, and her hair is all messy, too. If Mommy sees her like that she'll make her brush her hair. Bethany told Daddy she had to finish cleaning up the kitchen. It was already clean, and now she's sitting on the swing.

I think she just didn't want to go. Mommy calls that making excuses.

Joey lies on his back in the semidarkness under the bed, eyes still closed in concentration. He's thinking about food. Any food sounds good. His belly grumbles.

I hope Daddy hurries up with my Fruity Pebbles.

His eyes pop open when he hears noise outside. The thump of a car door. The front door squeaks and Michelle comes in, calling, "Joey!" He doesn't come out from under the bed. Instead, he grins and waits. Aunt Michelle is almost as good as Fruity Pebbles.

My Joey loves my sister because she's fun and funny. Knowing Michelle is with my family, in my place, gives me some relief. She'll take over for Bethany, feed Eddie, and hug Joey. She'll fill my empty spot for a while.

Michelle drops her pile of stuff in the foyer and takes the stairs two at a time and enters Joey's bedroom humming Bette Midler's "The Rose." She lies down in a pile of crumbs by the bed and lifts the edge of the blanket to peek under. She spills a shaft of light under his bed, and Joey smiles at her, reaches out his hand to touch her face. Still humming, she lays a kiss on his palm and crawls under the bed with him. She pulls my boy into her arms.

As she kisses his soft, dirty cheeks, he giggles and offers her his last Oreo, which she stuffs in her mouth. After a few minutes of hugging, Michelle gets Joey to snuggle in the covers on the bed with her. She grabs the top book in the stack by his bed and finds the bookmark holding our page from the last night I ever read Joey to sleep—the night before I died. That was just two days ago, but is feels like a lifetime has passed. How long is a lifetime, anyway? Mine passed like a blink, just like the first day of my death.

While Michelle reads about the adventures of Bigwig, Hazel, and Fiver, Joey falls into a deep sleep in her arms. Michelle drops the book and cries while she cradles my sleeping son.

| | | |

"BETTER NOW, ANNA?" my mother asks.

"I'm relieved that Michelle has my boy and he's not all alone under that bed waiting for me anymore."

"Good. Then you can start to consider your situation. Take some time. Look around on your own. Just call me if you get lost or need a nudge back."

"What am I looking for?"

"Watch your life. Watch your family for as long as you like. Go back and remember the good and bad. There is no reason to hurry here on the dead side. Just relax and absorb as much as you can."

As suddenly as my mom appeared, she leaves, and I know for certain I'm alone once again.

Look around. Watch my life. I can do that, I think, but I can't control it. I don't know how or why, but I'm pulled back to Eddie.

9

Running with the Dogs

"I WONDER if the dogs took away a part of my mind," I said to Eddie. He was driving the van. Behind us, six-month-old Joey snoozed in his car seat. We were on our way, as a family, to pick up Bethany from her first middle school dance.

That morning when I ran, I was chased by a small but intense dog. I stopped running, but I wasn't scared like when I was a little girl. My distress was comprised mainly of annoyance. I charged at the dog, and it backed away.

A woman was watching from her porch. I asked if it was her dog.

She said, "No, but you should report it. That dog's a menace."

I started jogging away, and the little rodent dog came barking at me again, nipping at my shoes. Then, out of nowhere, the owner was chasing her rat-dog. She was limping along with one shoe on. She swung her other shoe rather fruitlessly at her idiot dog.

The mutt ignored her and charged at me, so I stopped running and growled back at it.

The shoe-waving owner yelled, "You hear that, Nelly? You be nice!" Little Nelly turned on her and tried to eat her ankles.

"Is this your dog?" I demanded as the dog latched onto the cuff of her jeans. When she nodded, I said, "Well, it scared the shit out of me," not because it did, but because I was so mad that it tried.

She said, real sweet, as she attempted to unclench her dog

by spastically swinging the shoe at its flanks, "Oh, I'm terribly sorry."

Well, that fixes everything, right? I was supposed to back off from being a jerk about her obnoxious dog. But the incident challenged my admittedly shrinking mental control, and I heard myself say, "Does your rat-dog stink up 113 or 115?" I pointed at the two houses behind her.

She managed to look offended and offered no further apology but did not admit to the crazy runner where she lived.

I heard my mouth say, "113? Right! Get a leash," and away I ran with my mind somewhere off to my left.

I had relayed all of this to Eddie over the phone earlier that day while I stood guard on lunch duty in the cafeteria. He'd heard my complaints about dogs before. He listened patiently and then launched into his best rendition of Repairman Husband, earnest to fix every problem for me. "Why don't you do what my mom always did?"

"What was that?" I worried where this would go.

"Write a letter to the owners and complain," he said simply.

I thought he was joking, but I was clearly at the desperate stage, so I'd drafted a dog memorandum instead of grading tests during my break that day. I dug the pages out of my purse while we sat in the line of cars full of tired parents in front of the middle school. "Listen to this, Ed. I drafted my letter." His smile encouraged me.

I began, "Dear Neighbors: I have lived among you in silence and misery for a long time. I avoid confrontation. I'd rather be mad at you than have you mad at me. This is a costly way to live. Among other things, it appears to be costing me my mind. Granted, it is not the only thing wearing down my mental capacity, but it is one of the obvious things, and I have deemed it fixable, so I am compelled to write you this letter."

Eddie smiled and nodded, yet looked oddly saddened by my words. I continued.

"My husband is the true dog hater at our house. He yells out the windows and into your yards for your barking dogs to 'shut up.' He rides to your house on warm evenings on his bike and rings your doorbell at midnight to wake you up and tell you 'your dog is barking.' He calls your house in the middle of the night with the same message. Why don't you hear it? We don't know. Maybe your mind is missing, too." This made Eddie snort a laugh, which made Joey stir in the backseat.

We both froze. "Oops, sorry," he whispered. Laundry duty for a week was the consequence in our family for waking a sleeping baby. I was lucky: my voice never woke Joey. It just made him smile and gurgle in his sleep.

Eddie said, "Take that last part out, will you?"

I made a dramatic X through the offensive section that pinned the dog hate on him.

"Thanks. Go on. I'm still listening," he whispered.

"Your expressions of love have resulted in your dog behaving like a brat. He does not know or follow traditional, standard dog rules. He barks excessively. He does not stay in your yard because you have no fence. You do not leash him. You let him out the front door, and you stay inside. He runs free to my yard and craps on my lawn. He crushes flowers and runs through bushes. He has no idea where his boundaries are. You are happy because you love your dog. He is happy because he does not know any better. I am miserable because of you and your dog. The anxiety and frustration of your actions are overwhelming.

"I honestly have never lived in or even heard of a place where packs of large dogs ran free through neighboring yards. Where they barked and played and crapped wherever and whenever they pleased. It is baffling and has led to a partial loss of my mind.

"I feel better for having told you. Now you can be mad at me. Hopefully, while you hate me, you are also keeping your dog quiet and at your home. Then the cost of sending this letter was worthwhile and, maybe, part of my mind will return to me."

"Good!" he declared. "Let's stop at Kinko's on the way home and make copies. But don't sign it. Then tomorrow in the middle of the night, we'll drive around the neighborhood with our headlights off and put one in every mailbox. Nobody will suspect us." He was so brilliantly deadpan, I couldn't help laughing.

"I could never send it, Eddie. But it felt good to write it."

"I know. I'm glad you did." He put his large hand on my leg and squeezed.

"What other kernels of advice do you have for me, Mr. Fixit?"

"How about this? When Joey learns to walk, we'll get him a little shovel and train him to pick up poop in our yard and fling it into the street. If we start early, he'll think it's just naturally his job and never complain."

"Nope. My son will not be exploited as a pooper-scooper. Next idea, please."

"Then you could do it. Each day, pick up the piles of fresh dog droppings and dump them in a paper bag. Then deposit it on the dog-owning-neighbor's front porch, set a burning match to the bag, ring the doorbell, and run."

"No! I'll burn their house down!"

"I doubt it. They'll open the door, find the burning bag, and put out the fire by stomping on it."

I lost myself in giggles. He was crazy.

For the next few months, I developed my own strategies—which also failed. Daily, I called my neighbors or found their children outside playing. I reported the newest loads, and I asked them to pick up the poop, which, of course, they always did. But it was usually a big production and rather embarrassing for all involved. Often they came to my door and insisted that I come out and help them *find* the smelly heap.

Finally, without any real forethought, I tried a new tactic. After arriving home to find Goliath happily relieving himself by my garage door, I ordered the wind to hold my caution and all calls, and I abandoned my mind. I picked up the mess, gross and still warm, in a plastic bag and walked across the street to *deliver* it. I didn't intend to set it up in flames and run. Instead, I rang the doorbell with the stinking bag in my hand, a sick look on my face, and Goliath prancing around and occasionally sneaking a sniff at my crotch. Sometimes in life, I wondered how I ended up where I did. Exactly like now. How can I be dead?

That night, I confessed my impulsive strategy to Eddie over dinner, with Bethany groaning in embarrassment and Joey gleefully tossing mashed potatoes at the wall.

"It was a large load, Ed. Sorry, you're eating. But you're a doctor, so you're used to blood and poop, right?"

"Actually, no. The nurses are good with that stuff. I still have a weak stomach." He put down his fork and rinsed his mouth with milk.

"Anyway, Lisa didn't open the door. Her sister did, and she invited me to come in."

"With the poop?" Bethany asked.

"Yep, with the poop. She didn't know what it was—yet. Don't worry, I didn't go in. I said I couldn't come in with 'this,' so she offered to take it."

"Oh, Mom," Bethany complained, "why can't you just be nice?"

"Me? I *am* nice! I'm not the one pooping on their lawns!" It was impossible to make a teenager see justice when her primary goal was acceptance.

Eddie stepped in. "What did you do, Anna?"

"Well, it obviously wasn't going as planned. Is there a good way to effectively deliver poop? I considered whether I should just hand the bag to her. I thought about doing it."

"So you just lit it with a match and ran like I told you?" Eddie teased.

"You *guys*! What is *wrong* with you?" Bethany threw down her fork. "I have to live in this neighborhood, you know. I have to go to school with those kids!"

"No, I didn't light it up," I said to Ed.

"No, I didn't hand it to her," I said to Bethany.

I spooned mashed potatoes into Joey's open mouth. "You don't care *what* I did, do you, Joey?" He gurgled.

I took a big gulp of wine and continued with my poop saga. "I just shook my head like an idiot and told her she shouldn't take it into the house. Finally, Lisa came to the door all chipper. You know how fake nice she is? I smiled back, but mine was more a shit-eating grin."

"*Language!*" my daughter admonished me.

"Well," I continued, ignoring my teenage conscience, "then I just gave in and did it. What else could I do? I handed the bag of shit to her," I glanced at Bethany, daring her to correct me again, "and said, 'I believe this is yours.'" Eddie snorted milk out his nose. "I explained its origin, and asked, as sweetly as possible, that she keep her dog at her house."

Eddie declared, "Good for you, Anna!"

"Maybe. I'm not sure. It wiped that smile off Lisa's face, for sure. She said I didn't have to bring it over. She would have come to pick it up if I'd just called. Damn. She completely missed the point."

"Lang—!" Bethany started. Eddie cut her off by holding up his hand, palm to her. She would pick at me, but she wouldn't defy her father.

Mr. Fixit morphed into Professor Wixim. "Think about it, Anna. This has two distinct sides. Although we want Lisa's dog to *never* crap in our yard, *she* is confident that her mere willingness to clean up the individual piles at your daily request is sufficient to keep peace and harmony. No amount of explaining can fix this. It's just the way people are. Not people like us. But the rest of them."

Bethany groaned. "People like you two. I'm one of *them*."

"We know, Bethany," I said. "After dinner, you can pooper-scoop the whole yard for us. That might help you appreciate the Wixim perspective."

She ran to her room and slammed the door. Joey began to wail. Stink the cat licked spilled milk off the floor under the highchair. Eddie laughed and came over to hug me. As my mind returned to me, I realized that attempting to comprehend the reasoning ability, or lack of it, of the rest of the human race was exacting a huge toll on my own intellect.

Best to just give up.

| | | |

BACK ON THE DAY AFTER I DIED, Eddie sits alone on our driveway and throws a wet, chewed tennis ball for Lucy, our neighbor's black Labrador. Although we were declared "not dog people" by the rest of humanity, this sweet canine never got the memo. She adores Eddie. Lucy chases the tennis ball as it bounces through the trees and turns to race back to her friend. Although he's watching her, Eddie doesn't react when Lucy pauses to dump a fresh load on the edge of our lawn.

Whoa, he is really gone. No, I am really gone. Poor Eddie.

Then I feel the tug—so much like when he crept into our bedroom at night, no talking, in the dark, and got into the bed. That feeling of having him nearby, so close and quiet. Wanting to roll to him, my Eddie. But no, it hurts too much. I will not listen to him think. Keep me out of that head. I think he knows I'm here, but I will not go into that head.

Lucy romps joyfully back to Eddie, who sits on the driveway and wraps his arms around her neck. This playful three-year-old twitches with excitement whenever she sees him and wants to play fetch, but she settles down in his arms and lets him hold onto her.

Eddie is sitting still.

Lucy is sitting still.

These are things that never happened when I walked among the living. How did things change so fast? And why am I wasting time thinking about dogs?

10
Bookstore Shenanigans

"G'NIGHT, ANNA," Eddie whispered as he kissed my forehead. I opened my eyes in time to see him remove the book from my stomach. He picked up our sleeping baby boy from beside me and carried him to his bassinette.

Joey is an infant, barely beyond a newborn. My body is still pudgy with retained water. Great. I can't even follow the time line of my own life.

"It's all right, Anna," my mother's voice breaks in. "You're traveling on thoughts and associations instead of on a forward time line."

"Eddie looks good here. I always liked him in his scrubs."

She makes a noise like "hrmpff" and leaves me to watch my life, like old TV reruns from which I cannot turn away.

When Eddie came back to turn out the light, he saw me watching him. "Oh, sorry. I didn't mean to wake you."

"That's all right. I had a little nap. Come here and see me. I miss you." I yawned and stretched.

He sat on the edge of the bed and held my hand, and we whispered together.

"How's the new book?" He picked it up and checked my page. "Going slow? Do you like it?"

"I love it, but reading makes me sleepy these days. I have to keep rereading pages to remember where I was."

"What do you remember?"

"It's about a mom who disappears and her odd engineer husband. She used to be an architect. I like it so far."

Joey gave a content baby sigh and wrestled his strong arms up and out of his wrap. Eddie and I both froze and waited for him to settle back down. After a few little grunts, he did.

"Want a glass of wine?" Eddie whispered and pointed to the door.

"Oh, yes, please." I wiggled out of the covers. He took my hand, and we snuck out of our own bedroom.

We snuggled together on the couch in our quiet house and shared a whole bottle of wine. That's when I told Eddie about my bookstore adventure. My life with a new baby was in quiet, slow-motion, autopilot mode, with long days somehow comprising short weeks, so even a trip to the bookstore was fodder for analysis.

"It happened again. The guy at the bookstore asked me to buy a membership card."

"Huh. Too bad for them. Even I know you'll never do that. You're way too cheap."

"Well, yeah, there's that, and I like being anonymous. If I had one of those cards, they'd know every book I bought."

"They already do, Anna. You use your credit card, right?"

Oh, I hadn't thought of that. I drained my glass before I triumphantly reported, "Today, I got the discount without the card."

"What?" He refilled my wine glass. "How'd you do that?"

"By being very, very observant."

He laughed. "You? Observant? You don't pay attention to anything."

"Don't laugh at me. I was paying attention today, and it paid off. I saved eight bucks."

He took a slurp of his wine and covered us with the blanket on the couch. "Tell me all about it, please."

So I told him. I'd heard the cashier ask a customer ahead of me for her discount card. When the lady said she didn't have it with her, the cashier asked for her name and looked her up that way. He didn't even ask for identification.

So when it was my turn and I was asked for my discount card, I lied and said, "I forgot to bring it."

Then he asked, "What's your last name?"

I met Eddie's smiling eyes and confessed, "I said 'Muckenfuss.'"

"Seriously? *Muckenfuss?*" Eddie mimicked what the cashier was undoubtedly thinking when he'd asked me to spell it.

"Yep. Then I spelled it for him, but I was nervous that I would get caught. When he asked for my first name, I lost my nerve and thought I should just give it up and run. What if they were recording the whole charade on a security camera?"

"You're sneaky and paranoid. And like an onion. Year after year I just keep finding more interesting layers of my wife," he mused.

"You'll never know all of me. I'm way too complex." The wine was going straight to my head, which I rested on his shoulder.

"So, he found a Muckenfuss then?"

"Yeah. That's the funny part. I said something like, 'I think it's probably under my daughter's name,' thinking that would end the panic induced by lying. I was digging in my purse for some cash when I heard him repeating, 'Emily? Is it Emily? Ma'am, is your daughter Emily?'

"That's when I realized he was talking to me. I looked up from my mess of a purse with a dumb look on my face and mouth hanging open and said something smart like, 'Huh?'

"He said, "You can use your daughter's card. We allow family discounts. Is her name Emily Muckenfuss?'

"I said, 'Yes. That's her.' My hand shook as I gave him some cash, afraid to get caught if I used my credit card."

Eddie lost it. He doubled over laughing.

"Shh!" I giggled with him. "Don't wake Joey."

"Oh, man, that was so worth the eight bucks!"

I still felt guilty about it and asked Eddie's opinion, hoping for reassurance. "Was this petty theft? Did it cost Emily Muckenfuss anything that I used her discount card and I didn't even know her?"

Despite his laughter, he didn't disappoint me: Eddie took my side. "Nah. It's the store's fault that their lax discount policy doesn't require having the actual card." He hugged me and said, "Anna, the world is immensely improved by your presence."

My husband used to love me. And then, he stopped.

| | | |

A COUPLE OF YEARS LATER, I was in a different bookstore with my kids in tow. Bethany had Joey by the hand while we waited in the slow line to purchase a big pile of books. I switched to the other line, but my presence just made that one go slower and the other one speed up.

When it was finally my turn, the cashier asked for my membership card, and I was honest this time to make up for the Muckenfuss saga and said I didn't have one. He asked if I wanted one, and of course I asked if they were free. He said not for most people but it would be essentially free for me that day. He said the card cost ten dollars and gave a ten percent discount. Since I was spending almost a hundred dollars, the ten-dollar card and the ten percent discount would cancel each other out.

Well! This was an entirely new way of looking at things. No one had ever done the math for me before. I had no frugal card left to play, so I pulled out my privacy-freak trump card and asked, "Do I have to use my real name?"

From my shoulder, I heard Bethany admonish me with a two syllable, "Mom!"

The clerk smiled indulgently and said, "You can be whoever you wish to be." He sort of sounded like a wizard. Or maybe he was my fairy godmother. Bethany stood at my side, agitated and embarrassed, likely calculating the years until she could drive herself to the bookstore and avoid her mother's shenanigans.

As I considered my identity choices—Elvis, Elizabeth Taylor, Freddy Mercury—I glanced at Bethany and winked. She rolled her eyes when I said, "I am Martha Washington and I would like to buy a free membership card."

He asked for my address. When I asked whether that had to be correct, he grinned. He was on my team. Bethany pulled Joey away from me to look at a gumball machine—anything to escape from the hell of my presence. We settled on 1600 Pennsylvania Avenue, and the phone number I used was one from my old apartment in college.

Bethany didn't waste a minute to tell on her ridiculous mother to her sane father that night. "Daddy, Mom gave the guy at the bookstore a fake name to get a discount card!" she announced at dinner. Joey, wide-eyed two-year-old, nodded his agreement. Their mother was nuts.

Eddie looked up at me from his close study of the slab of shoe-leathery meatloaf on his plate. "Really, Anna? In front of the kids?" I caught the sarcasm, the sweet affection in his voice. Bethany did not. She raised her eyebrows, and her upturned chin made her neck double in length as she gave me the slit-eyed look she'd learned from my sister. *See? Even Dad thinks you're wrong.* I ignored her and addressed her father, my ally and best friend.

"It's no big deal, Eddie. I got a discount card for free and didn't even have to put my real name on it."

"Or her address. Mom lied, Daddy." Bethany never lied. She told the raw truth. Slapped you with it. Well, really only slapped me with it. Lately, I was the butt of all of Bethany's accusations.

"You can use the card, too, Bethany," I tried to appease her. "For a year. You can get ten percent off every book." I suffered yet another eye roll from my daughter. Joey tried to mimic her, which made me laugh. Nothing angered my daughter more than happy people. Note to self: remember you are the mom. Do not appease.

Eddie was grinning at me through a mouthful of baked potato, watching me struggle to avoid catching our daughter's bad mood. His anecdote was always laughter. He asked, "What's your name, Anna? Muckenfuss again?"

"No, sir." I smiled at him and said, "I am Martha Washington, my dear Mr. President."

He chuckled while Bethany stewed, stuck in the middle of two parents who enjoyed each other. Her parents, still in love, made no sense to her teenage mind.

11
Stupid Market

"YOU KNOW I have trouble in grocery stores," I reminded Eddie one night after work last May. With just a few weeks of school left, and the anticipation of summer break looming like a vanilla pudding-stuffed double chocolate cake, I was exhausted. "Come with me, Eddie," I pleaded. "Bethany can watch Joey. Come with me and help. You can pick the cookies." I knew how to get the man's attention.

My weekly trips to the stupid market, as my sister liked to call it, encompassed three things that I hated to do: shop, spend money, and waste time. When I was there, I brought a list, and I found my stuff with record speed and got the heck out. I learned the layout of the store and zip-zanged through it like the Road Runner. There was nothing I could do about having to shop for food. My kids loved to eat. But with Eddie helping, I hoped we could reduce the wasted time.

Eddie, the Cookie Monster, couldn't resist. He agreed to come, and we left the house with my long list in his capable hands.

While I drove, Eddie critiqued my list. I'm a good driver because I'm so patient. I talk to the other drivers, gently coaching them, helping all of them to drive better.

"Get the hell off the road, you blue hair!" I yelled out my window as I passed an older lady in a beige sedan.

Eddie knew better than to comment on my commenting. That's why I was driving. When he drove, I couldn't help but coach him, too. I drove him crazy from whichever seat I occupied, but he was tactful enough to bear me in silence and love me anyway.

"There are two kinds of cereal on this list. Is that a typo?" he asked.

"No. Bethany wants the Cheerios, but Joey needs the granola."

"Needs the granola? He's five."

"And I'm his mother. Have you been around the kid when he can't go?"

He shook his head and smirked as he looked out the window.

"Do you *see* these people? Driving like it's illegal to go the speed limit." I looked for a chance to pass the dented pickup truck; I was bored with his bumper stickers.

"Don't beep, Anna. Please." It was a lot like having Bethany with me.

"I'm not going to beep, Eddie. I'm just going to ride real close to let the idiot know he is freaking crawling."

Out of the corner of my eye, I could see Eddie's foot hit his imaginary brake, just like my Dad used to do when I drove his giant blue sedan. I smiled and slowed down just a little. My husband sighed.

"Um, Anna? Do you know we just passed Walmart?"

"I know. Didn't I tell you? I don't shop there anymore."

"But it's right there. What's the problem?"

"I can't believe I forgot to tell you. The old hag in the deli hates her job. She gets so annoyed when I ask her to slice cheese. And if I ask for it sliced thin, holy crap, she looks like she might cry. So no Walmart for me."

"Are we going to Bi-Lo?"

"Nope. You must've forgot, because I know I told you about the hairnet lady there."

"Hairnet lady, hmm. In the deli? Is she the one who wrapped the cheese with the fly in it?"

"Bingo! You do listen. I think she did it on purpose."

"Right. She caught a fly and flicked it in your cheese." He laughed and summed it up, "So it's all about the deli, then?"

"Yep. The deli is the bottleneck of this adventure, so I do it first. That way, if things go bad, I can just leave the empty cart and walk out of the store."

He didn't know yet, but one of the tasks I planned to assign to him today was the dreaded deli. Dr. Wixim, with his sweet bedside manner and charm, could run for mayor and win—so I expected the deli would be no big deal for him.

I parked the car at the side of the lot of the new, shiny Publix, grabbed Eddie's arm, and we embarked on our first stupid market date.

"I'll take the cart and send you on errands. Is that okay?" I asked.

"Sounds great. Deli first?" My Eddie. The man would do anything for me. I nodded, handed him the deli list, and off he went.

Ten minutes later, I was halfway through my list when he found me; he was holding a pile of meat and cheese in his arms. "Yikes!" I said. "That's a ton of meat."

"*That's* what you said to me on our honeymoon," he grinned and grazed my hip with his.

"Jerk." I slapped his arm while he loaded the cart. "Are you going to eat all of that?"

"That's what *I* said—"

"Don't even say it if you know what's good for you." I pushed the cart away, and he trotted after me.

"Hey, this is a date, right? Can't a guy flirt with his wife?"

I stopped the cart and stood on my tiptoes to kiss his cheek. "Of course. Just don't upset the blue hairs." I pointed and whispered, "I think that's the one I passed on the way here." They were everywhere. It must be old folks' night, when they bus them all in and give senior discounts. I planned to mark my calendar and avoid this next week.

"We'll eat it all, Anna. I have a plan. Sandwiches every day. Chicken salad one night. Pepperoni bread another night. Omelettes another night. I think we could just about live on produce, deli, and eggs."

God, I loved that guy. He handled the despicable deli and now he was planning meals. Why didn't I unleash him on the stupid market years ago? "Sounds great. I already did produce." He inspected the bags of fruit and veggies and announced that we needed zucchini, mushrooms, a purple onion, and fresh tomatoes. And he was off again, this time without my list.

When he met up with me again, with his arms full of food, he kissed the top of my head. "Anna, this cart is loaded. Let me push it." I was in heaven. Pushing the heavy cart at the end of a grumpy stupid market excursion was a mood killer even worse than the snide remarks by the baggers when I demanded paper instead of plastic bags. This date was going even better than our first date.

That's when Eddie saw the cookie aisle. "Ooh, Anna, let me look around." He got that same glazed-over look that blanketed his features in a hardware store. The same one I probably wore in a bookstore. Eddie in the cookie aisle was a beautiful thing.

I don't eat cookies, so I rarely buy them. I'd rather bake them. Eddie loves all cookies, quite possibly as much as he loves me and the kids. He didn't even check the coupon pile. He didn't even look for sales. He couldn't decide between chocolate and oatmeal so, like a little kid, he grabbed both and hugged them all the way to the checkout.

It became our thing during my last summer. Our date night. Eddie would escort me to the grocery store. He'd deal with the deli, push the heavy cart, and help pick food for meals. After a month of such excursions, I suggested he just take over and let me stay home. Let me mow the lawn or something. He shook his head slowly, his serious eyes locked on mine.

"No, Anna. That's the point. If I did it alone, I'd hate it as much as you do."

He was right. Even grocery shopping was improved by his presence. That equals love. Now, from my front row seat on the dead side, I watch as, once again, Eddie is tossed into my path. My Eddie: the collection of atoms that comprised the saddest and best parts of my life. If he only knew how much I loved him. Always loved him. The most. He was my best friend, my center, my compass, but he left me at the end of my life. He pulled away from me and took my heart with him, leaving me empty before I even died.

| | | |

EDDIE IS DRIVING MY CAR with my seat pulled all the way forward and his thighs hitting the steering wheel. He pulls into the parking lot of the Shop-N-Stop. As he walks in, he reaches into the back pocket of his baggy, old man jeans and pulls out a list. Where did he ever get a list? Eddie is not a list maker.

He pushes the cart at turtle speed, bent over like it hurts to walk, drifting through every aisle and studying the food in wonder. He keeps looking up and down at his list.

He grabs whole milk instead of skim.

Chunky peanut butter instead of creamy.

American cheese instead of provolone.

Things are going to change without me in charge.

With half a cart of preserved food, stuff we never eat, Eddie just wanders aimlessly around the store. I ache to be with him. To touch the soft hair on his forearm, kiss his stubbly cheek, and breathe in the musky smell of him in a hug. All I can do is watch him and let the pain burn down. In the cookie aisle, he leans over the cart, looking like he might pass out, when he sees the Oreos.

I feel a strong tug to listen to Eddie's thoughts, but my own are chaos. Swirling. Too many painful options present themselves, trying to pull me in. They flash by and force me to watch my life, the life I used to have, as it flows forward in time. Without me. I resist with a newfound energy. I push back on the force, exerting a will that I didn't know I had. I leave Eddie alone in the stupid market. Alone with his pain.

12
My Daughter

BACK IN MY KITCHEN, Bethany washes a mountain of dishes. She has occupied my space, the place where I was always found. Her bare feet stand exactly where mine always did as she sloshes around in the hot, sudsy water. My stained, yellow apron is tied loosely around her pencil waist. For the first time since she came home from college, I can hear her from the dead side.

Mom, I'm trying.

And Mom? I'm sorry. I guess I always knew it wasn't only your fault when you and Daddy fought. It was hard to be caught between you two, though. Easier to side with him.

I watch her dry and put away all of the dishes and pans. She even wipes down the counters and the sink. Just like I would, if I was there. This from a girl who left her dirty clothes on the floor wherever they landed at the end of every day. Then she blows her nose on the dish towel and tosses it on the counter before walking out the back door. That's my girl.

| | | |

I LOOKED FOR EVERY OPPORTUNITY to try to get Bethany to talk to me more. It was tough, but she was so depressed after that bastard football player showed his true colors and broke up with her. I saw my chance and dove in.

"No, Mom, you do not understand." Bethany dumped a third scoop of sugar into her coffee. It was two weeks before her high school graduation and one week before prom, almost noon on a Sunday, and she'd just emerged from her bedroom.

"Oh, honey." I tried to hug her. She pushed me away.

"Who ever broke up with you?"

She was right. I didn't date enough to suffer a break up. Eddie was my first, last, and only real relationship. In my daughter's eyes, I was lucky. I got it right on the first try. She considered me an overachiever.

"There'll be other boys, Bethany."

"You see?" she yelled. "You don't know anything! Nobody wants to think about the next guy when one just hurt you. That doesn't help at all."

"What I meant was—you'll survive this."

"I don't even want to, Mom," she wailed. "I just want to die." She slammed her coffee mug on the table and stormed out the kitchen door into our garage. I followed right behind her, afraid she'd get in the car and drive herself into a wreck. She wasn't a great driver even when she wasn't sobbing.

"I'm sorry, honey." She leaned against the side of the car in a crumple, her forehead on her crossed arms, her face hidden. "What happened, anyway?"

She spun around and grabbed her hair in two fists, holding the newly cut ends in bunches. "This happened. Billy broke up with me because I cut my hair."

Oh. He was an ass as well as a buffoon, then. I was not surprised, but at least I had the tact not to say this out loud. Men and hair—what woman could comprehend that twisted puzzle?

"So, I'm furious, Mom. You were right, okay? He's an ass and an idiot, and he didn't even care about me. But talking about it with *you* makes it hurt even more. Can't you just go away without saying 'I told you so'?"

I held my ground. No way was I leaving her like this.

"Then I'll go away," she said and left the house for a long walk.

Late that night, I was drawn like a bug to the line of light under her bedroom door. I knocked. I just wanted to hug her, I swear. I wasn't there to lecture or pry. I just wanted my baby girl, who was almost grown up, to know that I loved her.

"Go away, Mom."

"How'd you know it was me?" I asked the closed door.

Her muffled voice, sounding just like when she was little, answered, "Joey walks in. Daddy waits for me to come out. You're the only knocker." Silence. I was dismissed. I knocked again, trained in persistence long ago by her father.

With a heavy sigh, she yanked open the door. She stood before me, blocking my entry, chin up and eyes defiant above her red and swollen nose. Mascara hung in black shadows under her glassy eyes. Her blue sparkling prom dress looked lovely on her petite frame, even with the toes of her bunny slippers peeking from the hem.

I sighed, my gaze locked on her toes. When I looked up at her and opened my mouth to speak, she raised her palm to me, Eddie-style, and insisted, "Do not say, 'Oh, honey,' or I will lose it again, Mom."

I opened my arms and waited. She hesitated a tenth of a second before she dropped her eyes from mine and stepped into my hug. And she lost it again anyway.

| | | |

NOW BETHANY SITS ALONE, with my planner, the map and chronicle of my life, in her lap. She shakes her head and frowns. *Mom, how the heck did you do so much? I think my life is crazy, but you never took a rest. Kinda scary, but it looks like life could get even harder. College is kicking my butt. How will I survive life after it? I don't see how I'm going to get through all of this without you for backup.*

Bethany flips through the daily pages of my October, the last full month of my life. *Mom, I only saw you once last month. I wish I could've come home from school. You didn't answer most days when I called. I didn't know what was going on with you.* She's crying a little now, wiping her eyes on the corner of the blanket. She leans back on the swing and closes her eyes, hot tears leaking out. *Mom, I'm not ready to do this alone. Daddy is a mess. Right now he's pretty useless. I'm totally running the show around here and I'm just not qualified for the job. I'm going to have to go back to the dorm and my classes sometime, but how can I leave them?*

Oh, honey. I'm so sorry I wasn't there for you the last couple of months.

I couldn't face anyone or even cope with daily conversation while I was crushed by my fear that Eddie was going to leave for work one day and not come home. I was so consumed with my own agony, I could hardly breathe.

What would I do if he left me? If I held my breath and stayed quiet, would the funk pass again? Would he come back to me again? What would it do to our kids if we split up?

If I'd known I had only until early November to see them all, I would have found more time.

| | | |

ON THURSDAY, NOVEMBER TENTH, Bethany called my cell phone during the school day. I had it set to vibrate so I was startled by the buzzing sound, and then every single one of my students looked up from their tests to watch it wiggle across my desk.

"Sorry," I whispered as I hit the red button for silence.

After class, I listened to Bethany's message. "Mom, sorry to call at work. I know you're busy with school, but I really miss you. College is hard. I haven't made any friends in the honors dorm. I don't know why I let you talk me into living here with all of these geeks. All they do is study! Heh heh, well, yeah, so do I.

"Anyway, I have two free tickets to the football game this Saturday. Will you come? I know you and Daddy can't both come, but I hoped you could drive up for the day. I feel like a baby asking. I know Daddy would just say yes and show up, but you're the one I want. Now I sound like I'm seven. You know I'm bad at asking for attention. I'm actually glad to be leaving a message. Okay. Well. Call me back. Love you."

When I called back, she let it go to her voice mail. That's my girl: the queen of avoidance, trained by her own mother. I left a message. "Hey, Bethany, I'd love to watch football with you this weekend. Maybe after the game you can come home with me and stay over Saturday night. Joey and Daddy would love to see you. We can sleep in on Sunday and then I'll make you all a big breakfast. Thanks for asking. I miss you and love you. 'Bye, honey."

Now it is Saturday, November twelfth. Bethany isn't at her football game. I'm not there with her. Nobody is where they're supposed to be.

Bethany studies the full calendars in my planner, and then rifles through the empty pages of the months to come. *I think I need a planner now.* Despite her tears, she picks up the pen and writes in the days she has exams and papers due in November.

| | | |

ON THE MORNING of college move-in day last August, I woke Joey before dawn and carried his dense little body to the van. Bethany and Eddie were almost finished loading all her clothes and books into the back. Though it was early, Bethany wore full makeup and had curled the stubby ponytail of her half-grown-out hair. The makeup contrasting with the ponytail pulled on my heart. She was trying so hard to be grown up, yet she was still our little girl. I caught Eddie's eye.

"After I fill up the coffee thermos, we'll be all set," he said. "Bethany, will you wait out here with Joey?" He grabbed my hand as he rounded the side of the van and pulled me back into the house, muttering something about needing help.

In the kitchen, he turned to me and wrapped me in his

arms. I rested my head on his chest and let him pretend he was holding me when really I was holding him up. Bethany was her dad's girl. He would miss her, despite all of what he called "her drama."

"She'll be fine, Eddie," I said. "She's strong and smart. We did a good job with her."

He rested his chin on the top of my head and said, "I know. I just can't imagine leaving her there. All alone. It feels like we're taking her into the woods and leaving her for the wolves."

"This is what kids do: they grow up and they leave. We fought so hard to get her to apply to college, and all those hours you spent with her shadowing you at work, helping her find her own way to nursing—it'll all be worth it. She'll be stronger for it."

He was quiet for a minute and then said, "She's going to cry."

"No way. It takes a lot to make Bethany cry."

"This isn't a lot? You watch. I'm right. It's going to be a hard day."

"We'll see. Let's get that coffee and pack up some Pop-Tarts for a treat." I unclenched his arms from around me and found some snacks.

At the end of the day, Eddie was right. After we hugged her and she walked us to the van, our daughter, the new college freshman, looked stricken. When we got in the van and closed the doors and Joey suddenly understood what was happening, he started his hiccup crying and howled, "No, Bethy! Come home with us!"

That set her off, and she stood there weeping and looking simply pathetic. Eddie opened his window and reached to her. She took his hand and said, "Just go, Daddy. I'm going to cry whether you go now or later. It doesn't matter. Just go. I'll be fine."

We pulled away with both of our children in broken pieces,

Joey wailing and Bethany dripping silent tears. Eddie was strong. He laid his big hand on my thigh and left it there while I joined in and cried all the way home.

Less than a week after we abandoned our daughter at college, Eddie entered his yearly funk and deserted me. I lived the last two months of my life without my daughter or my best friend.

13
Mom, Again

EDDIE HOLDS the full glass of milk and spoon while Joey pours in a pile of chocolate syrup. The bottom inch of the glass turns brown, and still Eddie doesn't make him stop squeezing the bottle. Joey eyes his dad, who is oblivious and staring over Joey's head out the window.

Still holding the syrup bottle, Joey says, "Mommy wouldn't let me have that much chocolate," and walks away.

Eddie hands the glass and spoon to Bethany and then trudges to the garage to stare at his rakes and shovels. Bethany clanks the spoon in slow circles, watching the brown swirls dissolve. In one gulp, she drinks all of the dark chocolate milk down.

I always let her put in as much syrup as she wanted.

When she finishes drinking, she wipes away her mustache, and I see that my daughter, my firstborn, is once again crying. *Mom? Where are you? I miss you.*

I know, Bethany. I miss you too. I'm right here, honey.

She still doesn't hear me. This is the most frustrating aspect of death: the absolute isolation from communication with my family. I am no longer a mom for my children.

"Give her time," my mother answers out of nowhere, or perhaps everywhere. "Bethany's pain shields her ability to detect your presence." Our constant friction and head-butting had the same effect when I lived. I never could breach that towering wall.

Together we watch my daughter wander through the quiet

house. She picks up the fat cat and sits in her dad's blue chair to continue her crying.

I can't watch anymore. I decide it's time to find some answers. "I have a lot of questions," I tell my mother.

"Of course you do. I can answer some of them, if you like," she offers. "But most of the answers will come to you on their own. Relax and absorb. You already know more than you think you do."

I don't feel like I know anything yet, but bouncing ideas off her mind always gave me strength when I was young and she'd call home from England or Africa or wherever she happened to be that month. "Let's start with the very first thing you told me after I died. You said I could depart. Where will I depart to?"

"It's not a departure like leaving New York City on a train, dear. Your departure won't take you from one place to the next. You have the power to make the choice to join the fabric of the universe."

"What the hell is the fabric of the universe?"

To her credit, Mom doesn't sound as exasperated with me in death as she often did in life. "The fabric of the universe is composed of a complex weave of space, layered with matter, sprinkled with antimatter, and bound with threads of time." Her voice, confident and competent, is familiar and comforting, even though I cannot understand what she's talking about. "Your consciousness, what is left of what you consider 'me,' was a distinct piece of the antimatter of the cosmos, which, during your life, was combined with the matter of a special, quite misunderstood region of your brain to generate the energy that was your life force."

Misunderstood part of my brain? Though it was tempting to follow her down this rabbit hole of questions, I had my own long list of other mysteries to solve. "So if I depart, where will I be?"

It takes a long time to get my answer. In fact, I think she might be gone. Worlds rotate, galaxies revolve. I wait with my newfound patience, a trait recently added to my superpowers; I'd never been accused of being anything like patient before I crossed to the dead side.

Finally, my mother says, "Everywhere." I can hear the smile in her voice. It sounds just like when I was little, when she was always thrilled to do what she called her motherly duty—to reveal the wonders of the world to me.

"How is that possible?" It doesn't make a speck of sense to me, and I'm getting a bit irritated.

Mom refuses to let me go. "As antimatter, we're particles that act in harmony. We've shed the burden of our earthly matter, that body you claim to miss, and combined with the fabric of the universe where we become pure cosmic energy. That makes us virtually massless, so we may travel at light speed. It takes no time to travel this way. No time, Anna. Imagine it! We are simply everywhere, and we exist in all time."

"All time? No time?" No wonder she loves the dead side. My mother understands even more about everything than she did as a brilliant human during her life. But I still don't get it. "How can there be no time?"

"Honey, from the perspective of energy, there is no such thing as time. Think about it. On the dead side, there is no reality to the Earth concept of *now*." So far, her tone is coaxing, patient, with just the slightest edge of annoyance creeping in that this might not be crystal clear to her dense daughter. "Surely you read and tried to comprehend Einstein's theories?"

When my mother switched to her professor voice, it meant I had to be on my toes.

"Of course, Professor McElveen, you made me read it in third grade." She laughs at my whiff of sarcasm. "Time stops at light speed. Does that mean I can come back to Earth whenever I need to?"

"You won't need to come back; you'll always be there, and everywhere, at all times, for all of eternity." Her voice trails off into the immense silence that permeates the dead side, confident she has explained all that needs explaining.

I am flabbergasted by the logical complexity, hypnotized as Mom's intelligent voice continues, inviting my understanding. "You know our little planet is a special place. The energy of life on Earth has been successfully reproduced less than a dozen times in all of eternity in all of the billions of galaxies. During an immense majority of the millennia of our planet's existence, our world was uninhabited by any energy-life forms at all. After the blink of the lifespan of that energy, life as we know it will cease on our little rock. But life, that special combination of matter and antimatter existing in just the perfect conditions of atmosphere, temperature, and environment, has appeared in other times and places. The trick is to glimpse life when it happens."

"Glimpse life when it happens? Come on, Mom. How can you use words like 'when' if there is no such thing as time?"

"Good point. It is all too magnificently complex to be captured by the language of mere humans."

"So to recap: when I depart, I will be everywhere at all time. That's what you said, right?"

"That's the raw essence of existing as pure energy, Anna. The ability to travel at light speed allows a slower passage of time. Or a stoppage of time. Or even a reversal of time."

I can roughly comprehend what she's saying but need some time alone to dissect and digest it. It's all very intriguing, and I am relieved to get some help in this confusing death saga. Still, I need a break from the science, so I change the subject and ask, "Where's my dad?"

"Your father chose the Earth version of heaven." Her gentle voice indicates Mom is back again and the professor went on break. "He always loved nature and camping and gardening and having that pack of dogs with him. All that touchy-feely emotional stuff I couldn't care less about. It's a wonder we lived together for so long. But we are together whenever I am near Earth, which, as I've clearly explained, is always and never. This speed of light travel stuff is the best." This is really still my mom, atoms or no atoms.

"You say I need to absorb and answers will come to me, but you know I'm not a patient person."

"If you would just relax and try to think, you'll remember that you do understand this." I have exasperated and disappointed my mother in death just like I always did in life.

"I am thinking, Mom. That's all I seem to be able to do here. But I can't control my thoughts, what I watch, where I go. There is no focus. I just jump around and around." I'm frustrated. It's hard for me to admit my confusion to my mother.

I can feel a mom-smile and something like a hug in her voice when she says, "Try not to worry about how long things seem to take. Gaining control takes practice. You have to let yourself adjust. And when you're truly ready to depart, you'll know."

"Well, what I know for sure is that I don't feel ready to do anything like departing, whatever the hell that means. I want to watch more of my family as their time actually passes."

"I understand. These things are all in your power to choose. When you have decided to depart or need to ask more questions of me, I'll be here."

Mom leaves, I think. I feel alone again and a little guilty to be relieved by her absence. I get a break from the hot seat imposed by her presence. Free from her supervision, I let myself drift in time and space, curious about where and when I'll end up, but relaxed enough to just let it happen.

14
Baby Foot

THE SUN COMES IN through the sheer lacy curtains and lights the room. It's early, but the baby usually wakes by now. Under the frilly edge of the pink blanket all that shows is the seashell bottom of a tiny foot. I put my hand on her back, just a feather of a touch, the way my mom always did to just make sure the baby was breathing. Just a little pat to make her stir and make me relax.

But she doesn't move.

I reach down and rub the little foot and find it cold. I unwrap the rest of her tiny body and turn her onto her back. She is so still, like she is just sleeping. I lean down to her face and listen for breathing.

Nothing.

The scene plays like a slow-motion silent movie with viscous momentum. A man comes in the room. He is a grown-up version of my son. I hand the still baby to him. He begins CPR. I watch for endless minutes as he breathes into her tiny face.

Nothing.

We have lost another one.

| | | |

"MOM! MOM! WHAT IS THIS?" I scream into the endless void.

"Oh, Anna, I'm sorry. Looking to the future can hurt," she says.

"That's the future? I thought it was a nightmare."

"Quite like a nightmare."

"My Joey is only five, and I just saw him, and he must have been at least twenty-five."

"Of course, Anna, he must get older."

"I get that. That's not the problem. I mean, that was horrible. But, Mom, *I* was there in the future. I wasn't dead. Tell me how that's possible."

"I didn't think we'd have to get to this so soon, but you always were a questioner. Okay, get ready because you have to think. The last time we talked, you had questions about time and about your antimatter after you died. I thought you understood all of that quite well."

"I think I do, Mom. On Earth, time just marches on. Time stops on the dead side. There is no time. Without the constraints imposed by our faulty concept of time, we are free to travel through time just like we always travel through space. Time travel. That would explain why I could stay in slow time and watch my family in the day after my death, or speed up time to see the future. But I did not voluntarily do this. I did not speed up on purpose to see the future. It just happened."

"No, it did not just happen, dear. You decided to do it, whether you are aware of that or not. Light speed travel is instantaneous. The newly dead need many experiences to comprehend it and learn to navigate."

"Okay. Whatever. I'll get better at it." I'm flustered and confused. "But that's still not the point. How was I *there*? What was my matter doing in the future? I mean, I thought it was just my imagination, just a nightmare, but it was real? I want to know how I was *there*!"

"You must have chosen to be there," she declares.

"What does *that* mean?" I roar.

Silence.

Infinite silence, deep and chilling. This quiet is unfathomable to the living because on Earth, in life, when there is a quiet time that we call silence, there's always some sound. The wind. A cricket. Breathing. A motor. Someone burps. A bird tweets. But on the dead side, in the near vacuum that is the space between the densely packed particles of planets and moons and stars, there is so much nothingness, emptiness, that it is unimaginable until it is experienced.

Yet I can still read this silence: my mother is pissed.

She never dealt well with confrontation. Once when the principal called from school to report that Michelle and I had cut our afternoon classes, my mom hung up on him. I need to be more circumspect in my questioning.

"Sorry. Mom?" Where the hell did she go this time?

Nothing. Infinite black space twinkles its suns and stars and waits along with me. It's peaceful and tempting to just relax into it. But I need to understand. How was I alive in the future?

"Please come back, Mom," I beg. "I need your help here. This would make up for so many years when Michelle and I had to figure out everything for ourselves."

"What are you blubbering about? I always answered all of your questions!"

"Only if you were in the country to hear about them."

"Aw. I did travel a lot. Those were the best perks of my full professorship. Sabbaticals in Europe and Japan. That was my Earth-heaven."

Good, she was back. Time to charge back into it, this time without pissing her off. Tricky. I have to get her to focus. The woman is still brilliant but, oh, so exasperating.

"I just need to ask some simple questions. Little questions. Slowly. Can you give me simple answers?"

"I'll try. Shoot."

"Have you ever traveled to the Earth future?"

"Yes."

"Did you do it on purpose, or did it just happen to you?"

"I thought it was just happening at first. But after a few

terrifying trips, I wanted some control over it, so I tried to figure out what I was doing to make it happen."

"What were you doing?"

"Well, I liked to pop in to check on you and the kids and even that awful Mr. Ed you married."

"Good to know," I interrupt, "but what were you doing to make it happen?"

"Well, you see, when you flit around at the speed of light enjoying your personal exploration of the entire universe, it's easy to lose track of Earth time. My goodness, once I stopped back and the world was covered in a thick, black cloud. I didn't dare go into that mess. I hoped it was the far-distant future and popped away."

"Tell me about this popping that you do. Do you control that?"

"In a way, yes. I just think of where I want to be, and if I think of *when* I want to be, too, I usually hit it right. But if I just think of where, like Philadelphia with your dad, I could end up in the delivery room pushing out your sister. Ugh. That's a nasty place to find yourself surprised."

"So, if I want to be with Eddie and Bethany, but don't think of *when*, I could end up in the past, present *or* future?"

"That's right, dolly. See, you've been so focused on your death that you've been hovering within days of it. But when you asked about future travel, I figured you were onto it. I hope I warned you adequately. Peeking into the future can be appalling."

"All right, that's scary, but I think I understand a little better about controlling where and when I go. But you still haven't explained how I was there in the future. I was alive there. Mom, how did I do that?"

"Honey, the mysteries of life and death and outer space and all the contradictions of physics have baffled humans since they became a conscious species. They have invented myths to explain every natural phenomenon they have encountered, and they cling stubbornly to those myths well after they fully and scientifically understand. I tried to help you keep your mind open in life to every possible answer to all of life's questions. That was my motherly duty. It turns out there are even more questions to be answered in death. The universe is infinitely more complex than our beloved little planet. You are just beginning your journey of questions. Let the answers come to you. I can reassure you that the answers are there, but I cannot explain it all to you. Full understanding of your choices is a personal mission. And even when you do understand your choices, I can't help you make the right one. Each choice is right."

"What kind of choices? What are you talking about?" I demand. I know perfectly well that her professor speeches are cloaked in smoke and mirrors to cover up when she intends to deliberately dodge my questions. I also recognize that she is too stubborn to be forced out from behind the smoke when she wants to hide.

I feel a mom-hug in her voice as she assures me, "You're my smart girl. You'll see."

She leaves.

So I try it again. I let myself think of Eddie and wait, curious to see where these thoughts take me.

15
Nightmare in the Future

THE STREET IS SO CROWDED with people and filth that, though he has a firm grip on my hand, I have trouble keeping up with Eddie. On his other side, Bethany holds tight to his arm as he pushes through the crowd to the barred front door of a hotel. He bangs on the glass and shows his medical identification, and we are allowed inside. It is an enormous luxury to find a place to stay for the night.

We sleep in our clothes. Eddie wakes me before dawn. "Anna. We have to get out of here."

I drag my old body up, grab my backpack, and the three of us leave the safe shelter of the hotel. Bethany is older—maybe in her thirties. We find a crowded restaurant that serves weak coffee and toast. We stay there the entire day because the street is closed, barricaded by what appear to be military police. With no working satellites, our cell phones are useless. Eddie and Bethany will not be able to get to the wounded today. We wait, cold and hungry, listening to gunshots, worrying all afternoon.

An hour after dark, we sneak out a side door. We lose Eddie in a crowd. Men grab me and Bethany and pull us back into the restaurant. They throw me to the floor and drag Bethany away through a door to what must be the kitchen.

Eddie comes back and finds me on the floor.

"They took her, Eddie!"

He bangs on the door, yelling that Bethany is a nurse and is under protection for her skills.

I meet the eye of a stranger who hands me a gun.

The kitchen door cracks open, and Eddie is pulled in. I follow.

When they accuse Eddie of theft, he hurls an empty glass bottle at a burly man and hits him in the face. I slip past in the fight to where Bethany sits, bruised and crying, while two men argue about what to do with her. Without hesitation, I pull the trigger, blowing a hole in the wall. Eddie grabs Bethany and pulls her out.

I lower the gun.

We run.

| | | |

WHAT THE HELL was that?

"Quite like a nightmare, I know," my mother's voice soothes.

I demand, "Was that one real, too?"

Mom sounds exasperated when she replies, "What does 'real' mean? The meaning of the word is as elusive as always. Layers of time and reality allow for infinite possibilities, Anna. Not all of them are pleasant, and not all of them occur."

"Another nightmare on the dead side? Help me get away from it."

"The effect is quite like when you woke from nightmares in life. You have to rise up to full consciousness and will yourself away from it. Declare a time or a place, or both."

"Just bring me back to my real life." I almost laugh. What is real life?

"That's too vague. Pick a place."

"I don't know—how about just take me home again?" I don't care at all. I just want to get away. Far away from the dark feeling of that bad dream.

"Past or present?" she asks.

"Present. Let me see what Eddie's up to."

"Still hung up on that man, aren't you?"

"He's my kryptonite, I guess. I want to know if he's hurting or happy."

"There you go," Mom says as she leaves. It feels like maybe this time she nudged me in the right direction.

16

Another Lesson and a Palindrome

DEATH HAS NUMBED some of the pain of my crumbling marriage. It was lucky for Eddie that I kicked the bucket and relieved him of the nasty burden of me.

Now, he sits alone and quiet on my swing. He looks so formal in his suit and tie and stiff dress shoes. He also looks sad. I wonder if it's harder on him that I died while we were fighting. He was fighting; I was just playing possum and trying to survive. But he was ready for a fight any minute of any day or night. Tiptoeing around his moods was exhausting. I went to work on November eleventh because I needed to get away from him.

While we were fighting, Eddie and I had an unspoken contest to see who could withhold attention, and especially eye contact, the longest. For months, I never caught him looking at me. This made my life as desolate as our lack of touch. When your best friend won't spread his gaze over you, you become invisible. Eddie looked away or down, even during the few times when we spoke. The man was guilty of something. At first, I played along in self-defense. Eventually, I became certain that he'd never look at me again, so I began to study him. While reading, mowing the lawn, paying bills, tucking Joey in bed or watching TV, his sad eyes and downturned lips revealed his disgust with his life. With me.

I continue my self-torture and study him still, now from the dead side, trying to understand this man I used to know as well as I knew myself. I'm not seeing what I expect. If I'd died last spring, back when he was my prince, I'd expect him to be devastated. I died during his funk, though, when it was obvious that Eddie suffered from my mere presence in the room. I expected him to be relieved, like I feel. But he looks like a man destroyed by the loss of his wife. This baffles me.

"Yes, Mr. Ed does looks pathetic, Anna."

I'm startled by her voice in my thoughts. "Mom, did I call you?"

"No, dear, it's like cell phones. I can call you, too."

I haven't been interrupted by my mom in years. "You never liked Eddie, did you?"

"Not much, no," she says, point blank and frank as always. "He took you away."

"But getting married always takes people from their parents. What was the big deal with Eddie and me?"

"The big deal was that he changed your plans so drastically. You were accepted to the doctoral program in physics at Cornell. How could you turn away from that to become a high school teacher?"

She really didn't get us. "Those were *your* plans for me. I was following along because it was the easiest thing to do. Don't rock the boat. Don't make people mad. I have the same confrontational issues as you. But Eddie fell for me. Nobody had ever loved me before. Nobody had ever thought I was beautiful before. I was always the ugly, nerd sister."

Mom is quiet for a while. "I thought you were beautiful."

"That doesn't count. You're my mom; you *have* to think I'm beautiful. You probably thought so when I was a wrinkled, old-man newborn."

"I did. But something didn't feel quite right with you and that man. It all happened too fast. I wasn't convinced. Obviously, you were in love. You were delirious. But you were also incoherent—so different from my normal, level-headed, capable Anna. Do you remember what you told me when you said you were marrying this perfect guy? Do you remember why you were so sure, so soon, that Mr. Ed was the one?"

"I could just feel it. Love might be as hard to explain as this timelessness that I'm still struggling with."

"Well, you didn't express that feeling very clearly. What you told me and your father was that your fiancé had the perfect last name."

"I did?"

"You did. And that's about all you offered as justification for marrying Mr. Ed in such a hurry and for changing all of your—all right—*our* plans."

I think back to our discussion about Eddie's last name. It's my name now and has been for half my life. I take it for granted. Then, suddenly, I remember. Mostly I remember the dead silence on the other end of the phone when I broke my big news to my parents. "I told you his name was a palindrome, just like 'Anna,' didn't I?"

"Exactly."

"You know how I love palindromes. Oh! I remember you argued with me that Wixim wasn't a palindrome."

"Yes. And that was my biggest mistake. Instead of arguing that a palindrome last name is a weak sign that your love would last forever, I argued that Wixim wasn't a palindrome, as though convincing you of that would make you change your mind. Your father watched and listened in horror from across the kitchen table as I wrote W-I-X-I-M on a piece of paper and whispered to him that our brilliant daughter was marrying this strange man named Ed because she thought his name was a palindrome."

"I remember. You were going a little bonkers over the phone, yelling that Wixim is definitely not a palindrome, and then all of a sudden you went silent. I thought you'd passed out, or we were disconnected."

"That's when your dad rotated the paper upside-down to

me and showed me your unique rotational palindrome. What kind of mind notices these things? I was shocked into silence."

"That wasn't the only reason I knew Eddie was right for me. My feelings were so strong and undeniable, so right and certain, but, at the same time, I couldn't explain them. Not with mere words."

"Do you remember ranting about elevens?" Mom asks.

"Elevens?" Of course I remember, but I want to hear her take on it.

"You said Wixim has elevens both ways. 'Roman elevens! Roman elevens!' And you loved elevens. The time 11:11, the date November eleventh—you were a bit obsessed. And you insisted that the Roman numeral eleven 'both ways'," she mimics me, "in his last name was the most perfect married name for you."

She's right. I was a little crazy then. I decided not to remind her of how much I loved my first name back when she first taught me about element symbols when I was eight years old. I was thrilled that my palindrome first name was made from the symbol for sodium, Na, frontwards and backwards. Sodium reacts violently with water, forming explosive hydrogen gas, sparks, and flames. And, drum roll, please, its atomic number is eleven. No kidding. My obsession with elevens was my mother's fault in every way. I'm a geek, just like her.

With Eddie, though, I lost my head with my heart. I was just so caught up in being in love. But I did die on November eleventh, so the elevens of my obsession did turn out to be significant. Was that a coincidence? I decide not to push this sore spot with my mom anymore just now. I'm sure I'll need more of her help, and I don't want her mad or distracted. I avoid confrontation in death just like I did in life. Instead, I try to convince her that Eddie, the guy I almost divorced, was the right guy way back then.

"But look at him now, Mom. He misses me. We were

fighting two days ago, and now he misses fighting with me."

"Anna, I watched enough since I died to see that he loved you. I saw what I couldn't see while I was living. Alive, I just knew he had you, so I had to give you up. That's a hard lesson for a parent."

Once again, she's gone, just like a dropped cell phone call.

17

Getting Ready, Letting Go

BETHANY'S CELL PHONE SINGS an old Elton John love song and wakes up Joey. She lets it ring. Joey comes down the stairs in his Superman pajamas, humming "Rocket Man," and he goes straight to the bottom cabinet where he digs to find a big bowl.

"Hey, Joe-boy." Bethany grabs him to kiss the top of his head. I miss the sweaty boy smell of the top of his head. "Want me to make some pancakes?" He wiggles out of her hug.

"Nah. Daddy bought me Fruity Pebbles." He climbs up the pantry shelves and topples down the box. After a struggle to rip open the inner bag, he pours the cereal into the big bowl. He opens the fridge, holding his spoon up like a weapon, and stares into the bright box for a full minute. Without turning around, he says into the cold air, "Bethany, will you help with the milk? It's too heavy. Mommy used to leave me a cup on the bottom shelf."

Only a few days ago I left a cup of milk for my son on the bottom shelf of our fridge and already he's saying I *used to* do it.

"Sure. Grab me a bowl. I'm having some of these, too. I haven't seen sugar in the morning at this house since before you were born."

"What was it like before I was born?"

Bethany pours milk in his bowl, snorts, and says, "Quiet." She eats a spoonful of her cereal and gags. *Kid food. Ick.*

After she puts a bagel into the toaster and pours the sickly sweet cereal down the drain, she starts a fresh pot of coffee. *I'm gonna need some $C_8H_{10}N_4O_2$ to get through this day.*

My daughter tells my son, "Hurry up with that cereal, Joey. We need to get dressed for Mom's memorial service."

My memorial service. Cripes. I might just need some of that caffeine myself.

| | | |

EDDIE WAITS for the rest of our clan to get ready. He's all alone outside on my swing, not swinging. Just sitting still as stone, staring at nothing. Somehow, he found Joey's little blue suit and some dark socks and has them ready, all laid out on his bed to wrestle Joey into. Now, for a few minutes of peace, he just sits in the sun and lets his thoughts leave again. *Empty-headed is the best way to be.*

This time we agree. I wish I could stay empty-headed.

On the couch in the library, Michelle sips black coffee. The pile of used tissues beside her tells me she has not managed to reach Eddie's empty-headed state. She holds a pen over a page of scribbled notes and hums. A bowl of half-eaten Fruity Pebbles rests on the floor at her feet.

My family looks pretty good today. Everyone is awake, getting ready, and even eating.

Mom's voice answers me. "Yes. It doesn't take long. The energy created by matter's union with antimatter compels life to continue, even though your family will miss your atoms and your presence every day."

"And I'll miss them every day."

"Even Mr. Ed?" she challenges.

"Please stop calling him Mr. Ed. Eddie's a smart guy. Not at all like a talking horse."

My Eddie earned his doctorate in electrical engineering and then went on to medical school and worked as a pediatric oncologist for a dozen years. After all of this my mother still never gives him any credit.

"At least you could call him Dr. Ed," I say, wondering why

I am defending the man.

Mom considers this. "Hmm, Dr. Ed. D-R-E-D. I kind of like that. Do you think he'd rather be called Dread than Mr. Ed? I could be like you and endear him by calling him *my* Mr. Ed, if you prefer."

"Mo-ther," I moan.

"Sorry, old habits die hard—no pun intended. Did you know today is your cremation and memorial service?"

"Yes, I saw Eddie write it in purple ink in my planner."

"Ooh, purple ink. That sounds serious. He wrote it in your planner?"

"That's what Eddie does. He always read my lists. He liked to check what I did and didn't finish at the end of the day. I'd leave my planner out at night so he could look it over after I went to sleep. Some nights he started my list for the next day before he came to bed. We were a good match most of the time."

Again I hear myself defending him. Where is this coming from? Eddie drove me crazy and broke my heart, but I still defend him to my mother. After a long silence, she is wise to change the subject.

"I understand the need to linger nearby," she says. "But you will eventually have to make your final choice, Anna. It could help them all to heal and move on if you let them go and try to depart soon after the memorial service. Then stay away for a while."

How could I stay away? It all sounded so final. So over. The end. My finite little life reached its conclusion while I thought I was in the middle of the twisting plot of an odyssey. But it turns out I was the lead in a one-act play. The audience walked out when the director stopped the action. I always understood, in theory, that my body was only on loan to me, made up of borrowed, recycled, previously used atoms. Yet I am still bitter about giving it up.

"Cremation sounded like a good idea when I was alive. Now, the thought of such a rapid return and redistribution of my atoms, breaking down my proteins and amino acids to ash and smoke, seems the most final of all of the phases of death so far."

"Try not to worry about that. You don't need that body anymore, Anna. You can exist in death and make your choices without it. You have all you need at your disposal."

Death still doesn't make much sense to me. Especially the part about choices—I have no idea what she's talking about there. But I understand the grieving process from too much life experience. Memorials and funerals and wakes and the gatherings of family and friends afterward were always an unexpectedly comforting time. Dealing with the loss was harder alone, and being together, crying and hugging, laughing and eating, always helped. Maybe it would help me to be there, too.

"I'll try to depart, whatever that means, after the ceremony. I don't know if I can, Mom, but I'll try."

| | | |

"JOE!" Eddie calls from downstairs, ready to wrestle if needed, "time to get dressed."

"I *am* dressed, Daddy." Joey's innocent voice gives him away. The kid is up to something.

Eddie starts up the stairs. "No, buddy, you can't wear your baseball uniform to Mom's memorial service." A typical day in the Wixim house, except that I'm dead.

"Can I wear my cap?" That's my boy. Push and push.

"Nope."

"Can I wear my cleats? 'Cause Mommy loves my cleats and the clicky sound they make, so she'll know it's me."

"Sure, you can wear the cleats, but with your suit." Eddie gives in. He always did when I was alive. In the game of good cop, bad cop, Eddie was the so-good-he-could-hardly-be-true cop.

My protective shield has cracked. I got too close to Eddie, and he got into my head and I now hear him thinking. *You poor kid. You don't even understand what a memorial service is about. You still think your Mom will be there, don't you?*

I will be there, Eddie. But what do you care?

Joey smiles. *Only wanted the cleats anyway. Daddy's way easier than Mom.*

Eddie smiles back at him because he won't have to wrestle or bribe Joey to get him into the suit. *The tie could still be an issue, though.*

Ten minutes later, Joey charges into the kitchen in his blue suit and baseball cleats. He even has his tie on—in a knot around his head. Bethany and Michelle take turns hugging him and telling him how great he looks for his mom.

How come nobody's taking my picture like Mommy did on the first day of school?

Joey studies his adults and wonders about winning the cleat war. *Daddy looks funny in his shiny shoes with all that toilet paper stuck to his chin. Bethany won't quit crying.*

Aunt Michelle hugs me too much. She feels like Mommy, but she doesn't even know where the camera is. Mommy takes all my pictures. Without Mommy, there'll never be another picture of me ever again.

My poor family is a pitiful mess. I watch as they line up and trudge together to the car. Joey's cleats scratch at my hardwood floor, and I don't even give a damn. He has cookies stashed in his pockets. Bethany pours an extra mug of coffee, over sugars it, and brings it to the car. She hasn't showered in days. Michelle fiddles with a pile of paper scraps as she shoves dirty tissues up the sleeve of her sweater just like our mother used to do. She's humming to herself and crying her stupid mascara off.

Eddie, last out, hesitates at the door and turns back. He looks at my purse still on the floor beside the sneaker pile. He scans the kitchen, looks toward our bedroom door. *Still waiting for her.* Go ahead without me, Eddie. I'll be right behind you.

KIDS PARK their dads' shiny BMWs on the grass and boulevards. What a mess. People huddle together on the sidewalks in dark coats, and others push their way into the warmth of the stone building.

Since there is no body to view, the funeral directors and ushers quietly, but frantically, try to direct what looks like the entire high school population into the small chapel. They hand out programs and ask people to sit closer together to make room for more. Old Mrs. Smithers from down the street drove herself in her dead husband's pickup truck. She sits alone in the back row eyeing the noisy teenagers who fill the seats.

Programs? At a funeral? Well, aren't we special? That Anna was so full of herself. Thought she was so smart. Hmpff. If she was so smart, she wouldn't be dead. It's her own fault that she died.

How was it my fault?

Look at all those kids! So noisy in a church! Somebody should tell them to hush. She cranes her stringy neck around looking for an adult husher, but sees only ushers who are useless and the pompous principal of my high school parading in.

Mr. Carter walks stiffly down the aisle shaking hands and greeting students and parents. *Oh, my lord, this is horrible. Like a PTA meeting. So many people! Is it okay for a principal to genuflect in church? Well, this isn't my church, so I won't. We had to close school early again today so all these teachers and kids could come to this service. In the spring they'll forget they demanded this, and they'll all complain when we have to make up the school day. It's not my fault either way.*

He finds a single seat alone on the end of a pew and remains aloof, but the deep crease between his eyebrows gives him away: he is extremely worried. *How the hell am I going to find a science teacher this late in the school year? How can I explain to the media and the school board how this happened to our teacher? It isn't my fault what happened on Friday. It isn't my fault that we had to close school early today, either. Christ, they blame me for everything.*

My principal is worried that he'll be blamed for my death? What is going on? I can't remember how I died. Was it my fault? Why has that not occurred to me until now?

"Because, even though you are newly dead, you're my smart girl and you knew to focus on your family. The details of how you died are not important once you're dead. Not to the dead, anyway."

"Hi, Mom." Just when I begin to lurk around, to pick people's thoughts and snuggle in to revel in their sadness over the loss of me, spoilsport Mom pops in. "Thanks for coming."

"I wouldn't miss this, dear. Don't mind me. I'll be quiet and let you enjoy your misery. Oh, look at the lovely program—so formal. Your death is all organized, just like your life was."

~*~*~*~*~*~*~*~*~*~*~*~*~*~*~*~*~*~*~

Memorial for the internment of the soul of ANNA WIXIM
Procession of family
Pastor Jones—Surviving the departure of a loved one
Michelle McElveen, sister of the deceased
Chorus—River in Judea
Dr. Edward J. Wixim, husband of the deceased
Jazz Ensemble—Amazing Grace
Recessional

~*~*~*~*~*~*~*~*~*~*~*~*~*~*~*~*~*~*~

Melancholy organ music starts up from the balcony. People rise, unsure, in a hesitant wave that starts in the back of the sanctuary when old Mrs. Smithers lurches to her feet. My family walks down the center aisle. Bethany and Michelle hold each other up. Joey marches in his cleats, held in line by his father's large hand on the top of his head. Eddie's face is granite.

This hurts.

The music ends. Sniffles echo. Bodies rustle back into seats. The standing-room crowd maneuvers to lean on walls and pillars. I've been here before, but never as the dead one.

The minister talks for a while, but I don't listen so much to him. I just watch my family. Eddie's head is bowed, and his hand rests on Joey's leg, which kicks the wooden pew rhythmically to a beat in his head. Bethany sits straight and tall like a weeping statue beside Michelle, who keeps a protective arm around her shoulders.

Although I'm not listening to him, I do notice that the minister's comforting thoughts have made my students cry.

Little Wendy sits behind my family. *I loved Mrs. Wixim. Is it okay to love your teacher? If I didn't love her, this wouldn't hurt so much.*

Alex, a football player who graduated a few years ago, sits with other boys from the team near the front of the church. *Mrs. Wixim is dead. I can't believe it.* I remember Alex. He was the quarterback and homecoming king. So smart, but he didn't care at all about school except for sports and girls. *Man, little Tina Thomson is all grown up. She looks hot today. Heard she broke up with Brad. Maybe I'll get a minute with her later—hold her while she cries.* Crying, weeping noises dribble from the crowd of pretty girls sitting all around the football players. I wonder if they're crying for me, or just for attention from the guys.

There is James, one of my all-time favorite kids. Sweet blue eyes brimming with tears. He breaks my heart. If I had a heart. Can you cry when you're dead?

"Without the tears, but the feeling is the same." The voice of reason, my mother asks, "How're you doing?"

"This is rough. I might need to leave," I admit.

"I'll go if you will."

"Wait. Just a little more." I ignore my mother and concentrate for a few moments on this intelligent young man. When I taught James, I was pregnant with Joey. I was a cranky old pregnant mess, often grumpy, always tired. James wipes his nose on the back of his sleeve. *I remember when I came to Mrs. Wixim's class, I hated school. No teacher even noticed I was smart until she did. They only knew I was trouble. But Mrs. Wixim loved us even if she never said so. She was tough—just kept pushing and pushing. And those rules. She was a crazy woman with those rules. No excuses.* Yes, James, you were amazing. I followed your story and heard you are in graduate school. You'll make me proud.

I check on my family. Holding it together pretty well, I think, so I'll take a peek. What is Eddie thinking? *Anna. Anna. Anna. Anna. Anna. Anna. Anna. Anna.* Well, that's enlightening. He remembers my name.

Bethany? *They cremated Mom today. She's gone. Mom's body is really gone. There's nothing left of her. She's gone.* A steady stream of tears runs down her cheeks, leaving two growing wet spots on the shoulders of her jacket.

Joey? *They all said Mommy would be here.* He pivots his head like an owl and searches around the church. *I don't see her. Good thing I wore my cleats. They click real good on this wood floor. I get to do a lot of things now without Mommy telling me not to all the time. But I wish she would get here. I saved her a seat.*

Oh, my sweet boy, I'm sorry. I'm so sorry.

The song ends, and Michelle stands up. She watches the toes of her high heels walk up the three steps to the podium. I wait for it. And there it is. Gravity strikes again. She caught her toe on the top step. That's my sister. The chronic tripper.

God, Anna, I need some backup here. Or at least a hug. Help me with this one, will you?

"Mom, I need a break." I'm the one who needs the help.

"Sure. Let's get you away from here. We can come back

later if you want to."

"Take me somewhere and tell me how I died. And why it was my fault."

"Honey, I can take you somewhere, but I cannot tell you what you already know."

19
Last Lunch Duty

FRIDAY, NOVEMBER ELEVENTH, 11:00 a.m., first lunch. Like water escaping a high-pressure hose, hormonal teenage bodies blasted through the narrow doors into the cafeteria. They brought noise with their fragrant mass. I was accustomed to these attributes of the humans with whom I spent my working life. Teenagers are incessantly noisy, perpetually hungry, and relentlessly mad with hormones; I understood them. I even pitied them a little as I waited, impatient and unreasonable, for them to get on with their growing up.

Lunch duty was a dreaded event for me every Friday. I tried to trade for Mondays. I'd rather get this over with at the beginning of the week than have to face it, tired, at the end. I failed. Nobody would trade. Normal, intelligent college graduates do not become teachers because they have a burning desire to serve lunch duty. It is a shocking and hazardous fringe benefit for teachers to learn that they are expected to herd kids like cattle—to patrol them like a cop walking a beat, enforcing rules laid down by administrators. Lunch duty was comprised of too many moving parts: four hundred kids, one administrator, four grumpy lunch ladies, twenty-two minutes, 500 milligrams of ibuprofen, and me. It was a deadly mix.

I gave myself a pep talk. I only had lunch duty thirty-six times a year. Just twenty-two minutes each time. If I ended up teaching for thirty years, lunch duty would only consume about seventeen days of my life. Seventeen days. Ugh. Quit your whining, Anna. People spent more time in lines at the bank and grocery store and DMV. Some people are shoe salesmen. Some people scrape gunk off other people's teeth. Some people empty urine pans. This wasn't so bad. I said shut up to my calculating head and went in. I could survive this.

Two freshmen girls came in swinging their boyish hips, doing the look-at-me stroll. They dropped their book bags on a table to lay their claim and walked, showing their bellies and pierced navels, to the cookie line. They didn't even try to disguise their mission: they were prowling some senior boys. The boys ignored them, which of course made the flirts even louder.

The Goths sat together and didn't eat. Ever. One boy was busy pushing the end of a paperclip into his wiry, thin forearm. Another was reading a magazine with dark images on the cover. At least they can read. I held out my hand to Goth number one as I passed by. He looked up, non-confrontational. I glanced at the paperclip and nodded, and he dropped it in my hand. I tossed it in the trash on the way to the cookie line.

I wonder if these kids will be embarrassed one day to remember how they behaved in high school. It's agonizing to watch them try to figure out which version of themselves to be.

At the cookie line I made eye contact with one of the noisy freshmen flirters. She glared back at me, but I didn't look away. She became uneasy when I glanced down at her belly, which was not on display for me. She yanked down her shirt and gave me a sneer. I smiled a thank-you and walked away.

I was two-for-two and hadn't needed to yell or even speak yet. This luck couldn't hold up much longer.

At the pizza line, some of the free- and reduced-lunch kids were trying to buy pizza with their free tax dollars like they did every single Friday. The cashier was once again denying them this forbidden pleasure, and they were ganging up to argue with her. I stepped up to the leader at the front of the line and asked if I could offer my assistance.

He said, "What? Are you the Walmart greeter or something?" I wanted to backhand him.

I smiled my best fake teacher smile, glanced at his ID tag, and said, "It looks like you're in the wrong line, Pete. Let me put that food back for you so you can step over to the turkey-and-mashed-potato-entrée line."

He flipped over his picture badge and turned back to argue with the red-faced cashier. "Just ring up my pizza, will ya?"

"No, sir, I will not. You know the rules," she replied with a nod of her round, curly head. She crossed her arms the best she could across her flat, wide chest.

"But I don't want no turkey entrée. I want pizza."

"That's your misfortune," I said to the back of his head. "Come with me now, or I'll call the resource officer to escort you out of the cafeteria."

I'd dealt with this kid—I thought of him as Pizza Boy—for nine Fridays so far and was weary at the thought that I was facing a couple dozen more. Two months ago, when we first came face-to-face over his desire for pizza for lunch, I felt sorry for him. I took his side and pleaded his case with the cafeteria staff, while they explained the rules to me as they might to an imbecile—only the main entrée line was approved for subsidized lunches. It didn't make sense to me or to the kid, and I thought he'd appreciate that I went to bat for him. My efforts embarrassed him. On a subsequent Friday when he tried again to get the pizza, I offered to pay for him, which sent him over the edge. He flipped me off, and I had to report him to the administration. At this point, we had walked the tightrope of lunch rules together and frayed the line. It made no sense that we were fighting the same, futile battle again.

"Resource officer? Do you see him around here anywhere? Like he has time to deal with a freakin' lunch issue." Pizza Boy addressed me without turning around, posturing in front of his followers. While I watched the back of his greasy head, I heard him say, "Don't you know about the gangs in this school? And the drugs? And the guns?" He turned to me then, glaring into my eyes. "There are lots of guns, lady. You just don't know where they might turn up."

On my last Friday of lunch duty, I nodded to the cashier, and she pushed her button to call for the administration. I should have stayed quiet and waited for help. Instead, I was furious that he had the nerve to threaten me, and I said, "I don't care if you have a gun." I could barely get a full breath I was so furious with him. "It is time for you to stop blocking this line. If you're hungry and have a gun but no money, your only lunch option is the turkey. I expect to be obeyed. Immediately. Now, *move!*" A bit loud, even in the noisy cafeteria, I managed to get the attention of a hundred students, but there still wasn't an administrator in sight.

He didn't talk back this time. Somehow in the last few years I had managed to disregard my small size, and I never backed down to any kid. They were all children, no matter how tough they seemed. My poor Pizza Boy realized he'd lost again. He dropped his tray of pizza on the floor, ducked between the bars, and stormed to the back of the cafeteria.

Well, at least he was gone. Still no administrators. I sighed.

Seventeen minutes to go. The ibuprofen wasn't working.

I grabbed a cup of water and trudged to my designated post by the door. Technically, once the lines of kids died down, my job was to keep them penned in, to stand by the door and just say no. This was the best part of lunch duty because there was no need for discussion. The rule was no students were allowed to leave through my door and no one could enter. Simple. It was no longer a door, just an extension of the wall.

A big girl with long, oily hair approached me, and I wondered why kids didn't wash their hair anymore. Hairs, I corrected myself and smiled. I liked plurals with and without the extra s. She asked, "Hey, can I go to the math hall and use the soda machine?"

"No."

Insistent and craving sugar, she whined, "Why not? Come on. I can't drink that crappy milk again."

"Sorry. Nobody leaves the cafeteria during lunch," I said with a smile. She deserved a smile at least, if I had to deny her a caffeine fix.

She gave up and walked away with a groan. While I was busy with her, two other kids approached with requests. I dealt with one—I said no—while the other tried to sneak out the door. This was a blatant, coordinated approach to escape. I turned in time to see the door closing on him and chased him into the hall. He came back in.

Fifteen minutes to go. When did I sign up to be a cop? All the science and math rattling around in my brain served no purpose on lunch duty.

There was a commotion by the wall of windows. That meant I needed to abandon my door to investigate. Two girls were in each other's faces and ready to brawl. Girl fights were the worst. They'd claw and scratch and pull each other's hair and would not let go. I once saw an administrator get a bloody nose trying to break up a girl fight. At our last professional development training, we were ordered to avoid confrontation or contact with students. Basically, we were expected to wait for the kids to fight it out. The mom in me couldn't stand that, though. I always thought of my own kids when I watched one student hurt another and felt compelled to act in their parent's place and try my best to stop the pain. In prefight, especially with girls when they're just warming up and yelling, I could usually break it up by yelling louder.

In my giant teacher voice, I roared, "Girls! That's enough!"

My interruption made them step apart enough for me to get in the center of the battle. I knew one of them and turned to her. "Ashley, how are you doing on those hurdles this year?"

"Fine," she said, without taking her eyes off the other girl for an instant.

I turned to the other young lady. "You don't know me yet, but if you fight in the cafeteria on my lunch duty, you will never be rid of this face. Saturday after Saturday we will sit together while you do algebra problems until the end of time. Sound like fun?"

"I thought you got expelled for fighting, not just a Saturday detention?"

I lowered my voice and privately said to her, "I like you. You're a smart one—too smart to fight at school. Please, go and sit down."

She glared at Ashley, and I thought she'd take a cheap swing. Instead, she turned on her heel and walked away, head held high. I felt myself exhale and realized I'd been holding my breath.

"Thanks, Mrs. Wixim," said Ashley before she sauntered the other way.

Good fight. They both thought they won.

This lunch duty was never going to end. I was getting hungry. No lunch for me on Fridays. There might be a crumbled granola bar at the bottom of my purse. Or maybe I could eat a spoonful of peanut butter before my last class if I could get out of the cafeteria in time to beat the crowds to my room. But I'd need a plastic spoon. I could see them across the cavernous room right beside the grumpiest cashier. Maybe I could grab one on the way back to my guard post.

I was deep in my snack planning and making a beeline for my spoon when I heard screaming from my door. The panic on the faces of the children stunned me. Then, someone screeched, "Gun! He's got a gun!" and hundreds of kids were all running, panicked, across the cafeteria toward the other door. The noise was deafening.

I didn't hear or see a gun, so whoever had one hadn't used

it yet. Instead of joining the throngs running for the far door, I ran to my door. I still didn't see anyone with a gun. That didn't mean it wasn't there. Then I saw my pizza-not-turkey boy. He was walking fast.

Right toward me.

In the middle of this terror I checked my watch again.

It was 11:11.

20

How Did I Die?

"MOM, THAT'S ALL I REMEMBER. Why can't I remember what happened next?"

"That's all you can remember about Pizza Boy, honey, because that's all he let you see. I've watched him from here, though, and the perspective is enlightening. He was hungry and sad, lonely and so frustrated. He wanted to show you that you could not deny him what, in his mind, was rightfully his. This unfortunate young man had a terrible morning. His mom stayed out drinking all night. He rocked his baby sister until four in the morning, when she finally settled down and went to sleep. He overslept, missed the bus, and was late for his math test first period. He was assigned detention on Saturday for being late, which meant he'd be late for work and would lose some pay. He uses his own money to support his little sister when his mom doesn't get hold of it first to spend on gin. Every aspect of his life spiraled out of his control. Your little confrontation made him snap."

I tried to remember his face. It was a blur. He was just another kid to deal with in the duties of my day. One hundred and eighty days, a couple thousand kids a day. It was an overwhelming zoo. Compared to the students in my classes, who I knew personally and became completely invested in, the kids who misbehaved in the hall and cafeteria were just part of the duty of my job. They weren't encompassed in the joy of my job, the real reason I pulled my body out of bed before dark each day to come back to the brilliant students I loved. I didn't

laura lanni

teach the hallway kids or the lunchroom kids; I corralled them. We were all just trying to survive the best we could.

Assuming they would do what I said cured a lot of my headaches and worries. Masses of kids always did what I said, so I didn't have to see them as people, as individuals, only as kids to be dealt with while I skipped eating my own lunch. It seems Pizza Boy got caught in my radar that day. I certainly registered on his.

I try hard to sift through the chaos in the cafeteria to remember what happened to me. It must have been Pizza Boy. He must have had a gun. Did I make him so mad he killed me? I have a chilling flash. "Mom, I remember something else."

"Now, honey, it's probably better not to dwell on that day too much. Separation of matter from antimatter is a stressful event."

"Stressful?" My mother is still queen of the understatement. It wasn't emotionally stressful. That can't be what she means. It was physically stressful. Like a trillion forces pulling on a single point. The rippage was brilliant, like the blazing white energy of burning magnesium.

"Let me tell you what I do remember," I insist. "You already know it, I can tell, but I just need to say this. I remember an ambulance. Eddie is beside a bed, and a paramedic is calling for help, and another paramedic climbs in with a tube, and Eddie yells, 'No! No! Do not resuscitate!' Eddie is just kneeling there, crying. Eddie is a doctor. So why is he crying? Then I look down, and the dead body is me. Oh, God, they didn't try to resuscitate me. Why not, Mom?"

"You were bleeding heavily from the main artery in your left leg. And you had a severe concussion—probably from falling—and you were unconscious. You had lost so much blood before anyone got to you. They were worried about brain damage. They believed that if you recovered, you wouldn't run again, maybe not walk again, and there was a chance you would be in a coma indefinitely."

"Oh, Eddie. Poor Eddie."

Mom is quiet for a long time while I agonize over what I made Eddie endure—both before and after I left him.

"Mom? Are you still here?"

"Oh, Anna, couldn't you hear me?"

"You were talking?"

"Here we go again. I'm talking, and you can't hear me. There's some glitch here. Either you don't want to hear what I say, or a greater power is blocking us. The effect is the same: you cannot or may not hear the details about your death from me. Your dad explained these silent voids to me like this: the answers to some questions cannot be supplied by anyone else. These answers must be realized by the newly dead."

I died. I bled out. I have choices. I can find answers hidden in something called voids. It's all too much. "When have you noticed these voids before?"

"When you asked about the future, those nightmares, and your choices. Apparently, you are only permitted access to this knowledge in some specified order so that you find the answers on your own."

"Well, here's my current wish list. I don't understand those nightmares. I haven't a clue what you mean by choices. And now I want to remember how I died. You're my guide. You have to help me."

"I'm trying, but it's a process that you must drive. I can push, but I can't lead. You have to steer."

I go to the person who was always honest with me, who gave the best advice: my sister.

21
Good-bye, My Sister

I MAKE MY WAY BACK to my memorial service to find Michelle at the podium, shaking. No makeup left on her pretty face. She has cried it all off. No jewelry. My invincible sister looks fragile. She stands alone at the microphone and looks out over the heads of the crowd. She lets the silence draw out. I wonder if she's going to pass out when she bows her head and closes her eyes. Quietly, she starts to sing. It's difficult to make out the tune, and the crowd strains to hear. I realize before the rest of them that she's humming the first few lines of "The Rose." She can never remember the words. I hum the harmony that only I can hear. But Michelle stops abruptly, and noisy silence from all the crying engulfs the chapel again.

She opens her eyes and looks from face to face. She looks down at the scraps of notes in her hand, and then she says, "If Anna was here, she would have sung the words to the song for me because I can never remember them. Something about love and razor blades that makes your soul bleed. Anna's soul can't bleed. Bleeding is for the body. What a strange line. I guess it's poetic and has deep meaning. But Anna and I were brought up to be analytical by a brilliant mother. Just the facts, sir. See, Anna was my sister. She was the other half of me."

How did I die, Michelle? Give me a hint.

She hums again and shakes her head. "The next line is about being afraid of dying. But Anna was never afraid of dying or anything else. She attacked life."

If I'd been afraid of dying, maybe I'd still be alive. Is that what Mrs. Smithers meant? Was I reckless with my life?

Michelle doesn't or cannot hear me. She focuses on the scribbled words on the paper clenched in her hand. "My sister's favorite quote was by Jonathan Swift." Michelle smiles, her eyes shiny with tears. "'May you live every day of your life.' Yep. That's what she'd want to leave us with. A sound bite. An easy out. Not this jumble of pain and memories. She'd tell us to go on without her, but to carry her with us." She takes a swipe at her wet nose with the palm of her hand and looks at Eddie, who shakes his head and looks away.

I love my sister.

She continues, "It feels like Anna is gone, but I know she's not. Only her atoms are gone. One thing our professing mother always taught us—in life you need your atoms. But in death, matter doesn't matter. Let those atoms go. Give them back so some other life form can use them. We are all made of recycled elemental particles. Some of our carbon used to be wheat. Before that, those same atoms were in carbon dioxide. Before that, they were exhaled by some other animal or person or dinosaur. When we die, we simply stop participating in the endless spiral of atom recirculation. We leave our matter behind. Cremation has returned the atoms of my sister to the world to reuse. That's what she'd want."

Maybe that's what I wanted before I died. Now I wish I had my atoms so I could make you hear me and talk to me, Michelle. Help me understand.

Michelle ignores me. She hums again, still trying to recall the lyrics of our song. "Anna was strong, and lucky to have all the love she experienced in her life."

She hums the next few lines and looks at my family. "Eddie, the nights will be lonely. Bethany, the road will be long. But, Joey, I feel like your mom is here with us to help us learn to live without her." Joey points a solemn nod at his aunt before he resumes looking around the church for me.

I'm distracted by Joey and go to him. I sit beside him. He can't see me or feel me.

My sister pauses and shakes her head, smiles at Eddie while tears stream from her eyes. Then with a quick nod, she whispers, "Good-bye, Anna. I love you."

She hums the last line from our song, and I remember the words but I'm powerless to give them to her. And then she breaks down and sobs her way back to her seat.

That's enough for now. I need another break. I wonder where Mom went.

"I'm right here."

"How did you get here so fast?"

"I thought we went over this already," she answers, once again annoyed with me. "I am everywhere, at all time. So 'getting' to you is almost effortless. Making you aware that I'm here, wherever 'here' might feel like to you, takes a little of my energy."

"Mom, this is all too hard for me. I need to leave again."

She catches me in my devastation. "Of course, dear. Let's go."

WE JUMP AWAY AGAIN. I'm still a bumbling amateur with this navigation at light speed. I don't know what I did to bring me here or whether, maybe, Mom nudged me this way.

On the dresser in my bedroom there's an old, faded soccer picture of Bethany. Five years old, shin guards, ponytail, gaping grin from missing front teeth.

The sight of the picture catalyzes a time leap, another one out of my control.

In the autumn when Bethany was about six, I had to leave her soccer game early to go to parent-teacher conference night. Eddie was the assistant coach of her team. He'd run up and down the sidelines screaming instructions for the entire game. The players didn't listen to a word he said. Bethany-the-Bruiser just wrestled with whoever had the ball. The games and Eddie-the-Coach were so much fun to watch that I hated to leave.

I pulled our big white van onto the dirt road by the field and made the first left onto Harden. A car up ahead slowed to make a left turn and had to wait for oncoming traffic, so everyone in the line of cars slowed down and stopped. The license plate of the car in front of me was BL 123, which reminded me of my birthday. I was contemplating what the BL might stand for—Birthday List, Be Lucky, Big Laugh, Broken Leg—when I caught a glimpse in my rearview mirror of a truck coming fast behind me.

The sixteen-year-old driver of the pickup truck didn't see the long line of red brake lights. Was he playing with his radio?

Combing his hair? Reading a book? He was going about fifty when he rammed the back of my van.

The rear and right side windows shattered, and the back end of my van caved in. My chair broke, and I was flipped onto my back. My foot came off the brake, and the van was pushed across the yellow line in the middle of the road. As I was falling backward in my breaking seat, I saw a red car coming at me from the other lane.

My van stopped on the other side of the road. I was flat on my back.

A young kid came running to my car. "Lady! Hey, lady, are you all right?"

"I don't know. My neck hurts," I said.

"Oh-god-oh-god-oh-god," I heard from the poor kid.

He disappeared and was replaced by two older ladies. One patted a wet towel onto my forehead and said, "I live right here, honey. Thank you for not driving into my kitchen!"

The other said, "Now you just lay still, dear. They said an ambulance is coming for you."

"No!" I yelled. I couldn't go in an ambulance. I needed Eddie. "Somebody get my husband."

"She's going a little bonkers in here, Jim," one of the voices reported to somebody else. Another head appeared, apparently Jim. He reached in and put the car in park and pulled the keys out of the ignition.

"Hey, little lady. You did a right good number on your van back there. Now you need to stay quiet till help gets here."

The crash happened many years ago before cell phones. I handed Jim the wet towel that had fallen into my eyes and asked, "Will you get my husband for me? Eddie Wixim. He's right down the road at our daughter's soccer game."

"Sure thing, missy. How will I know him?"

"He's the assistant coach on the pink team. Walking the sidelines in a neon pink soccer jersey. Yelling the whole time."

"All righty, sweetheart. You just sit tight." And he was gone.

Minutes later I heard a siren. Then paramedics were pulling me onto a stretcher and taping down my head and chest. Eddie's face appeared. He looked wretched.

"I'm all right, babe. Just come with me, okay?"

No answer.

"Eddie, who has Bethany?"

"Uh, she's—uh—Sue will take her home." He kissed my forehead before he began inspecting me—my private doctor. "What happened?"

"I got hit from behind." A large female cop appeared at Eddie's shoulder. She looked me over and asked the paramedic for a minute with me.

"I know you're hurting, ma'am, but I need to ask you a couple questions," she said.

"Okay." Eddie held tight to my hand.

"Why did you stop so suddenly?"

"I didn't. The cars in front of me were all slowing to wait for the first car to turn left. We were almost stopped when I got hit."

She frowned. "Kid who hit you says you stopped suddenly and that caused the wreck."

"I did not! He must've been flying. I—none of us stopped fast. We were never going more than fifteen miles an hour after the last light because this first guy was slowing down right away to turn left. The kid wasn't paying attention."

"Okay, I got it. One more question, though."

"What is it?" I asked, weary and foggy, but tethered to Eddie. My head clouded up, and I needed a quick nap.

"What stopped you on the far side of the road? Did you hit your brake? There aren't any marks on the front of the van, so we don't know what stopped you."

"Maybe I hit the brakes. I don't remember. There was a red

car coming at me when I crossed the center line. Didn't I hit him?"

"No, ma'am. Not a scratch on his car. You musta' hit the brakes."

She nodded and started to walk away, but I stopped her. "What about the kid. Is he hurt?"

"Nope. His airbag opened up. He didn't feel the impact at all."

"He's getting a ticket, right?"

"We'll see. I still have to check with a few more witnesses. Thanks for your help." She wandered away.

They loaded me into the ambulance. Eddie came with me, looking pale. I smiled at him and said, "Don't worry, I can move my toes." I showed him, and he smiled back.

"That was also November eleventh," says my mother's voice.

23
Deathday

"ARE YOU KIDDING ME? How many times can a person almost die on the same day?" I demand.

"It's simple math," she replies. "Once a year, so just count up the years of your life and there's your answer."

"Did I almost die every year on November eleventh?"

"Not 'every' and not 'almost'," my mom answers with a snort.

"What is that supposed to mean? And don't give me any of that crap about having to figure it all out for myself. If you're my newly dead guide, sneak your way around the voids or I'm going to find another guide." I'm about to lose it.

"Okay, let's start with every year," she begins, calm as a clam. "No, you didn't even have a near miss every November eleventh. You had one three or four times that I know about. When you were tiny and Molly bit you, that was November eleventh. Your car crash was November eleventh. There might have been others. You'll certainly think of them yourself, sooner or later."

"But why November eleventh, over and over?"

"That's your deathday," she states simply, as though she was telling me the time.

"My deathday?"

She continues, "Just like January twenty-third was your *birth*day, your *death*day is predetermined. We all have one. My deathday was August fifth. I didn't know it either until I died. Your deathday is a crack in space-time where your antimatter can slip through and escape from the dawdling speeds of Earth and go back to the universe. Every soul has a deathday and a birthday."

This makes sense. I always knew 11/11 was a special day for me. I just never knew why. "What about the rest of it? What did you say? 'Not almost'?"

"Yes, that's what I said. I wish I hadn't though because it's harder to explain than it would be for you to just reason out on your own."

"That's just too bad for you, then. Tell me what you know!" I demand.

"Anna," she says in her soothing tuck-into-bed voice, "you did not *almost* die a couple of times. You did die."

"That's not possible."

"Think about what you know about speed of light travel and what you know about time and space. Think about all that you have rationalized, remembered, and learned since you died on November eleventh."

So, I think and think. Nothing fits together, though, so I start rambling. "I saw the recent happenings after my death. I saw a lot of the past." Then it hits me hard. "And, oh God, I saw the future with me in it. I thought they were nightmares." This stuns me. "And you wouldn't explain it to me. So I can travel back or forward in time . . ."

"And when you die," she helped, "if you have lived a balanced and good life, have not hurt others, loved whenever possible, then your antimatter has choices. Choices of what your heaven will be. Choices of reuniting with your matter."

"Reuniting with my matter?" There are sayings in life that almost apply here, and they all portray shock as a physical blast. I was blown over. This knocked the wind out of me. I was blindsided. This blew my socks off. Yes, I know I can't be knocked over since I have no mass; wind can't have any effect on my bodiless self; I can't be blindsided, and with no feet, no socks can be blown off. Yet all of these human maxims compound like a factorial to almost describe the feeling of disbelief that overwhelms me.

Reuniting with my matter means I can go back to my body, I think.

I can go back to my life? Incredible. Maybe I'd done it before. Why don't I remember that?

Mom reads my thoughts.

"If you go back, you go to the instant when your antimatter separated from your matter and consciously will it to stay put. After such a reunion, you'd have no memory or knowledge of the conversations you had with me or any of the experiences you had on the dead side."

"Have I gone back before?" I'm still stunned.

The long pause before her answer illustrates her reluctance or inability to explain this one. Maybe another one of those blasted voids. Her voice reaches me. "Honey, your memory of your car crash is not how it happened the first time. When you saw that red car coming at you and when you crossed the yellow line, you slammed on your brake and he hit you. Hard. The collision snapped your neck. When you went back, you didn't hit your brake, and the momentum of the car pulled you across the road where you stopped in some bushes."

The crash was a dozen years ago. "So who was my guide then? You were still alive."

"Somebody who loved us found you on the dead side and helped you find your way back. Maybe it was Daddy."

I miss Daddy. He might be a better guide than Mom. I hope she didn't hear that.

Finally, Mom says, "Honey, you need to start thinking about your options so you can make your choice. There is no real rush. Time stops for us—but it would help to make the reunion of your antimatter and matter smoother if you work this out. You need to take over and steer and decide for yourself what to see."

"I feel like I have other choices."

"You do, Anna. You have infinite choices. You must identify them yourself and decide for yourself. No one, no force, can make the choice for you. It is the loneliest path in the universe."

And to emphasize her point, she leaves me. I am alone and drifting in space. It is peaceful, but not lonely. I knew the feeling of loneliness in life. There is no sense of it in death. The rush of traveling at the speed of life is gone when the matter leaves. Traveling at the speed of *light* feels like standing still, held as solid and safe as alternating ions, locked in the crystal lattice in a patient block of salt. And I think Mom was right. I don't have to rush. I have eternity to think.

I exercise my right to make a choice, and I think about Daddy and Molly.

24

Space-Time Cracks Open

IT WAS A SURPRISING, yet welcome, warm day in November. The sun was bright. The sky was that deep autumn blue. A woman in her midthirties walked on the sidewalk on a quiet street pushing a baby carriage through the carpet of crunchy leaves. The pink-cheeked baby lounged on her back drinking a bottle of milk. She held it lazily with one arm as she watched the trees and sky go by and rubbed the fringe of her blanket with her exploring hand until the bouncing of the carriage lulled her to sleep. She dropped the bottle by her cheek.

"That was you and me, Anna," says my Mom. "You were nine months old, and I was pregnant with Michelle."

"Mom, you were old!"

"Thanks, dear."

"No, I mean—why'd you wait so long after you were married to have us?"

"Oh, you know me. I was still busy learning and trying to become me. I was certain for a long time that I'd never have babies. I was too worried about population explosion and killing the rain forests to reproduce without careful consideration. Your father worked on me for years to convince me that his obsession with his dogs might lessen if he had some kids to play with."

"It didn't work, did it?"

"No. He still loved those dogs."

When they returned home, Mom left the carriage in the warm sun. Inside a screen door, Mom talked and laughed quietly on the telephone. She dropped the phone and came running when her baby cried out. She'd never heard me wail like that before.

The dog, Molly, was Daddy's favorite. The neighbor's cat, Isabelle, jumped onto the carriage and licked the spilled milk beside the baby. Her long tail dangled over the side of the carriage and was too tempting to ignore. Molly leaped at her and jumped onto the side of the carriage. Somehow the baby's arm ended up in Molly's teeth. In the confusion, the poor old dog thought she had succeeded in catching the wretched feline. Instead she crushed the baby's wrist. I forgot as I watched that the baby was me.

Mom says, "That was such a sad time. Poor Molly. You probably don't need me to tell you: that was November eleventh."

My first deathday.

| | | |

DAD HELD MOLLY in the veterinarian's office. The chocolate lab looked asleep, but she was dead. The community uproar over the dog attack gave my Dad no choice but to put his beloved Molly down. Dad was crying.

Later, on the swing in back of the old house, Dad sat with his two other dogs at his feet. He always had a mess of dogs around him. They walked together in the woods for no reason except to think and be outside. Daddy was happiest with his dogs. Mom carried the sleeping baby, me, out from the house to Daddy and laid the bundle in his arms. Her peaceful, long eyelashes and pouty lips projected a calmness that contrasted with the stark, white cocoon around the infant's tiny hand and arm. Mom sat down beside Daddy. She wrapped her arms around his neck and rested her head on his shoulder. Daddy stroked her belly where my new sister had started to kick. Surrounded by his girls and dogs, Daddy smiled and cried some more.

"Mom, how can I watch this? I don't remember it."

"You are watching it by traveling back in time. While we watch, it is actually happening all over again, just as I remember it," she explains.

"I want to see more."

"Just think of the people you want to be with and try to pick an age and see where it takes you."

I think: Daddy and Michelle and me. Little girls.

We were on a green, wet baseball diamond on a shiny spring day. Michelle stood way out in left field wearing a too-big baseball glove pulled up her arm and hanging in the crook of her elbow like a purse. Her big ears stuck out under the sides of one of Daddy's old caps. She alternated between hopping on one foot in circles and picking dandelions to poke into the buttonholes of her blouse. Twin braids framed her freckled face, and her high-pitched humming of "Jingle Bells" reached me at home plate.

Daddy pitched softball after softball at me, and I wailed them into the outfield. Michelle didn't make a move to retrieve them. Daddy just kept smiling and encouraging me to swing.

"Wow, look at that one go!"

"I want to try to switch hands, Dad," I said as I swung the bat right-handed for a change. "I think I can hit this way, too."

He squinted in the sunlight and said, "It's tough, Anna. Not many boys are good switch-hitters."

"I bet I can do it. Throw me some heat." And he did. The first few swings were awkward, but then I got the hang of it, and I smashed one right toward Michelle, who was bent down studying a line of black ants. She never saw the ball. It rolled by fast, not three feet to her left, and went all the way to the fence.

Daddy roared a laugh and yelled, "That's my girl! You *can* do it!"

Mom's voice: "Before Molly bit you, you were right-handed. Even though you were so tiny, I knew. You held your bottle and grabbed my hair with your right hand."

"It's so odd to see these things. It's like part of me remembers, even though I was so little. I miss Daddy."

Mom is quiet before she answers, "Your dad has been waiting for a turn. Why don't you go to him?"

25
Daddy's Love

I WAS ONLY FIVE YEARS OLD, and I knew to be quiet in the mornings. I knew how to get my own breakfast and let the family sleep. When I was alive, my kids still woke me up for food each day. Why did I allow this? Likely because I remembered how lonely it was to eat breakfast by myself as a child.

It was a weekend morning, so early it was still dark gray with fringes of light around the curtains, and I was the only one awake in the house I grew up in. I was a tiny thing with long hair and a chubby face. I wanted peanut butter for some bread, but the jar was closed tight. Way back then, peanut butter came in glass jars. Everything came in glass jars because humans hadn't yet discovered how to turn petroleum into plastics, but we sure knew how to melt silica. It was a full, new jar, and it was heavy.

I carried the peanut butter jar, cradled it tight to my chest with both arms, while I walked in my nightgown and bare feet to my sleeping Daddy. I didn't wake him up. I just sat on the cold wooden floor with the jar in my lap and my belly grumbling and watched him sleep—for a really long time. He snored a little. Finally, he opened one eye and tossed a sleepy smile to me. I held up the jar. I didn't even have to ask; he just took it and cranked it open. He wasn't even grumpy. I kissed his cheek, and, as I walked away with my open jar, he whispered, "Anna, don't drop it."

"I won't," I whispered back.

Then, I did.

It crashed to the wooden floor. I stood frozen amid the shards of peanut butter-covered glass. Daddy jumped out of bed and rushed to me, gaining consciousness, swearing under his breath, "Goddamnsonofabitch."

I thought he was mad at me for dropping the jar after he told me not to. I thought he was mad at me for making a mess. I thought he was mad at me for waking him up.

Daddy picked me up in my nightgown and bare feet. I tried not to cry. In his arms I understood, in my five-year-old mind, that he wasn't mad. He was just being my daddy and protecting me.

When he put me down far from the glassy mess and knelt on the floor, he let me cry on his shoulder for a while. Then I wiped my nose on my sleeve and whispered, "Sorry, Daddy, for making you swear."

"Sorry I swore, punkin'," he whispered back.

"Good thing Mommy didn't hear, huh?"

He shook his head and smiled before he began to clean up the mess. Mommy was still asleep in a lump on her side of the bed. Over his shoulder he said, "I think Mommy heard. But it's okay to swear sometimes if you have a good reason."

"Like that time you stepped in the poop in the living room?"

"A very excellent example, my dear. A lesson to remember: if you step in dog poop in the dark in your living room in your bare feet, it is okay to swear."

"Can we get some more peanut butter today?"

"Of course, sweetie, and I'll remember to crank open the jar for you before I go to bed so it's nice and loose in the morning. Okay?"

"Okay."

For the rest of my life, I never again asked for help in opening a tight jar.

Now, however, I feel like I'm stuck inside the jar of death. Daddy, I need help.

26

Driving a Car

I WAS SIXTEEN, invincible, on top of my game and learning to drive. Why was this car so damn long? It was like a boat on wheels. The lane was impossibly narrow. If I tipped up my chin and craned my neck, I could just see over the dashboard. It was my first time on the highway. Actually, it was the first time I ever drove faster than thirty miles per hour. I was busy calculating in my head how fast sixty miles per hour would be in feet per second, and I almost had it divided down to the hundredths place when Daddy's voice interrupted from the passenger seat.

"Anna, why don't you pass this guy?" How odd to hear his voice from over there. I, the new Queen of Sheba, was in the driver's seat.

"Okay." I hit my left turn signal, checked my mirror; the lane was clear, so I swung the wheel left and then zipped it back right, and somehow the car was in the left lane.

Daddy made gasping noises.

"Don't have a heart attack, Daddy. I did it." Jeez, he was so nervous.

When he recovered his breath he said, "Stay calm, Anna. I need to give you some advice. Now, don't take this as you would the daily advice you get from your mother—not at all like a suggestion to be briefly considered and then discarded. Take this as advice from your dad. Consider it an order. Got that?" This was quite a long speech for my dad. I just nodded.

He continued, "In a minute you're going to have to get

back in the right lane. From here on, you should not consider a lane change as a succession of two opposing turns. Ever again. Are you with me on this? There should not be a sharp right followed by a sharp left. It should be a slight turn of the wheel in the direction of your desired lane. Kind of ease into it. Do you see the difference?"

I nodded. I tried not to smile.

He said, "Okay. Right lane is clear. Blinker on. Good. Eeeease over." After I steered the boat-car back into the safer and slower right lane, he heaved a heavy sigh and said, "Good. That's enough practice on that. No more lane changes for this trip." We had an hour to go, so I guessed we'd be spending the whole ride behind the chicken truck.

I drove for about ten more minutes in silence as the chicken feathers wafted down on us like snowflakes. My dad was a quiet person. Silence and thinking were his normal modes of operation. So when a spider spun a string and dangled from the roof of the car in front of my face and I started waving my arms and screaming, the silence shattered like glass. Daddy was lightning quick. He grabbed the steering wheel with one hand and killed the spider with the other. So much like a superhero: mild mannered, ordinary guy springing into action to save my life. But after that episode, he was breathing heavy again. I hoped he didn't intend to have a heart attack while I was driving.

Once the spider was dead, I asked to turn the radio on. Daddy said, "No, Anna. Just concentrate on the road, please." Then, under his breath, I heard what sounded like, "Please, God." We had about twenty more miles until our exit—the horrible chicken truck was still pooping white feathers and a nasty odor at us—and then fifteen more minutes on the back road. Though I was getting tired, I knew I couldn't complain or he'd never let me drive again. I concentrated on staying awake, keeping my eyes wide open for the elongated minutes until we reached our exit. I pointed to a hitchhiker with a backpack on the exit ramp, and once again, Daddy started that pained, heavy breathing when I slowed down. I opened Dad's window with the cool power controls that the driver gets to use. I leaned across Daddy and yelled out his window to offer the guy a ride. He hopped in the back and we drove him about five miles down the road.

Daddy was steaming when he managed to speak. "Pull over, Anna. Driving lesson's over." Then, hitching his thumb over his shoulder, he told my passenger, "Free ride's over for you, too, buddy."

| | | |

"YES, ANNA, driving lessons were a special part of being your dad."

"Hi, Daddy! Where have you been?"

"I've been here, watching. You know me, not much to say."

It is such a relief to have him with me. He was my rock. I still have so much to figure out.

"Now you do know the rules, right? I expect your mother remembered to tell you all about this guide stuff? I'm not usually a guide. But, apparently, you need more guidance than your mother can give. Is that right?"

I don't want to make Mom seem like an inadequate guide, but there are other issues I need to cover. So I just say, "You were always good at helping me change lanes, Daddy. Will you help me with this?"

"I will," he says, "as much as I can."

27
Dogs

WHEN I WAS LITTLE, my fear of dogs made me tremble. As an adult, I was never afraid of dogs, or anything, anymore.

Then I met those three dogs on my long run and my old fear boiled back up. The six-mile training circuit was my favorite before half-marathons. Once I could do the six miles without hurting, I'd add two miles every two weeks until I got up to twelve miles. That's how I'd know my legs could carry me for the race.

The long loop had it all. Winding, lazy hills. A pond with horses. Lots of shade. A few houses. A toilet in a ditch. A small farm with a rooster that always crowed for me. A creek beside the road. Once I was warmed up, if nothing hurt or distracted me, I'd dive deep into my thoughts. My brain would just go and go and leave my body. I'd solve physics problems, contemplate science and religion, ponder the number of stars and galaxies in the enormous universe, and agonize about personal problems, like my crumbling marriage and what to do about Eddie. Lately, running was my favorite way to get away from Eddie's funk.

Back to the dogs. One day after dropping Joey at a friend's house, I found myself driving on the last two-mile stretch of my running route and saw three dogs at a mailbox up the road from the horses. I'd never seen them before, and I wondered whether they lived there or if they were a pack of strays. Either way, their presence on my quiet running path disturbed me, and I was glad to be safe in my car.

The next time I ran, I remembered them as I approached

the horses by the pond. When I got closer, I picked up a stupid little stick that I planned to use to defend myself against three large German shepherds who looked like wolves. Thank God they weren't there. And again, a week later, I took an early turn before their mailbox to avoid them, but I peeked around the corner and again they weren't there. So I had years of running data showing no dogs on this route, considered together with a couple more runs without them. My statistical brain concluded that the dogs did not live there. It was a fluke that I saw them when I drove by. Hence, my run was theoretically safe again.

I decided that I was not even scared the next time I ran the cycle, and I didn't even bother to pick up a dirty old log for protection. I said hello to the horses like I always did. As I started up the long hill and approached the dogs' mailbox spot, I saw movement through the trees. I saw one dog lounging on the driveway. He didn't move, but I was so spooked I turned around and ran halfway back down the hill toward the horses. The dog didn't chase me. My mind did the calculation of "five miles if I backtrack, one and a half miles if I can get by." The big dog seemed to be alone. I turned around and risked it. I ran by him, exuding the stench of fear, with all of the hairs on the back of my neck standing at attention.

His ears perked up as he studied me with sharp, black eyes. I stared back. The other two dogs were resting in the sun behind him. One heaved himself to his feet and paced when he saw me. When the third dog stood up, I almost peed myself. They didn't chase me, but their eyes followed me. They barked while they weaved an agitated dance in the high grass. I held my breath until, without warning, they all turned and ran toward the house. Away from me. My heart was beating in double time. I sprinted up the hill. The dogs barked from the woods but didn't chase me.

"That's not exactly how it happened."

My dad's voice.

"Daddy? What do you mean?"

"You should go back again and watch more carefully this time. Watch how the details change."

"The details can change? That doesn't make sense."

"I know, doll. Just let me show you. If you can manage to get through it on your own, you'll understand much more about time travel and your choices."

I jogged past the horses and approached the black mailbox beside the driveway where the dogs were spotted weeks ago. Movement through the trees. One dog, the biggest one, rested in the shade on the driveway. He didn't move, but I was so scared I backed away, slowly, down the hill. His ears perked up as he studied me. I stared back at him. Sweat streamed down my spine. I looked around for a stick, and found one that was both too heavy and too brittle. The other two dogs walked past the chief. They inched closer to the road, closer to me. My heart was beating so hard I could feel the blood pulsing in my temples. I turned and sprinted up the hill. They were too fast for me, barking close behind me. I ran as fast as I could, fighting gravity, blindly waving the branch as they nipped at my heels. The barking stopped. I felt something rip into my thigh. The ground rushed up to meet me as I fell fast, and my head hit a rock in the ditch beside the road. More barking. Pain in my leg. My head throbbed. And then there was nothing.

My body is by the side of the road. Blood is everywhere. Maybe I'm not all the way dead yet. The dogs stare at me from across the road.

The air is still. The birds are quiet. The dogs trot up the driveway, back to the house. The runner gets up and wipes grass and dirt from her hands and legs. She looks up the hill and begins to run. She is me.

The dogs did not chase me but acted spooked and ran around each other barking and then turned and ran toward the house. Away from me. My heart was beating so fast. I sprinted up the hill. The dogs barked behind me but did not chase me.

They did not chase me.

Did not chase.

They ran the other way. They did not bite me.

I took a full breath and ran for my life.

Now they chased me. I ran faster. Not fast enough.

I fell. I bled. I heard music. Eddie cried.

It was a nightmare, rewinding, replaying, and changing each time.

"Now do you see?" asks Daddy. "It was fall. You were training for a half-marathon. It was November eleventh."

Another November eleventh. Space-time opened up for me. I must have passed through. My matter and antimatter had separated. I died and came back. How many times? Different each time. Why do I have no memory of this?

"What year was that?" I ask him.

"Oh," he says, "it could've been any year. The year isn't important. What's most important is that you see the various versions of the incident, each influenced by the innumerable choices you made that day, before that day, and even after that day."

"I see the event has many layers. That's because of different choices?"

"Yes, honey." My dad is gentle with me. "Once the space-time gap opens on your deathday, the opportunity to pass through beckons you. But to pass *back* through to your life, if your atoms of that part of the core of your brain are even strong enough to take your antimatter back, is a solitary choice. It's a decision that the individual must make."

I'm stunned as Daddy continues to explain, "When you go back, you must leave all of your death memories behind on the dead side. Imagine how life would be if living humans remembered their deaths and reentries. People survive in the space and time of their lives because these variables are distinct entities at earthly speeds. They vary directly and the proportionality constant is the speed. You know all of this, right? Speed is the magnitude of the velocity vector. Velocity equals distance over time, so distance or space in one direction equals velocity times time. Right?"

"Daddy? You understand physics?" This makes me laugh. This was so my mother's realm. In life, my dad shunned technical explanations of any natural phenomenon. He and my mother thought and spoke different languages. It was amusing to watch them communicate, he with emotions and she with facts. It worked for them, but Michelle and I knew to go to Daddy for hugs and support and to Mom for homework help.

"I always understood. I just didn't enjoy applying it." He's quiet for a while. Silence hugs us. What I'm beginning to understand in death is so crystal clear that I wonder why the living can't comprehend it.

Daddy answers my thoughts. "It isn't so much that they can't. Living humans don't want to comprehend it. It wouldn't fit in with the energy that is life. You should think about this, Anna. I'm sure you will see why it is so."

And once again I am alone. Oh, so alone, but not lonely. Now I know that I can go and do and see whatever I choose.

Regardless of how I died, I can go home again. I can live. I can kiss Joey's head again. I can hug my Bethany and vent to Michelle and yell at my students. I can continue fighting and loving Eddie. Or maybe I could just skip past that last part.

I can remain dead.

As antimatter, I can consider the universe forever. The freedom of thought that almost always consumed my fourth and fifth mile of a six-mile run is mine for eternity if I choose it. I can loop back and reenter my life just by deciding to do it. I can reconnect my antimatter to my body and continue my life. Or not.

Death doesn't hurt anymore.

28
Friday, November 11

ONE MORE TIME TRAVEL, just a little side trip, and then I'll decide. I'm in better control now, and I know exactly what day and what people I want to see. I even think I can get there all by myself.

On the morning of Friday, November eleventh, the day I died, I rolled over in bed and cracked Eddie on the nose with my elbow. Not the best way to start my last day on the living side. It was still dark, too early to get up, but Eddie got out of bed and started sneaking around the room the way he did when he thought I was asleep. He was horrible at being quiet. Even when he managed to avoid running into things in the dark, his ankles cracked with each step.

When I asked what he was doing, he said he was checking the time.

Though it was ridiculous for me to crave his attention, I hoped he'd get back into bed. But he didn't. A few minutes later, I heard him whispering with Joey. I smelled coffee. I stumbled to the shower where I washed my hair for the last time and scrubbed the last sleep from my eyes.

In the kitchen I ignored Eddie and went straight to Joey. While I sipped my last cup of coffee, which was sweet and strong, I rubbed Joey's morning hair and sensed the guilt vibe hovering near Eddie. He was acting even stranger than normal. Our last morning matched our last two months together—we didn't communicate or acknowledge one another.

Watching now, it seemed I was ignoring him. Eddie's eyes

were fixed on me.

Joey had all of my attention, especially when I saw the chocolate crumbs in his teeth. My little boy complained of a bellyache, and he leaned to me for a hug. Our last hug.

I wasted it.

When I said, "Show me those teeth," my boy giggled and my husband gasped.

I looked up at Eddie, caught him staring at me and saw him look quickly away. "Hey!" His eyes locked on mine. They were the same eyes as Joey's, green and wide, but sad. On the last day of our marriage, we had our last fight before I turned my back on my best friend and huffed out of the kitchen with my coffee.

I was still crying behind my sunglasses when I left for work. I couldn't stop. I was relieved and even eager to leave my own house. I had to get away from my husband.

Until he called me "honey" and made my hope bubble up again.

Eddie leaned his head in the passenger window of my car and knocked me off my guard. I breathed in his soapy-clean morning smell, felt his gravity reaching for me. His face was shaved close. He smelled so good. I should have reached out to feel his face one last time.

He asked, "Honey? How about a day off today? You and me and Joey. Let's all play hooky."

My heart leapt, skipped a beat, and then hid down in the dark, afraid to take the bait. He would hurt me again if I gave in. I knew not to trust Eddie with my fragile heart, so I threw up the gates and defended myself with my furious offense.

"You're calling me *honey* now? Where'd that come from? I'm going to work." I was glad the sunglasses blocked my wet eyes. Then, the last thing I said to my husband on my last morning alive, as a renegade tear of weakness snuck down my face and dripped from my chin, was sarcastic. I said, "See you tonight, *honey*," and I fled.

I wish I had kissed him good-bye and felt those arms around me one last time. I wish I had stayed home and played hooky. I wish I knew how I died. I wallow in my many ungranted wishes drizzled with regret.

Suddenly, out of the unending nowhere all around me, I have that odd sensation which I've grown accustomed to on the dead side—the uneasy feeling that I'm not all alone.

"Mom?" I try.

Nothing.

"Daddy? Who's here?"

"Maybe Old Man Eddie finally lost it and just snuffed her?" This wasn't Daddy or Mom. A new guide with a sick sense of humor?

"No, you fool. Eddie would never hurt me. He wasn't even there when I died," I said.

"How do you know?"

That's when I recognize the voice. His voice. How is this possible?

Eddie

29
Invitation

I LIVED WITH THE KNOWLEDGE for a quarter of my life. It ate me alive. I knew Anna would die. I even knew *when* she would die, but I was powerless to stop it. I tried but failed to keep her with me.

Now she's gone, and I find it's quite impossible to move my body out of this chair. My arms and legs are liquid. My neck and back ache. Head throbs. Eyes are scratchy, dry sockets. The only functioning part of me is my mind, and it won't stop flashing numbers and memories, taunting me with a running commentary of *I toldya so, if, and should've*, reminding me that my life is now deficient of the billions of trillions of precious atoms that comprised my wife.

Anna did it. She left me right on schedule. I never deserved her. I could rarely comprehend the complexity of her mind.

Anna. I give up the fight and let my trolling mind go to her, engulf her, remember her. I embrace the pain with doses of her, letting them simultaneously sting the open wound in my heart and wrap me up.

Despite its frequent short circuits, my Anna's mind didn't rest. She was endlessly entertained by her fixation with numbers. When she saw 1:23 on the clock, she'd call out, "My birthday!" Her fascination with 11:11 was broadcast twice each day. Although she didn't often or intentionally stay awake until after eleven at night, she had the time on the alarm clock by our bed programmed twenty minutes fast so she could trick herself into waking up each morning. So when she called out, "Eleven

eleven, again!" to me, as she turned out the light by her side of the bed every night, I knew she was delighted that her favorite time was when she always went to sleep. It didn't matter if I argued that it was only 10:50. To her it was 11:11.

Every fall she anticipated November eleventh like a kid waiting for Christmas. She was so naïve. She had no idea how inextricably those numbers were linked to her death. Through the years it became more and more difficult for me to refrain from explaining it to her—11/11 would be her deathday.

When I met Anna she was a student in Particle Physics and I was the graduate teaching assistant for her section. I held recitation on Tuesday mornings during that spring semester while I wrote and defended my doctoral dissertation, took the MCAT, and applied for medical school. There seemed no time for a love interest during that insanely busy time of my life. I was so self-absorbed that I almost didn't notice when Anna's light threw a shadow over my life.

She was young and lovely and intelligent. Wildly, unstoppably intelligent. Self-assured beyond her years. And she was independent, in need of no one. But all of her self-esteem was fueled by her confidence in her intellect. She had no idea that she was a beauty.

I couldn't look away.

On a Saturday in late March, a week before my birthday, I found Anna's apartment and boldly knocked on her door. She seemed confused by my presence.

"Um, hi. Mr. Wixim, is there a problem? I did turn in the last problem set. Didn't I put my name on it? It was the one in green ink on the pink grid paper." She smiled hopefully. She had an animated talking face with a furrowed brow, her chin down, her head turned to one side while she looked at me out of the corner of her eye. She also nodded while she talked in rhythm with her words. Her eyebrows never stopped moving, and I just about drowned in her big eyes.

"No, Anna. There's no problem with your assignment. I'm sure you turned it in," I stammered and stopped. "Could you, um, could you call me Ed, instead of Mr. Wixim?" I lost my train of thought, distracted by the summation of details that comprised this girl. She wore plaid shorts, a little tank top, tube socks, and a bright yellow apron.

"Sure, *Eddie*." She tipped her head to one side, studying me back, pulling my attention back up above her neck. Her auburn hair was bunched in a loose pile and held in place by a pencil. Flour on her right cheek. Some wet white cream, maybe toothpaste, on her chin. "If my assignment's okay, then why're you here?"

I smiled. Well, I tried to smile. It probably looked more like I was in some abdominal pain. I gathered myself, shook off her spell, and charged ahead with my prepared speech.

"I'm going to take the MCAT next Tuesday, so I won't be at recitation. Then on Wednesday afternoon, the first draft of my dissertation is due to Dr. Hornsby. It doesn't need to be perfect, just presentable, and the data and graphs have to be clear and all. Anyway, it'll be a hectic week, and if I survive it I plan to celebrate." I paused, out of breath.

Anna's dark eyes studied me, the uninvited enigma on her porch. "Oh. So. Um, do you want my problem set rewritten on white paper, then?"

I needed to get to the point before I lost my nerve. "Anna, listen. I've been watching you in class. You are very intelligent, and I like the way you help explain things, even to the guys who hate girls telling them anything. You are a very take-charge person."

I paused. She waited with her head tipped to the left and her eyebrows scrunched together.

"I wondered if you had time next Friday to celebrate the end of the week with me. That is, if I actually survive."

Her mouth fell open. I held my breath for the rejection that was sure to ensue.

"You're asking me *out?*"

I looked down at my Converse high-tops, thinking what she must be thinking: I was way out of my league with this girl. My next thought was *What the hell?* I met her unbelieving wide eyes, nodded once, and said, "Yeah."

Anna shook her head and put her hands on her hips and said, "Can you do that? I mean, you're my teacher."

"I think I can," I said. "I just did. I've wanted to for a couple months." She didn't answer. Her intent stare somehow hindered my muscular function. My brain threatened a shutdown as well. My mouth still worked, so I continued to plead my case. "I'm not really your teacher. I'm just the teaching assistant. Dr. Hornsby is the teacher of record. He establishes grades and writes the tests. Do you see the difference?"

"That's not the only difference," she laughed. "He's old and bald and fat, and I would never go out with him."

I held my breath and asked, "Will you go out with *me?*"

Her smile and reply of "Yes" were a blur because my heart was beating so hard I was sure she could hear it.

Anna wasn't the first girl I dated. I was pretty old when I met her. I was about to turn twenty-five. But no girl had ever flung such an instantaneous, magnetic attraction on me before. We dated for the next two months. Then we both graduated. I earned my Ph.D. and she earned her master's. She intended to move north and pursue her doctorate, but I messed all that up when I asked her to come with me when I started medical school. My happiness at her acceptance paled in comparison to the fury her mother expressed at our plans.

Now, I finally understand her mother's pain. I took Anna away from her, and now Anna is gone from me. Gone. She's really gone.

Anna.

30
April 1, First Date

THE DAY BEFORE MY BIRTHDAY in the year we met, April first, was our first date. It was unseasonably warm. The first tempting day of spring had continued into a clear sky on a night made for watching stars. The cool air was so clean and crisp you could cup it in your hands and gulp it down. A perfect night for a first date.

I planned our date as meticulously as the circuitry of a motherboard. We were going to dinner at a steakhouse and then to a movie on campus. The film club was showing old Abbott and Costello movies for free from eight until midnight. If I was lucky, Anna might agree to a walk through the campus after the movie. In the dark. Who knew what might happen?

I rang her doorbell at six-thirty that night, right on time and in a haze of déjà vu. My week had been hectic and painful, as expected, but when I awoke that morning and found myself still alive, my anticipation of time with Anna made me giddy. A giddy graduate student is not a pretty sight, so I stayed home alone most of the day getting ready.

Obviously, Anna had spent part of her day getting ready, too. When she opened the door and shined her smile on me, my gaze fell on her newly cut and permed hair. I had loved her long, shiny, straight hair. It hung down her back and was one of the first things I'd noticed about her. That cape of silk was gone. All gone. I was so shocked that I couldn't help it—the first thing I said was, "Your hair."

Her fingers brushed a wavy strand. She smiled, chin down,

head tipped, and looked up expectantly with those big eyes and said, "What?"

She anticipated compliments and praise. Instead, I said, "I liked it better the other way."

Well, the silence was deafening. Her rage was palpable. Her face clouded up, and she shut the door in my face.

Things were not going well.

I stood on her porch for a full ten minutes trying to work up the courage to talk to her again. I knocked timidly, three staccato taps, and waited. I was afraid when the door didn't open for quite a few minutes. When it finally opened, just a crack, I heard Anna say, "What?"

"Do you, um, think we could get going now? If we don't get to the steakhouse by seven they'll cancel our reservation, or else we might be late to Abbott and Costello. I hate to be late for movies. You know how it is. The lights are out and you have to find your way in the dark to some seats and climb over people who weren't late who're trying to see the screen." I stopped for breath.

From behind the door I heard, "What?" and realized this was the third time she'd asked the same question, and it was the only word she'd said to me so far on our first date. See, I still expected a first date and was still hopeful about the walk in the dark at the end of it. Only, this "What?" was louder than the others and sounded even madder.

I charged ahead. "You might want a sweater. It's supposed to get cooler later." I leaned my forehead against the door and started to worry.

Then I heard laughter, so I started to hope.

After two hundred long seconds, which I watched tick by on my sturdy Timex, Anna came out with a sweater and her new curly hair. She didn't speak to me. She just walked to my car with me trotting behind like a puppy. I was afraid to look at her, but I think she was smiling.

At dinner she started to make some intermittent eye contact, which made her silence louder. I had trouble with my salad with her watching me eat the large hunks of lettuce. She noticed my unease and intensified her stare. Slicing my steak was troubling—I was all elbows. She finally spoke to me when the waiter offered dessert.

"Eddie Wixim, I decided to come with you to get a free steak dinner. Now, I want chocolate cake. But I don't want to go with you to Abbott and Costello in the middle of campus where everyone can see us. This is our first and last date, and I don't want people thinking there's something going on here. Got that?" The waiter beamed at her, pen poised over his pad, and waited to see how I would get out of this mess.

My heart was pounding. What could I do? I asked the only person who knew. "Anna, what can I do to make you stop hating me?"

"I don't hate you." That was encouraging. I glanced at the waiter, trying to will him away, but he just raised his eyebrows higher and held his ground.

"Well, then, how do you feel about me?"

She pinned me with her glare and said, "I have never been insulted in the first five seconds of a date before. That makes you a special, unforgettable date. And, I haven't been on many dates. That also makes you special and unforgettable. But even if I have to live the rest of my life alone, no dates, *forever*, I will never be so desperate that I will have to be with a guy who is mean to me. Got that?" The waiter snorted.

Now I got it. She thought I was mean to her. I was just in shock because she messed up her hair so bad. But I still found her irresistible, so I said, "I'm sorry I was mean. I didn't mean it. Please go to the movie with me?"

I was hyperventilating a little, and my anxiety seemed to give Anna some smug pleasure because she smiled when she said, "I think you are begging me." She gave her head full of new curls a shake of disbelief. The waiter nodded. He was getting on my nerves.

"You bet. I am. Really I am. This cannot be the last time I see you." What would I do if I blew this?

"Why not?"

She was waiting. Waiting for some perfect thing I could say that would fix everything.

"Because."

That wasn't my best work, but Anna laughed.

"Convincing argument, Wixim. Is that all you've got?"

"It's a very loaded 'because.' Because I——. Because you——" I stalled and cleared my throat.

"Because I'm already crazy about you, and I would be even if you shaved your head. Got that?" I reached across the table and took her hand. And she let me. I smiled at her, and she smiled back. And I knew. I just knew. We were going to make it.

"Chocolate cake for two," I said to the waiter, who nodded curtly before walking away.

31
Wedding

I PROPOSED TO MY WIFE without asking. It wasn't planned. It just turned out that way. Actually, I had no plan, but I felt more confident that day in the drive-thru than ever before. I knew, for certain, that Anna would choose me. And I was right. Without even asking, she knew what I wanted, what the ring meant, and she didn't surprise me—she just accepted me the way I was, the way we were. At the beginning of our marriage, I could predict her every move. Now that Anna is dead, though, I ache with worry about the choices she'll make. At the end of our marriage, all of our insights about one another had vaporized. And so I have no inkling, now, of whether Anna will choose me again.

A lousy ending shouldn't follow such a perfect beginning.

We were married in August, less than eight months after we met. With so little time to plan, we decided to have a small wedding. It was outside on a grassy, sunny hill on campus. One of the philosophy professors was a justice of the peace and agreed to perform the ceremony. Anna found a dress at an antique shop, and I rented a tuxedo because, according to the mothers, that's what you're supposed to do. Somebody ordered the tent and food. A friend from the lab played guitar in the corner. It was supposed to be a simple and easy ceremony, perfectly suited to us. I should have known it wouldn't be that easy.

When Anna's mom lost it at the rehearsal dinner and announced that she did not approve of our marriage and would say so during the ceremony, Anna fell apart. With my Anna in pieces, I feared I might lose her. I decided to reason with her mom.

"Mrs. McElveen?" I said when I called her on the phone late on the night before the wedding.

"Who is this? Are you trying to sell me something? Because I don't want any." Slam. She hung up.

I called back.

When she answered, I rushed in with, "Mrs. McElveen, this is Ed. I really want to talk to you about tomorrow. Please don't hang up."

"Oh, Lord. Ed, listen to me, there is nothing you can say to change my mind. You want to marry my Anna. You have her brainwashed into thinking she wants to marry you. She is out of her mind and is giving up all her dreams and goals for you. I don't see any way it is possible for you to make her happy when marrying you means giving up so much of who she is. Therefore, you must see why I cannot endorse this union!"

"Oh." This was the clever rebuttal from my end of the line.

"It absolutely infuriates me that you're going to win this battle and your brilliant response to my side of the argument is 'Oh'." On that note, she hung up on me. Again.

I didn't sleep at all that night.

At the ceremony the next day, I was exhausted. And starving. I'd cleaned out my fridge and whole apartment in my frenzy to prepare for our move and our life together after our honeymoon. There was absolutely nothing to eat. For breakfast I contemplated a half-dried jar of mustard with a spoon, gave up, and drank the dregs of the old milk. The ceremony was at eleven in the morning. I wouldn't be fed until the afternoon.

Unlike Anna, who talked about our wedding every year on our anniversary and cried at every wedding we ever attended after our own, I don't remember many details about that day. I don't remember who was there. I don't remember what we said.

If I broke any wedding vows through the years, I am innocent due to ignorance.

I do remember Anna's face. It was pale. She looked like she might faint at any second during the ceremony. Holding her breath, she didn't just hold my hand; she clenched my forearm with her icy hands like a vice-grip. I was aware that I was holding her up. A nasty grumbling sound came from my abdomen during a pause in the action of the ceremony. My hunger made me feel like I might puke. If Anna fainted, I decided I might as well hurl. I watched her closely for her cue to begin the festivities of our falling apart as an almost-married couple. She held herself together, barely, so I managed, too.

Somehow, Anna's dad kept her mom muzzled during the part of the ceremony when the justice asked if anyone had any reason to stop the union. I'm not sure if he physically gagged her, but I appreciated whatever means he employed to make his wife forever hold her peace. In this case, forever can be defined as about thirty minutes. Anna was wound as tight as a spring until that moment passed. After that, all I wanted to do was kiss her. I waited as long as I could and then laid one on her.

At our forty-minute reception in a tent on the field, the temperature soared to almost one hundred degrees. Anna and I smushed red velvet cake into each other's faces. It was delicious, and the cream cheese frosting sent sugar buzzing to my brain. I can't remember why the cake came first. Probably because no one was in charge. We chugged huge goblets of cheap champagne, and my odds of puking spiked again. Then we ate real food—some kind of chicken—tossed the bouquet, jumped into the limousine, and escaped to our honeymoon.

The clearest detail of the day is burned in my memory as the first of many cryptic conversations I was to have with my new wife during our life together. We were on our way to the airport.

"Eddie, do you remember what everyone said when you kissed me?" she asked.

"People said something?" I hadn't heard a thing.

"Yeah," she insisted. "They all said the same thing."

"Sorry, babe, I didn't get it," I admitted.

"They said 'Aw.'" She was beaming.

"Oh. That's great." I was lost.

But Anna wasn't finished. "If you think about it, little boys say something *different* when they see people kiss, like in movies, you know? While I was smushing cake into your face and you were chowing it off my arm—that's when they all said it."

Still lost. Being married to Anna was looking like it might be intellectually challenging.

She filled in the gap. "They said 'Ew!'" Her eyes were big, and she started to laugh. My diagnosis: too much champagne, too little sleep and food.

I just smiled a little and tried to get her to come closer to me. If I couldn't understand her thought process yet, it was okay. I knew I was nuts about the rest of her. She pushed me away and said, "You don't get it, do you?"

I shook my head in mock despair. "But can I get something else instead?" I begged.

Anna shook her head and laughed again. "You have to get this first. What are your initials?"

"E. W."

"And that spells?"

"Ew."

"Right, like what they said when I smushed the cake into your face. Got that?"

"Yep."

She continued down her personal brain path, dragging me along by the hair. "And what are my new initials?"

"A. W."

"And what does that spell?"

"Aw." Finally got it. "Like what they said when we kissed."

"Isn't that cool, Eddie? You are Ew and I am Aw, now. We sort of go together." My wife was so happy in her own strange-thinking world.

"We definitely go together," I said, and pulled her to me and silenced her lips.

When we came up for air, I said, "Aw."

And my new wife said, "Ew."

ON THE DAY BETHANY WAS BORN, my job was to run interference. It didn't matter that I worked at the hospital as an intern in pediatrics. That day, I was just the husband, the frantic first-time dad. I was enraged that my wife was in pain and frustrated that I couldn't bear it for her. She was going to try to have a natural delivery—her choice. It was the "in" thing to do. No drugs for Anna—just controlled breathing to ride out each wave. I became her slave. I did whatever she said. I pushed on her back. I wiped her forehead with a cold cloth. I brought ice chips. I supported her when she insisted on walking. I saw why they call this labor.

"Ow, ow, ow, ow, ow." Under her breath, Anna reported the pain. She didn't yell. She didn't cry. She breathed and said "ow" all afternoon.

"You're doing great, honey," I crooned.

"Don't *honey*, me. I'm not your honey." Anna lay on her side, the only position she'd tolerated for the last hour. Her hands gripped the stuffing of a rough hospital pillow. The paper-thin gown was pulled up above her giant belly. "Untie this damn thing, will you? I'm boiling."

I pulled the strings apart behind her and yanked off the gown. She was splendid. Huge and full of life. Red-faced. Mascara smudged under her eyes. Hair in a flopping ponytail on top of her head.

She gripped my forearm for the next contraction, and I remembered our beginning, our wedding day when she clawed my arm the same way. She needed me, and she centered me. While I watched helplessly for hours as she writhed in pain, somehow it helped her to have me there.

"Dammit, Eddie, get me some ice. I'm on fire. If this kid doesn't get out of my body soon, *I'm* getting out!"

As I scampered out to refill her ice cup the nurse smirked at me and said, "Transition's starting. It won't be long now."

"Hallelujah."

Anna didn't remember the details of that day. Not the way I did. We never remembered things the same way. I remembered what she said and did, and she remembered what I said and did. We each saw ourselves reflected off the other. I laughed to myself as I ran to gather up a cup of solid, crystalline water that normal folks call ice.

I thought about our baby, the one that Anna insisted was a boy. She'd resisted the medical tests that would verify the sex of the baby because she'd read that the test could hurt the fetus. So I was surprised when she insisted that she felt like the baby was a boy, because I was so certain it was a girl. From medical school, I knew that no statistical studies supported the fuzzy claims of women's intuition. Likewise, there were no words to explain why I was expecting a daughter, so I humored my wife. We joked about it.

"Good thing this baby is a boy," I said, just a week before Bethany was born, "because I don't think I could survive in a hormonal house of two women."

Anna whacked me with a pillow and said, "I'm not hormonal, you jerk. Can I have some ice cream?"

"There's only vanilla left."

"Aw, Eddie, I want chocolate. Your boy wants chocolate, too."

I went to the store late in the night for more chocolate ice cream. Just the way I ran for ice on Bethany's birthday. I'd do anything to make my Anna happy.

In the early evening, as the sun was setting through the tinted hospital window, they told Anna she could push. My relief was physical. My heart rate slowed. It would end soon. It would start soon. The pains would end. A life would begin.

In the first moments after Bethany's birth, I was acutely aware of the low frequency hum in the room. A soft, almost imperceptible magnetic field pulsed the molecules of the air into frantic motion. I had that hair-standing-up-at-the-back-of-my-neck feeling while I watched, in awe, the raw beauty of new life. My wife, my world, held our daughter as her brand new antimatter hovered above them. I stroked her downy cheek. I touched her tiny fingers. Her antimatter latched on while we mere mortals stood in awe. There is no other word. We can marvel in awe. That's all we can do when the power that is life blows us down and holds us up.

Unaware that she was crying, Anna leaked a steady stream of tears while she smiled, as happy as we'd ever be in our lives together in this bubble of a moment, at the edge of the crevice from which the energy of our daughter's life emerged and converged. I could understand it all, in theory, more than a typical dad. But at the edge of the abyss, at the beginning or end of a life, the passage of the antimatter through the space-time gap will always leave me breathless and awed.

33
Hitch in Time

I KNOW WAY TOO MUCH. Much more than I could compassionately tell my patients, or their parents, about the rapidly replicating murderous cells that crowd out the good ones in their young bodies. I know even more about the boundary, the elusive and delicate perimeter, the membrane that divides death from life. The deathday. The heaviest burden I've borne during my medical career has been struggling for acceptance that, as a doctor, I can only do so much. I offer support and medicine to the children in my care and to their families, yet their final choice, the ultimate decision, is utterly beyond the scope of my power.

Despite my frustration, I would not change my choice to spend my days with the children in my care, especially the time I've spent with them on the edges, the borders of their lives. Obstetricians bring children into the world and I, sadly, often help them leave. Quite an emotional career for an outwardly stoic geek of a man, yet I cherished my work enough to share it with my own, healthy daughter.

When Bethany was little, I brought her to the hospital with me some days after school. She played with the kids who were my patients in the pediatric oncology ward, particularly a little boy named Ben. During our ride in one day Bethany asked, "Dad, how do little kids get sick?"

"Same way as adults: bacteria and viruses and cancers and things like that."

"Do you think Ben will be awake today?" she asked

hopefully. Sometimes when she visited, Ben slept the whole time.

"We'll see."

"I hope so. I want to beat him at War." She smiled in anticipation. Ben was my patient, part of my work, a child I worried about. To Bethany, he was a normal kid and a friend.

Bethany was a miniature replica of my Anna. Just like her mother, she carried my heart in her small, innocent hands. I willfully avoided finding out her deathday. I decided, in Bethany's case, to behave as a normal parent. It was a much healthier, more human way to live. It allowed me to worry about her *every* day and sort of spread the angst out into three-hundred-sixty-five bearable doses instead of the annual nuclear bomb I experienced in the third quarter of each year from knowing Anna's deathday.

Professionally, I was aware of the deathdays of many children because I was with them and fighting to keep them alive when they died. Forever died. These kids' bodies were usually so weakened by their illnesses that they most likely had no choices when they passed through to the dead side. Even the most resilient antimatter cannot sustain the energy of life when its corresponding matter is too weak. Sometimes, I witnessed a child's return by being present when his heart stopped and restarted. I had a keen awareness of their journey to the dead side and back. I enjoyed spending time with these kids who traveled round-trip through their space-time gap. They saw the world through shining eyes and were brimming with life.

I never directly questioned them on their experiences, but sometimes the children remembered little bits of the journey, which they would unconsciously share with their family, brothers, nurses, and even me. Most often, they just thought they'd had a dream—a long and convoluted dream.

Bethany's friend, Ben, had an obvious deathday on

February ninth. His small-cell lymphoma cancer had succumbed to medicine and his own strong will multiple times—once with radiation and chemotherapy when he was three and once with a bone marrow transplant from his older brother. The third time, he came back to us from the dead side on his own. There were no alternative treatments, and he was too weak for more chemo. I had no faith that his body could sustain a reentry, but he'd made it back somehow.

I remember the day when the first code was called on then three-year-old Ben. I excused myself from my consultation and started my run. Nurses and doctors universally describe this race in the same manner: it is a slow-motion sprint. No worldly speed is ever fast enough; gravity amps up to exert an additional negative force vector—like iron chains on your ankles—as you run. Your legs pump, muscles burn, like your own life is on the line, with death trotting at your side, taunting you, all the way to the room with the dying child.

I arrived at Ben's door and found two nurses and a resident surrounding his bed. They were listening for a heartbeat, adjusting his IV, watching the monitors, calling out what they found—a symphony of medical professionals working to keep the body's trillions of molecules oxygenated and viable in case the patient came back. When the patient is three years old, thirty pounds, and limp, the symphony plays its beat in all eighth notes. This is the essence of what we do—provide maximum time, extend the workability of the body, the matter, and keep the space-time gap stretched open to give the soul a nice wide window to make its choice. We give the hitch a chance.

The code cart came in right behind me. I absorbed all of the information from the team in seconds while my eyes scanned the monitors that showed Ben's pulse, oxygen, brain waves.

"Pulse forty and dropping. BP eighty over thirty-five."

"Oxygen at fifty percent."

We were losing him fast.

"He stopped breathing."

"Beginning CPR." A nurse got on the bed with Ben and bent over his tiny body.

This was the process. CPR, then intubate if there was not a DNR order. When his heart stopped and the brainwaves stopped, we had five minutes to bring him back with the defibrillators. All of the equipment was here. It was my call.

Although I was working frantically with my team, I felt myself stepping away and watching the action. I often had this sensation when emergencies galloped at light speed. Somehow the five minutes lasted hours. Time warped and slowed. The feeling of doing the same things over and over and over was common. That was the hitch in time. I believe this was when the antimatter came back.

Ben came back.

When one of my little patients did not or could not return to us, there was no hitch or slowdown in the emergency room drama. Time slammed forward at a breathless pace and relentlessly beat us to the finish line. Even the best medical teams could not keep up. Afterward, when the time of death was called, the tender absence of the young soul was physically evident. In those cases, I knew the child's antimatter departed quickly and painlessly. No decisions. No agonizing. A clean break. What lay beyond to greet the antimatter in death was all good. The child would be cared for and comforted by the entire universe.

Ben's mother sensed his deathday and made a point of having her son in the hospital every year in early February. A few years after his first death, I was called at home about him by the head nurse.

"Dr. Wixim, Mrs. Martin is here with Ben. She's insisting we admit him. There is no medical basis—his temp and oxygen are both normal, white blood cells slightly elevated but not alarming—so her insurance refuses coverage. She won't take him home. What should we do?" Sandy was one of my favorite head nurses. She loved the kids and supported their parents through the worst living nightmare: watching their children die. Ben and his mom depended on Sandy for consistent pain management and middle-of-the-night jokes. Right now, dealing with a panicked mom and a stubborn insurance rep, she was all business.

"It would help if I could talk to Mrs. Martin. Is she there with you?"

"Sure is. Hold on."

"Dr. Wixim? This is Candace Martin, Ben's mom?"

"Yes, Mrs. Martin. Tell me what's going on with Ben."

"Well, it's hard to explain. So far everyone has told me to just take him home. But I can't." She paused, and I heard a sniff. Then she stated this as a fact, "Dr. Wixim, if I take him home, he'll die." She rushed on, "I know this sounds crazy. But I also know that I'm right."

That's how it was with the space-time gap. The deathday was a mystery to almost everyone. Those who had some inkling of it were puzzled by it. Parents who knew their child's deathday were paralyzed, even when they had no idea how they knew, or even what it was they knew. They suffered from relentless and mysterious anxiety, both physical and emotional, when the planet revolved to the proximity of their child's deathday. Ben's mother felt his deathday pulling her son away and knew that he'd almost died this week in February twice before.

"All right, listen. I have some questions for you. I could ask Sandy because they are medical issues, but it will help me know what to do if I hear the answers from you. Okay?"

I heard a small gasp of hesitation. "It feels like I'm about to take a test that I forgot to study for. What if I give the wrong answers?"

She was a mess and didn't know I was on her side. I was also certain Ben's deathday was coming up and that he was dangerously susceptible to the force it would exert on him in his weakened state.

"Candace, if your son is going to die soon, being in the hospital might not help him. But I'll fight with your insurance to admit him. Just help me find a reason."

"I'm ready." She didn't sound convinced.

"Does he have a fever?"

"No."

"Is he complaining of any pain?"

"No."

"Diarrhea or constipation?"

"Always one or the other—from his meds."

"Is he sleeping?"

"Yes."

"Is he disoriented or—"

"Wait!" she interrupted. "Sleeping. That's it. Actually, he isn't sleeping well. He falls asleep easily but he wakes up four or five times a night."

"Does he stay awake? Insomnia?"

"No. He goes back to sleep."

"Does he complain of pain at night?"

"No," she said, "let me think a minute. See, Ben doesn't even wake me up when he does. He tells me in the morning that he was up. He worries that I need *my* rest. In the morning I always ask, 'How'd you sleep?' and his standard answer is 'Like a rock' or, when he's feeling silly, 'With my eyes closed.' He learned those from his dad. But lately, he just talks about his dreams. His dreams are waking him up."

"Are they nightmares, did he say?"

"No, not nightmares—he never seems afraid. Well, you know Ben isn't afraid of anything. No nightlight, none of that jazz. He's good at falling asleep. He likes to sleep." She paused.

I didn't interrupt her thoughts. I waited. Then she said, "He's dreaming that he's talking to my mom."

"Is Ben close to his grandmother?"

"He was," she said, "before she died."

Then he was hovering nearby, feeling the edges of his space-time gap. She was right that he could die. I didn't know what I could do about it, except grant his mother's request for support. "Candace, I need to examine him right away. Put Sandy on the line."

"Oh, thank you so much." She was crying.

Sandy's voice said, "I don't see how this will fly, Ed. You can't admit a kid for nightmares."

"I can. And I am. Admit him for gastroenteritis and insomnia. I'll wrestle with the insurance later, and I'll be there in an hour."

"Insurance will deny it," she insisted.

"Of course they will. That's what they do. But you know at the end of the battle they'll always cave and pay for the care of a dying six-year-old." I hung up and told Anna I was going to the hospital for a couple hours.

The Thursday I brought Bethany to see Ben was February tenth, one day after his deathday. His mother had been right. The day before, his heart had stopped. No pulse. No brainwaves. We called a code and worked on him for minutes that felt like days. And he came back to us. When I walked in his room with Bethany, he was napping. The room was dark.

Bethany heaved a noisy sigh and whispered, "Who will play War with me, Daddy?"

Ben rolled over and saw her in the doorway and, still groggy, said, "Whatcha' doing here, Beth-Bomb?"

She snorted and said, "Came to smell ya, Ben-Bomb." They both burst into giggles.

I opened the blinds to let in the winter light. I patted Ben's foot and read his chart while Bethany jumped up onto the bed with him.

His chart indicated hourly checks of blood pressure and temperature. He was steady and strong. Lungs were clear. Other than being tired, he was ready to go home.

"Wanna play War?" Ben asked as he pulled a double deck of cards from under his pillow.

Bethany beamed and nodded. They split the cards to shuffle. No dealing required. They made two piles of agreed-upon equal heights and started warring.

I kissed Bethany's head and messed up Ben's mop of new hair and continued on my rounds. He was doing great. He was going home again.

As a pediatrician treating terminally ill children, I could predict who would come back based on whether there was that hitch when they died, whether I had the stepping-away-from-things feeling and the incredible second-by-second déjà vu. This was when the antimatter would return. Their space-time gap opened, and I am convinced everyone in the room would have felt it if they knew to expect it or knew what it was. I watched my peers for evidence of this knowledge. But, even in this, I was isolated.

The times that I'd died were not easy for me. My experiences from the dead side made me a better doctor, but also served to alienate me from normal humans. I knew that it would be impossible to explain what I knew to anyone who'd never survived death, so I never tried.

When Anna died, I felt the hitch. I'm sure I did. That was two days ago, and I'm still waiting for her, trying to be patient, hopeful but helpless. Everything I could've done to influence her choice to return to me is now in my past. On the living side, there's no going back in time to repair mistakes. They gape open like rips in our relationship. Maybe Anna can look past our last few months. Maybe she'll forgive me.

Maybe not.

34
Hair Farming and Parenting

MANY OF MY KIDS IN ONCOLOGY lose all of their hair during treatments. They don't just lose their headhair, as Bethany used to call it, they lose eyelashes and eyebrows, too. Though it bothered Bethany at first, she became accustomed to it. After accompanying me on my evening hospital rounds, I was surprised when our first-grader, with glorious chestnut hair, asked me about my bald young patients.

"Daddy, Jess doesn't have any hairs. Katie, too. Aren't old men the baldies? Little kids—little girls are 'sposed to have hairs like me, right?" She sat up like a puppy in the front seat of my truck, watching every detail of the world go by.

"Yeah, Bethy," I said as I rubbed the top of her little head, "they're supposed to have beautiful hair like you. But the medicine to make them get better takes their hair away." It was a tough concept to explain to my healthy little girl.

"Hey! There's my school! And there's the swing that Maddie wouldn't share!" She frowned at me. "Medicine takes away hairs? Why do you give them that medicine, then?" She absently stroked her long ponytail.

"It's called a 'side effect.' The medicine fights the bad cancer, but also eats up their hair."

"Ick. Hair-eater," she pondered with a sneer. She looked out the window and announced, "Look! A field of cow!"

"Cows," I corrected her but immediately regretted it.

"No, Daddy," she argued. "Mom said we don't have to add s to cow. She said they're like deer and fish. My teacher marked it wrong on my spelling test and Mom wrote her a note."

Bethany never doubted a word her brilliant mother said and wouldn't believe me or her teacher, so I didn't argue. She turned back from the field of future burgers and asked, "Will they always be baldies now?" Like her mother, my daughter was capable of multiple, simultaneous, unrelated conversations—from a field of cow to the side effects of chemotherapy to who knew where we'd go next.

"It takes a while, but usually the hair grows back." If they live long enough.

She held up her long ponytail. "I have lots of hairs. Can't I give 'em some of mine?"

Ah, there's that missing s. I smiled but didn't correct my daughter this time. This was her mother's territory. I'd heard Anna, while tucking Bethany in one night, try to explain why, even if there are a hundred pieces in a bowl, we still call it "popcorn" but we never say we have a bowl of "potato chip" unless there is only one left. Bethany had argued if there was only one potato chip, we wouldn't even need the bowl. They giggled together over that and plural words became their bedtime game—to s, or not to s.

"Actually, you can give them some of yours. There's an organization that takes hair donations, mostly from little girls like you. They make wigs for sick kids. Would you like to do that?"

"Yes, Daddy!" she squealed. "Let's go to there right now!"

So that's where we went next. I was so caught up in her enthusiasm that I brought her to my barber and had ten inches of her silky hair chopped off. My girl was delighted as she carried the long hank of her hair to my truck—to bring home to show her mother.

I should have known how Anna would react. She was always a bit sensitive about hair.

Bethany ran in from the garage screaming, "Mommy!

Mom! I need you *now*!"

Anna appeared right away, saw our little girl and screamed, "Who scalped you?"

When I walked in behind Bethany, Anna's huge eyes landed on my smiling, guilty face.

"Eddie! I will *kill* you! Why did you do this?" She sank to her knees in front of the still beaming Bethany and gingerly touched the ends of her butchered hair. "Oh. My. God!"

There was nothing I could say, so I didn't even try. It would be like arguing about whether to add an s to cow or popcorn. Besides, any comments from me about hair had been forbidden a decade ago on our first date. It was my number one No-Go zone. Fortunately, I didn't have to say anything because I was saved by the six-year-old wizard.

"I'm donut—danish—giving it away, Mommy!" She bounced up and down and squealed with delight, her face all smiles. Anna wept silently, but there was no denying this little girl. "It's *okay*, Mommy. It's for the sick kids at Daddy's hospital." She wrapped an arm around her mother's shoulders and patted her back. Anna wiped her eyes, smiled, and pulled Bethany to her in a bear hug. Perhaps I was home free.

Over Bethany's head, I ventured a single line in my defense, "It's only hair, Anna." It was a risk, but worth it when she let out a snort. I still had it. I could still make her laugh.

Thus began Bethany's hair cycle. She'd grow her hair all the way down her back and then hack it off and give it away—like a hair farm. She managed a donation almost every eighteen months for the rest of her life.

35
My Joey

JOEY WAS MY PAL. I'd tiptoed around in Estrogen World with Anna and Bethany for more than a decade when, suddenly, I had a little boy in my life. My Joey was quiet, like his namesake, my grandfather. He liked to fish and look at books, to draw and think. He'd learned his numbers and letters before his second birthday and was reading when he was three. The kid was a genius. He spent hours under his bed. He was always thinking and had endless questions, none of them about adding s.

"Dad, tell me about the moon."

This was at bedtime, six months before his mother died. I figured he was stalling and wanted to draw me into a long discussion that I couldn't escape, to prolong the tucking in process and put off sleep. I told him, "Our moon is a big rock that orbits our planet." Simple statement. Answered the question. Case closed. Right?

Wrong. "What's 'orbits'? Like the gum?"

"No. Not gum." I scratched my head and sat down on his bed. "The moon orbits the Earth, um . . ." I had to define the word without using the word. "It means the moon travels in a path around the Earth."

"Oh, okay. A big rock, huh? Can we go there and touch it?"

"Well, I guess, in theory, we could go there. We'd need a big rocket though." I tucked his blankets in tight on the sides the way he liked, but left them loose on his feet.

He snuggled down with his black bear, wiggling his toes,

ready to chat the night away, and said, "Cool. Let's get a rocket and go. Does the rocket fly us there?"

"Mostly the rocket part is to help us escape the gravity of this planet and to steer the spaceship in space."

Anna came in to say good-night. She kissed Joey and sat down beside me on the edge of his bed. "What're you guys talking about?"

"Mom! Me and Daddy are going to the moon! We'd have a spaceship, too, right, Dad? How does the gravity thing work? Could we go other places besides the moon?"

"I guess. It depends on how much fuel we bring along. Fuel can be heavy. We'd have to balance the weight of our fuel with our rocket-thrusting capacity and the distance we wanted to cover. We'd have to bring along food, too, because there's no food in space." Yeah, he sucked me into his imagination again. Joey made life fun.

"Hmm. We'd have to balance our fuel with our weight in Oreos. I'd need Oreos. We could leave Mom's granola cereal here, though."

Anna laughed. "Leave it here with me. I'm not going to the moon."

"And what's gravity?" he asked like a dog with a bone. Joey had an incredible mind. He had excellent short- and long-term memory and never forgot a thing. Well, except for where he'd left his blue plastic cowboys. But I always suspected he was just too lazy to look for them. Or else he enjoyed watching his Mom find where he hid them.

Anna took a turn. "Gravity is what holds us all on the Earth. It's an attraction between the world and each of us. There's a gravitational force between every two objects, even you and me. Here, give me a hug—that's the force at work, pulling us together."

While he endured a hug from his mom, Joey dug his index finger two knuckles deep into his left nostril and tried the word "gravitational."

My boy wiped the boogies off his finger on the sheet, out of his mother's view. "Daddy, where can we get a rocket?" I realized he wasn't just stalling. Maybe he was at first, but now he was really interested in this. I shouldn't have misled him into thinking it was a possibility.

"Listen, Joey. I was just talking in theory here. I don't have a rocket, and I don't have enough money to buy one or the brains to build one." His face fell.

"It's okay, Dad. I'll figure it out."

Anna kissed his cheek and said, "I love you to the moon, Joey."

"I love you too, Mom."

After she left, Joey started a dig in his other nostril as I turned out the light. I kissed his forehead, and when I turned to leave, his voice asked from the darkness, "Is 'in theory' the same as when Mom says we could eat Oreos for every meal?"

"Your mom says that?"

He laughed. "Yeah. Then she says I should eat my granola, or peas, or mashed potatoes, or whatever thing I don't like that day."

"I guess that's the same 'in theory.' It means it's possible but not likely. Got that?"

"Got it. 'Night, Daddy."

"Sleep good, Joey."

36

All Roads Lead to Dogs

EARLY IN OUR MARRIAGE, Anna and I did everything together. We even ran together. That's how I first learned about the dogs, which eventually led to finding out her deathday.

We were jogging on a country road behind the high school football field when two frisky Dobermans chased us. Anna panicked and took off sprinting and screaming. She was hysterical. I kicked at one of them and the dogs ran away, but she was still shaky. When we got home and were cooling down with water on the swing, she told me all about her life with dogs. Her dad had a pack of dogs that worshipped him and followed him on his long walks, but Anna was always afraid of strange dogs when she was little. Although her fear faded with time, a barking dog that she didn't know always scared her silly. I tucked this information away for further analysis.

I asked Anna's dad about her fear of dogs. That's when he told me about Molly and the attack that occurred when Anna was just a baby. He said Anna didn't remember much about it, and they rarely spoke of it, but he always felt that it was the root of her fear. I questioned him, rather extensively, about the timing of the attack. He remembered that Anna's mom was pregnant with Michelle. He thought it was sometime in October or November. From then on, like a paranoid hypochondriac, I watched Anna every fall for any signs of danger. And I relaxed, floating carefree, the rest of the year. To my wife, I must've seemed like two different husbands.

When Bethany was eight, mid-November was verified and

the actual date revealed. Anna had to go to a meeting in the middle of one of Bethany's soccer games and was rear-ended by a speeding sixteen-year-old driver. Our totaled van leaned in the ditch at the side of the road. I ran like a madman from the soccer field and thought, damn it, now I know the date for sure. I was astonished to find my Anna still alive.

It was November eleventh, and Anna had avoided her space-time gap like a champ.

Afterward, I didn't know how I'd missed it. Anna always loved November eleventh and 11:11 on the clock. The parallel ones, the symmetry—she loved everything about elevens. The number is a palindrome. When doubled or squared, it makes two more palindromes. She even took her obsession a step further and declared a special affection for the number fifteen because it is written as 1111 in binary. November eleventh became the black hole of each successive year of our marriage.

When Anna began to train for her distance races, she did it with a single-minded fury. There was no stopping her. Each time she left the house to run alone on the country roads, she was gone longer and longer. She never decided how long to run until she was up the church hill. Then she'd analyze how she felt and decide on her route. It was futile for me to ask her how long she'd be gone when she wiggled her feet into her pre-tied sneakers and checked the batteries in her MP3 player. It made her mad to be questioned. She didn't like to tell me a certain planned distance and then have to admit when she returned that she ran less.

I didn't care how far she ran. I just wanted to know when to start searching for her body—especially in November.

I tried to pull off this questioning as a joke.

"Anna," I tried to sound nonchalant as I followed her to the door, "I just need to know how long to wait before I come searching for your body in the ditch."

She flashed her scariest teacher glare at me and said, "Don't be mean to me, Eddie."

This, of course, caused a vivid flashback to our first date—that day when she first warned me never to be mean to her. As she slammed out the door, I tried to salvage myself by yelling, "Your hair looks great!"

One day I'd learn. But not too soon.

I tried not to ask about her running schedule but failed. I tried not to worry about her. I failed again.

She came home from one run in the spring and told me about the three large dogs on her six-mile course. I lost all control; I broke out in a panic. This was her favorite path to run. There was no way I could talk her out of it.

I got out her sewing machine.

It was a Saturday, and there was no one home but me. I had no idea how to use the thing. It looked like the thread was in it already, so I plugged it in and put the pedal to the floor like Anna always did. My attempt at high-tech sewing was a disaster. The machine jammed and wouldn't turn. After almost an hour of mistakes, I found out why that little knife thing is called a seam ripper. Finally, I gave up with the machine. I threaded a needle and sewed by hand. Not much different from giving a kid stitches, really, minus the tears and wiggling. I sewed little white felt pockets onto four pairs of Anna's running shorts. I filled two-ounce spray bottles with diluted ammonia and slid them into the pockets.

I was working on the last pocket, bent over like a pretzel, when Anna walked in from the garage. I was busted.

She gave me a crooked smile and tipped her head to the side. "Eddie? What are you doing to my shorts? And what's that smell?"

"Ammonia. Sorry, I spilled some. Well, quite a bit. I don't smell it anymore. I wonder if that's bad."

"Yes, it's bad," she said as she walked past me to open the window. She came back and leaned over my shoulder. "Tell me,

Ed. Why are you ruining my most favorite shorts on the planet?"

Rather than try to explain, I held up my best effort—one pair even looked decent, the other three were drastically crooked—and, proud of myself, proclaimed, "Pockets!"

It came out more like a question. Anna frowned and took the shorts from me. She stuck two fingers into the felt pouch and asked, "For what?"

"For safety." I nodded and tried to sound authoritative.

"A safety pocket?" She shook her head and came up behind me. She wrapped her arms around my shoulders and said into the side of my neck, "Running is safe, Eddie. My resting pulse is fifty-eight. My blood pressure is one hundred over sixty. Running cannot hurt me. It might be the safest thing I do all day long. It's peaceful. Why do I need a safety pocket? To carry a condom?"

I held up a pink spray bottle of ammonia and asked, "How about carrying this to spray mean animals? The ones who chase and bark. And *bite*."

"Eddie, you are so sweet, but I'm not afraid of dogs anymore. That was twenty, no—cripes!—that was *thirty* years ago. I'm not afraid of dogs anymore. I'm not afraid of *anything* anymore. And, honey, this stuff reeks. I couldn't run with it on me." She hugged me again before she walked away and said over her shoulder, "Please get that smell out of here."

In the end, I convinced her she couldn't run without some protection. I think I convinced her. Maybe I just wore her down. I failed at convincing her to be afraid, though. She conceded that she would use my pockets to carry her cell phone when she ran. I tried not to call her, but sometimes she was out there way too long.

"Eddie—*huff*—what do you want?" she demanded.

My heart lightened and my shoulders unclenched. "Just making sure you're still alive," I said happily.

She was alive, but not happy. "Ed—*huff*—the reason I have the cell phone with me in—*huff*—this ridiculous pocket—*huff*—is to call *you* if I need you—*huff*—*not* for you to call me. *Got that*?" and she was gone.

Those pockets were great.

37

Approaching the End: Memory Leaks

IN GOOD TIMES AND IN BAD, in sickness and in health—
marriage provides all of these scenarios in an unpredictable
medley. During our bad times, the months right before her
deathday, there was nothing I could do to make Anna smile.

On a morning in late September, back on the wrong side
of the sun, I was acutely aware of the path of the Earth as it
zoomed toward my wife's deathday. We'd been avoiding each
other for weeks, so I knew when Anna voluntarily spoke to me
that she must have felt desperate.

I caught her in a rage, throwing keys and her purse to the
floor while she emptied the junk drawer and dug under the
couch cushions while Joey waited for her in the car.

"Anna, what's wrong?"

She glanced at me, pissed. Then she said, "Hold on, will
you?"

I did.

As she rushed past me, she barked, "I'm late, Eddie."

She was like the Tasmanian devil. I should have known
better than to step in her path, but I am a fixer. I couldn't help
myself, but maybe I could help her. "Can I help?"

She glared at me, and I felt guilt creep up between my
shoulders, like whatever she'd lost had been hidden by me.
"No. Just leave me alone and I'll find it myself." She marched
into the bedroom.

I followed her because I'm an idiot.

"Just tell me what you lost," I offered.

"Can you hold on?" she asked. "Ed, I don't have time to talk about it. I'm late." She swiped everything off of her dresser with one hand. "Picture twenty kids bouncing off the walls with no teacher in the room. Their day won't start until I arrive. And when I get there," she tossed the pillows off the bed, "first I have to explain to the pissed-off principal that I'm late again because I couldn't find my damn—" she paused, stopped yelling, and whispered, "cell phone."

She stopped and straightened up, silent and still. Stricken. She turned her back on me and said, "Okay. Sorry." A deep ragged breath, then, "Yeah, Michelle, I'll talk to you tonight. Yeah. Yeah. Love you, too. 'Bye."

As she lowered it from her ear, Anna stared in disbelief at the cell phone in her hand. The cell phone for which she ripped our house apart. One half of my mind told me this should be funny. It *would* be funny if I didn't know why it was happening. Anna couldn't keep her thoughts unscrambled with her deathday approaching and exerting its gravitational force field on her.

My sad wife looked up at me, met my eyes full on for the first time in a month, pleading with me to help her laugh this one off.

I couldn't do it. We weren't in our time when we could laugh together. We were on the bad side of the sun. I watched a tear drip from her chin. I shook my head and walked away. I'm sure I just looked disgusted with her. Inside I was falling apart right alongside her.

| | | |

I KNEW things were getting even worse when she called me on that same cell phone later that week while she was out running.

"Hey, what is it?" I was neutral and guarded when I picked up.

"Eddie. I need a ride." She tried to sound like it was no big deal for her to need a ride home from her run. No big deal for her to call me and actually ask for my help.

It was early October, a whole month away from her deathday, so I knew she wasn't in real danger yet. "Are you hurt?"

"No." I heard her sniffle. "I'm lost."

"How can I find you? What do you remember?"

"I'm on one of those back roads where I run, all trees and hills, but I can't remember which one." Silence for a moment and then she said, "I zoned out."

I grabbed the car keys.

"Let me get Joey, and we'll come find you. Okay?"

"Yeah. Call me back." She hung up.

We found her half an hour later sitting on a fallen tree trunk on the side of the road, about three miles and two wrong turns off her regular running route. She wiped her eyes dry and said she wasn't paying attention while she ran. I'm a distance runner, too, so I could relate, but I'd never lost track of where I was like that.

She sat beside me in my truck, weeping, and I didn't comfort her. I couldn't. Instead, in my blind fear, I admonished her for running so far out, as though she got lost on purpose.

"Anna, you have got to be careful!" I yelled at her and banged the dashboard. Joey sat between us, eyes wide.

"Careful, Ed? Careful? I was *running*."

"But you could get hurt!"

"No, I could not! And what do you care, anyway?"

"Anna, listen." I lowered my voice. "There's a gap, a hole. It can pull you in, take you away. Stay away from it. Stay still. Stay home," I pleaded.

She sniffled, and I knew I'd made her cry again. She wasn't listening to me. Or maybe she couldn't hear these words.

"Anna?"

"Don't be mean, Eddie.

"I just want you to be safe."

"What?" she barked at me. "Am I supposed to thank you for rescuing me?"

"I just don't want you to get hurt," I said. Lame. Weak. Helpless.

"You're like a broken record, Ed. You already said that. Just shut up, will you?" And she resumed her weeping, head turned away.

I shut up. My warnings couldn't get through. Damn the universe.

In my frustration, I treated Anna like an ignorant child instead of my brilliant wife. I hurt her because I was hurting. Weeks from her deathday, she was disintegrating before my eyes. I couldn't even hug her because I could not function. I could not breathe. I could not talk. I staggered through the days as they whipped past me, out of my grasp. It felt like my wife was already dead. I knew I couldn't live without her, and yet I had no way to protect her. I was paralyzed by the dreadful idea of life without Anna and by my growing certainty that she'd choose to leave me and not come back.

Taken all together—her cooking, her vaporous memory, and losing her way—it was apparent that Anna was coming unglued. Her matter and antimatter were separating.

It was only a matter of time, a finite and definite amount of time, until she left me.

38
Anna's Deathday

A WEEK BEFORE ANNA DIED, I came home from work at the end of a long day at the hospital. I'd lost a favorite patient that day. They were all my favorites, I'll admit, but watching sweet Selma die was tough on the entire staff.

I walked into our house, disheveled, and badly needing a hug and a few minutes alone with my wife, but certain I couldn't have either. Joey came running to greet me. "Daddy!" he yelled. I squatted and he launched himself into my arms. I took the available hug. So healthy and strong, he smelled like grass and chocolate. I couldn't lift him; he was too big for that, so I sat with him on the floor in my wrinkled scrubs while my boy chatted about his day.

"I kicked a homerun in kickball today, Daddy. And I learned to count to ten in Spanish. Wanna hear?" He didn't wait for a response. He just launched into, "*Uno, dos, tres, quatro, cinco, seis . . .*" and got stuck.

I prompted, "*Siete?*" and he jumped back in and finished.

"Know what else I know? Your shirt is *rojo*, and Mommy's skirt is *negro*! How's that?"

I kissed his forehead and said, "Amazing, champ!" The house was quiet. "Where's your *madre*?"

"On the swing. She wanted some peace. She was talking to Bethany on the phone, but now she's grading papers." He pointed out the back window, and I saw Anna outside. She looked peaceful when she didn't know I was nearby.

"What do you want for dinner?" I asked.

"Mac and cheese!" he yelled. No surprise there.

"Coming up," I announced. I pulled some hotdogs from the fridge to complement the cheesy noodles.

Twenty minutes later, I sent Joey outside to announce dinner to his mom. "Tell *tu madre* that *dinero es* ready." That's how Anna and I communicated—through our Spanish-speaking son.

"Dad," he said with two accusing syllables, "*dinero* is money, not food." He giggled and ran out the back door to his mom.

I saw Anna look up when she heard the door slam. Irrational jealousy stabbed at my heart when she gave Joey her smile. I wished I could hear her voice but couldn't through the closed windows. She shook her head. Joey turned to run back inside, but she caught his hand and said something to him. He tiptoed to her. She bent down so he could kiss her cheek. This made my wife smile again, but made me cry.

| | | |

LATER THAT NIGHT, I walked in on Anna, quite innocently, as she changed into her pajamas. Her clothes were strewn all over the floor in our walk-in closet. She didn't hear me come in. The sight of her bare back, so familiar and beckoning, stopped me cold. I hadn't seen her skin in months.

"Anna . . ." I sighed, forgetting everything and just seeing my best friend, my other half.

She froze. She didn't turn around. In March, she would have removed the rest of her clothes and greeted me with a hug. That night she said, "No, Ed. Just get out."

I was not permitted to touch her unless I was nice to her. It was an agreed upon stipulation from early in our marriage when we were learning to live together. Since I couldn't meet her eye without looking like a fox with bird feathers in my teeth, she didn't trust me. I didn't blame her. But I was dying right beside her.

I had no logical defense for my behavior. Nothing I could say that she would understand, and so I remained silent. She cried alone in the bathroom with the door locked every night before she came to bed. We slept side by side but separated by a gaping chasm. Bad days followed bad nights. She hit rock bottom and proclaimed that her mother was right about me. How could I hurt her so much, and why couldn't I stop?

| | | |

MY RELIEF at finding Anna still alive on November twelfth every preceding year for almost a decade was like coming up for oxygen after months of drowning. This year, I couldn't see beyond her deathday. I couldn't imagine that we would survive this time as we had so many years before.

November twelfth had become my favorite day of the year, a personal holiday of sorts. Last year, when I woke up beside Anna on the morning of the twelfth, she was already awake. I could tell by her breathing. She lay on her side, facing away from me, curled up into a ball on the very edge of the bed. I rolled to her and lay an inch away without touching her, marveling that she wasn't gone. She stiffened at my closeness, unaccustomed to it.

"I'm sorry," I said to the back of her head. "I've been an ass."

"Yes. You have."

"It's over, I think."

"Well. Good for you." She wasn't giving an inch.

"Can I fix it?" I asked.

She didn't answer, so I said, "I really miss you."

"Then why did you leave again?" She turned around and faced me, tears running down her cheek into her ear.

"Because I'm an idiot."

"I know that better than anyone."

"I'm sorry," I said again.

"You've been an ass."

"Anna," I breathed out her name and cautiously stroked her cheek, wiping away the tears. I remembered catching a single tear on her face on our wedding day. A surprising memory since I didn't remember our wedding day under normal circumstances. "No more crying." That made her cry even more. She'd missed me, too, and could no longer resist our mutual gravity. It was easier now because her deathday had released her. She crumpled into my arms.

Although she never understood my strange behavior, why I pulled away, Anna always welcomed me back. Our lives carried on.

Most people live their lives as though they have forever, an infinite supply of minutes and hours, weeks and years. They never imagine that they could die tomorrow, or even today. Knowing that my deathday is April second gives me a superhuman feeling the other three hundred and sixty-four days of the year. I know I won't die any other day. With my knowledge of the significance of November eleventh, I could function for about ten months each year after Anna's deathday passed. But as the planet's orbit approached the end of summer, every year my dread knocked me down and pinned me there to watch and wait.

| | | |

EACH FALL, in the midst of our annual cold war, I longed for the simplicity of our early days. Despite my awkwardness, even our first date had shown such promise. At the end of that night, I managed to get Anna to take a walk through campus with me. It was cool, and she put on that sweater I suggested she bring. We talked about everything: family, hopes and dreams, God, population explosion, politics, our fears, and just *everything*. She was my perfect match, and I knew it well before she had any idea that I was in crazy love with her and would propose as soon as I reasonably could without scaring her away.

We were walking through the rose path, her hand small and warm in mine. I suggested we sit down for a while on a bench. My intentions were completely dishonorable. I wanted a kiss, had a peculiar feeling I would get one, and yet I was petrified.

Anna sat down and said, "Do you bring all your first dates here?"

"No," I gulped. Could I tell her that I rarely had time or interest in dating, or would that just reveal me as a loser nerd?

"Just the ones with awful hair so you don't have to be seen in public?" she asked.

I hoped she was joking. I hoped she would someday forgive my comment about her hair. "Actually, it has nothing to do with their hair."

"Oh?" she asked. "Then what prompts you to bring a girl in the dark to a bench on the rose path?"

I decided to risk my life and said, "I just bring the ones I want to kiss."

"Really?" she asked warily. "How many times have you been here?"

Still out on a limb, torn between impressing her with my lady-killer skills and risking my self-esteem with the truth, I said, "Never before tonight."

Silence. We sat side by side in silence and the minutes danced around us. I could hear Anna breathing. I know it was her because I was holding my breath, every muscle tensed. I wished I could hear what she was thinking. What thoughts swirled in her head and why was she looking at me like that? Then she took my hand and brought it to her face. She spread open my hand on her cheek and turned her head to press her soft lips to the center of my palm.

The incredible pounding of my heart blocked the silence of the night.

Still in control of my hand, she placed it on her heart and said, "Not the best first kiss, but look what it did to my heart."

Her skin was warm and soft. Her heart was beating wildly and she was breathing as though she'd just sprinted a mile. I felt the stirrings of something that resembled hope. Maybe I had a shot with this girl because it seemed she might like me back.

My mind was a blur, so my body took control. With one awkward arm around her shoulders, I pulled her to me. And she let me. I lowered my face to hers until we were sharing the same molecules of air. I touched her curly hair and said, "I love your hair."

She said, "Baloney."

"I do," I insisted.

"I'll grow it out for you."

"Good," I said. I think I sighed too loudly.

She laughed and said, "Just kiss me already." She was smiling when I finally did.

39
Mood Swings

I CALLED HOME FROM THE HOSPITAL on November ninth to tell Anna I would be stuck there late and would miss dinner. She answered the phone in a huff. Her "hello!" was like a command.

It didn't sound like my Anna. Even when she was in a mood, she would fake it on the phone and do that singsong, three-syllable "hello-oh" that always sounded like her mom. When we were dating and I called her at her parents' house, Anna's mom would answer the phone all sweet like that—until she found out it was me, and then she'd turn into the drill sergeant.

I said to my wife, "Mrs. Wixim?"

"Who's calling?"

Amused that she didn't recognize my voice, I lost my mind and turned a little into my dad, dropped my voice an octave, and said, "Mrs. Wixim, you are the lucky winner of a free in-home pest inspection." Anna loved to torment telemarketers. Her goal was to harass them until either they lost it laughing or hung up on her.

When she didn't reply, I rushed on, hoping in my disguise that I could make her laugh. "Our highly trained bug engineers will come to your home and look for black and brown and green insects. How about that?"

She sighed and said, "Can you hold on a sec? There's a three foot cockroach crawling up my skirt, and I have to whomp it." She whomped something. With the phone. Then there was a thud.

"Mrs. Wixim?" I tried to get her back. "Hello? Are you there?"

"Yeah, yeah, yeah, I'm still here. But the sucker isn't dead yet. Can you send your guys over right now? I need backup." Then she let out a blood-curdling scream that ended in a cackle, and with a final grunt, she hung up.

When I got home that night, she was in a fine mood and didn't even complain that I hadn't called to tell her I'd be late. I went out on a limb and risked it. I told her it was me on the phone.

"Hey, Anna, did you know it was me? I'm the bug guy!" I offered an attempt at a laugh. She'd found it funny when she thought she was dealing with a stranger, a telemarketer. I missed her and us, terribly. Maybe we could have a little reunion over this one.

"What?" Her crumpled face told me I was repulsive. "Now you're calling me and taunting me and *making fun* of me?" She smashed the laundry basket down on the counter and, instead of walking away, this time she turned on me. "I told you not to be mean to me. I wasn't kidding, Eddie."

Utter failure. The wall between us was too high. I should have kept my mouth shut and just let her enjoy her little joke. Then I could have held it for myself, too.

She took two steps toward me and repeated, "Didn't I tell you not to be mean?"

"You did. Many times," I said in retreat. "I'm sorry."

Together, we had no humor. I'd killed it.

Less than two revolutions of the Earth separated us from Anna's deathday, and every bridge between us was shattered. I had absolutely no hope. I opened the back door and stepped into the rainy night to get away.

40
November 11

WHEN ANNA FIRST BEGAN TEACHING high school, she was in charge of a tough bunch of students for the first few years. Apparently that's what they do to new teachers. They stick them with the "bad" kids until they learn the ropes and gain some seniority. For the last few years, Anna mostly taught the higher-level classes and didn't have to directly deal with the discipline issues abundant in lower-level ones. She dealt with delinquents in the halls between classes each day. But her time in the well, as they called it, taught her to alter her kindhearted, everybody-is-nice ways and handle the rougher kids harshly. That's what they responded to. Don't back down, hold your ground, believe you are right and tell them what to do. My little Anna would stand up to anyone. She had no fear.

I carried a truckload of fear for her. As November eleventh approached this year, my mind ran through all the dangers she'd face that day. It would be a school day, so there was the added possibility of an attack on campus. Could I possibly convince her that her horoscope said she should be nice that day? Doubtful.

I decided my best hope was to keep Anna home all day.

On the morning of Friday, November eleventh, I awoke with a start. Anna wasn't awake yet. She was lying close to me in our bed. I leaned over, quiet as a mouse, held my breath, and brought my ear dangerously close to her face to check if she was breathing.

She rolled over just then and cracked me on the nose with

her elbow. Ow.

Definitely breathing. But she remained asleep, I thought.

I carefully got out of bed and walked around to her side. I was pretty sure I couldn't talk her into staying home, so I decided to turn off her alarm clock so she would oversleep.

"Eddie, what are you doing?" her groggy voice asked.

Busted. "Just checking the time?" I offered.

"What time is it? Did you make the coffee yet?"

I left the room to make coffee, and I heard the shower turn on. Joey was up early, too, and greeted me in the kitchen.

"Hi, Daddy. Is Mom up?"

"In the shower. Hungry?" I asked.

Joey's sleepy eyes lit up. "Can I have breakfast right now, right away?"

"Sure," I said. "Whatcha want?"

"Oreos, please."

I looked up from the coffee grounds and caught the grin on his face. If this was indeed his last morning with his mom, I didn't want them to have their traditional breakfast fight. I wanted him fed before Anna came out of the shower. But Oreos would ensure that, although Joey would be happy, Anna would crucify *me* on what might be our last morning together. I thought about it and decided to take my chances.

"All right, Joey. Two Oreos, with a big glass of milk—"

"Chocolate milk?" he suggested.

"Don't push your luck. Two Oreos, white milk, and then toast and orange juice when Mom gets out of the shower. Deal?"

"Deal." He climbed up on the stool and pulled down the Oreos. Then he asked, "Why?"

"Why what?"

"Why can I have Oreos for breakfast?" That's my boy. Questions all day long.

I took the plunge. "I need your help with something. I want

you to stay home from school today."

"Cool! Can we ride bikes?"

"No, Joey. I want you to tell Mom you don't feel well so she'll stay home with you." This would be a tough sell. The kid never got sick. And when he was sick, he never complained. Snot running down his nose, cough and fever, and he'd be out playing in the snow.

"Why?"

That word was gyped out of its fourth letter. "Don't worry about why. Will you do it?"

The little shyster saw he had something I wanted. His brain gears were rolling. He smiled his cat smile at me and said, "For three cookies, no milk."

"Deal." I delivered the goods, he scarfed them down, and we were moving on to toast and juice when Anna walked out of the bedroom with a towel on her head.

She walked straight to Joey to pat down his morning hair and wordlessly accepted the cup of coffee I had ready for her. She was taking her first slurp, nose buried in the cup, eyes momentarily closed, when Joey looked up at her with his grimace face. In that split second, I regretted the absence of the milk. It would have helped to wash the chocolate crumbs from his teeth. His mother opened her eyes and saw the remnants of Joey's forbidden breakfast. That's when he began his fake whining, and he leaned to her for a hug.

Anna wrapped one arm around him in what appeared to be a hug, but she was just getting a firm grip on him so her free hand could tilt up his chin. Joey was nose to nose with her when she said, "Show me those teeth."

I held my breath and hoped he'd keep his mouth shut. When he giggled, my heart burst open. His mother was going to kill me and then leave me.

With an accusing glance in my direction, which I shamelessly avoided, Anna released Joey and grabbed her coffee cup. She stole all the air out of the room when she marched back to the bedroom to get dressed.

Joey and I looked at each other. He smiled, showing big brown chunks of Oreo between each pair of his little teeth. I couldn't share his amusement. My plan was unraveling.

I watched in horror as Anna packed her school bag and headed out the door. I had failed to trick my wife into staying home, staying safe. I tried one more desperate tactic as she was starting her car. I was going to tell her the truth. Universe be damned.

"Honey?" I said as I leaned my head in the passenger window and boldly asked my wife to stay home with me, to stay safe with me, to live. Breathless, I reached out across our dividing line and held tight to her wrist while I pleaded with her to choose me. I glanced around, scared shitless, like a fugitive on the run, and told her this day would be dangerous. She could get hurt. She had to be careful of forces acting on her today, every second of this interminable day. This damned day. She didn't hear me. She couldn't hear me. My words spilled unheard from my lips and were sucked into the void.

"Anna, honey, please be careful today." She heard that.

My wife looked at me with a quivering chin. She wrenched her arm from my fingers and slowly, repeatedly, shook her head at me in wonder, left eyebrow raised, surely thinking *Why is this man such an ass?* "Enough with the *honey* crap. I'm going to work," she said curtly as a tear crept from behind the dark glasses that hid her eyes.

In a pained whisper, "Good-bye, Anna," came from my lips. Solemn, final, defeated.

She pulled down the glasses, and her sad eyes met mine one last time. She blew out her breath as she said, "See you tonight. *Honey.*"

And she left me.

Oh, please, I begged, *please let me see her tonight.*

41
My Deaths

ON APRIL FOOLS' DAY the year I was born, my mother called my dad at work at two in the afternoon to tell him she was starting her labor and needed a ride to the hospital. Dad was a famous jokester and was certain Mom was playing games with him. I wasn't due until late May.

Dad's reply was, "Call a cab, babe."

There was no way my mother could pull an April Fools' joke over on him. He had one planned for her that night. He was going to make her get all dressed up to go out to a fancy dinner, makeup and jewelry and all that girly stuff. Then he was going to pull into Jack's Drive-In and order her a hot dog and chocolate milk shake.

Dad loved April Fools' Day. I heard his stories every year. They were the background music while I ate my birthday cake.

So when Mom called him, in labor for the first time, and asked for a ride, Dad didn't fall for her old tricks. When she started protesting about a cab, he said, "Right. I'll meet you at the hospital." Click. Dial tone.

Mom cried for a little while, and then she called her mom and her sister and they drove her to the hospital. It wasn't until Dad arrived home that night and found the house empty that it occurred to him that something was up. The phone rang as he unwound his tie.

"Jack, are you coming to the hospital or not?" demanded his mother-in-law.

Dad snickered. He was impressed. This was good stuff.

Mom was taking this charade pretty far to have her mother call and get in on it. Before he could reply, my grandmother said, "I told Debbie not to get involved with you. You are never serious. Poor girl is a mess of worry over this baby coming so early, and you ignored her." Then she hung up.

With a jolt, my dad doubted himself. Maybe Mom really was at the hospital. He drove like a maniac and arrived in time to see her and beg for forgiveness before I was born.

Mom was in labor all night, and I was born at 3:57 a.m. on April second. Premature babies back then were not expected to live. I heard the story of the odds of my survival and my valiant struggle so many times it's almost like I remember it. Obviously, I lived.

When I died again six years later, my guide on the dead side helped me look around, and I got to spend some time reliving my birthday and my perilous loitering at the edge of my two-way portal.

I was diagnosed with leukemia a week before I started kindergarten. The chemotherapy treatments knocked out all of my hair and left me physically weak, but I loved to go to school. It didn't matter to me if the kids thought I was a freak. One little red-haired girl cried whenever she had to sit by me. It didn't help that Jimmy, the biggest bully, always made her rub my bald head and told her that it would make all her long hair fall out. I liked getting my head rubbed. It felt good.

Kindergarten was the coolest place to be. We colored and played and counted and learned to read. It was the best thing that ever happened to me. Everyone around me was concerned that my life was ending, but I don't recall any fear of my illness. Although I was weak, I was able to play and learn. Hug my mom. Sit on my baby brother's head. Roll in the wet grass with my big, smelly dog, Beau. Eat ice cream and chocolate cookies and licorice. Life didn't feel so different to me sick. I loved being a kid.

A week before my sixth birthday, I was hospitalized for a dangerously high white blood count. I was still in the hospital on April Fools' Day, the day before my sixth birthday, so Dad stayed with me, pulling jokes on the nurses. He had me giggling so hard I couldn't catch my breath when he held down the call button for Nurse Edna, but acted surprised each time she came to the room to ask what I needed. Dad was perfectly straight-faced when he was in a prank. The third time he hit the button, he made me hide under the bed and he got in it. When Edna came in the room, fuming that he wouldn't stop calling her for nothing, he was cowering under the sheets. When she yanked them down, he pretended to be asleep. She shook him again and again, and he wouldn't budge. Then she heard me laughing under the bed and pulled me out and sat me on top of Dad.

That night I turned six years old and I died.

Dad was devastated. I watched him for whole days and missed him. I'd never seen him cry before.

Mom was all business after I died. She took care of my little brother and arranged for my funeral. She angrily tossed away my birthday cake and candles and balloons and streamers. Dad was a puddle.

Maybe because I was so young, it wasn't hard for me to understand the matter and antimatter stuff. It was obvious that I didn't have my body anymore, but I knew I was still me. I couldn't feel anything, and it seemed like I was flying, but I remained still most of the time. I just hovered among my family. They didn't seem to know I was there. Well, I think maybe my Mom did.

At four o'clock in the afternoon on the day after I died, the doorbell rang. My friends from kindergarten arrived for my birthday party laden with gifts. Mom told them the party was canceled and sent them home.

42

First Guide: Grampa

I WAS FOUR when Grampa died, just a few months before my little brother Billy was born. Grampa was my pal and taught me to be quiet while we fished. He also taught me to stay quiet when Grandma was yelling at me and to smile when she was yelling at someone else. That's how Grampa dealt with any conflict. He was quiet.

Grampa was so quiet in death that I didn't even know he was with me when he found me on the dead side. Then, when I felt his presence, I asked, "Grampa, is that you?"

"Yep," he said. "What in the world are you doing here already?"

"I don't know. I was playing with Daddy, and then I got here and everything was so quiet."

"Yep," he said, again. "I like it quiet. But I bet you'll find it a bit boring after time with your Dad."

"Grampa, how come I can watch them, but they don't know I'm there?" One thing about Grampa, he knew everything.

"Well, boy, they don't know you're there because your body doesn't work anymore. See, you got real sick. Without a working body, you can't be alive anymore."

"Oh." I thought about it a little while and then asked, "Your body doesn't work either, huh?"

"Nope. Listening to Grandma complaining all those years wore my old body out."

"But my body wasn't too old. I was only just turning six."

"That's right. It was your birthday, eh? I guess I should say happy birthday then."

"Guess not. I been watching Mom, and she threw out my happy birthday and sent my friends away."

"Yep. That's your mom. She can deal with stuff if she keeps on moving. Your dad's not doing too good, though. Did you see him crying?"

"Uh huh. He's real sad."

Grampa hid in his quiet for a long time. I watched Daddy, and I felt like I was alone. He sat by himself with the old TV on but without the sound. He didn't even change the channels or adjust the bunny ear wires to make the picture better when it started to flip. Mom came in, looked at him and turned off the TV, and he didn't even yell at her.

Late that night when the house was dark, I was still watching them. Mom got up from bed. She walked through the house without turning any lights on and wasn't even scared. She went into my bedroom and took my blanket. Then she sat in the dark at the kitchen table. I wished I could be with her and have her hold me like when I was little.

And then, in a flash of sparks, I *was* little. Even smaller than little. Mom was in the hospital and Daddy and Grandma were arguing in the hallway outside her room. Mom was crying and grunting and sometimes yelling bad words. A doctor and two nurses were talking to her, trying to calm her, but she stayed real mad. After a while, there was different crying in the room with Mom. It sounded sort of like a kitten. Daddy started to go into the room, but a nurse came out fast and stopped him on her way by. Then two more nurses ran into the room and came out with a teeny tiny baby and ran down the hall with him. Daddy and Grandma stopped arguing.

I followed the baby.

That's when I realized he was me.

They named me Premature. When Mom finally pushed me

out, I was blue, and the doctor was worried. But my antimatter rushed to my body, and I started breathing and cried out. The matter was weak, though, and the antimatter hesitated. That's the minute they all thought that I would die, and the nurses started running around. Down the hall in the new room there were oxygen tents and machines. The nurses hooked up my tiny body to a respirator, and I started to breathe with help. That's when the antimatter, which was hovering just above the matter, reattached, and my pulse started again.

This was my first clear understanding of matter and antimatter. Body and soul. I was six years young, newly dead, and watching my own birth.

In the eight weeks after my physical birth, the doctors wouldn't give up on my body, and my antimatter was never far away. Gradually my body became stronger and the antimatter didn't dislocate anymore. They renamed me Stable then and sent me home.

Now, at six years old, I was dead again, and it didn't hurt. It wasn't scary. But I missed my mom and daddy. I missed my smelly dog. I sort of missed my baby brother. I could be with them, but they didn't know I was there.

It was Grampa's idea to send me back.

I asked him, "How come I kept almost dying after I was born?"

"Well, Eddie, it seems your antimatter wanted to join your matter real bad. They were a good, strong match, but they weren't ready for each other. The matter, a special group of molecules in your brain, had more growing to do, and your antimatter wasn't expecting to join it for a few months. Once your body was born, the antimatter accelerated to it at the speed of light. I know you don't understand how fast that is, but it's way faster than your dad's car."

"Dad's car is superfast! On the highway, when we go for rides without Mom, he really gets her going."

"I know. I've spent some energy watching you. Now your antimatter joined your body with some incredible force."

"Like a punch?"

"Yes! Quite a lot like a punch. And it bounced back off right away, then landed again and popped away sort of like a bouncing ball—each bounce gets lower until the ball stops bouncing. Do you see what I mean?"

I thought about a bouncing ball, and that made sense. I liked to play with the balls on the playground at school.

"So then what made my antimatter finally stick?"

"Well, a good match between matter and antimatter makes a strong attraction for each other. Kind of like two magnets. Once the antimatter slows down its bouncing, it can feel the attraction for the matter better."

"Why was my antimatter coming in so fast? Is it always that fast?"

"The antimatter of you is what you are now, Eddie. It's your soul. It doesn't weigh much compared to the atoms and molecules of your body, and naturally travels at the speed of light. When your body arrived early, your antimatter whipped in fast to get to it. That caused the force and the bouncing."

Grampa was so smart. I think he knew everything. "Once it stopped bouncing and stuck, I didn't die anymore?"

"That's right."

"Well, how come I died on my sixth birthday?"

"That has puzzled me. Your body was getting stronger in the last months, until your white blood cell count went back up a week ago. It's possible your body was just weak enough that when your deathday, which, in your case, happens to be your birthday, came along, you just slipped through the crack."

These were some big ideas for a little kid, but I got the gist of what Grampa was saying. "Eddie, your crack in space-time is still open. You haven't traveled far since you died." He paused for a long time then said, almost in a whisper, "Why don't you slip back in?"

It sounded like he was telling me a secret, so I whispered, too. "Back into what?"

"Back into your life. Go back. Be a kid. Live a good, long life. I'll enjoy watching it."

And that's what I did. Grampa helped me travel back in time about half an Earth day. Then he helped my antimatter cling to my body during the night that I died. He sort of hovered above me and used his antimatter force field to push down on mine and keep it in my body.

The next morning I woke up. The doctor decided my white blood count was low enough to send me home for a few days, and my mom threw the best birthday party I ever had.

Although I was so young, I instinctively knew I couldn't make my living family understand what had happened to me. Mom would say it was just a dream, and Daddy would make a joke about it. I also had a strong feeling that Grampa wasn't supposed to do what he did for me. The next time I died, I found out I was right about that.

It might be because I had these life-death crossovers so young that I remember a lot about them. They gave me an insight into what life and death really mean, but they isolated me from the rest of humanity who were blissfully unaware of it all. At times, for the rest of my life, I felt lonely and joked with the few close friends I found that I wanted to return to my home planet.

43

Another Birthday-Deathday, Another Guide

WHEN I TURNED TWENTY, it happened again: I died in my sleep on April second. I didn't wake up on my birthday-deathday. I was on the dead side. That's when I met the little red-haired girl from kindergarten.

This time I wasn't sick; my antimatter just detached. Luckily, my new guide joined me right away and clearly explained my situation.

"You're dead," she said.

"Oh. Again?"

"Yes. Mistake this time, though. Just a little slip-through, so they sent me to do a Rebound. Looks like your space-time crack is wider than normal—a bit flexible, not zipped up too tight—possibly because your birthday and deathday are the same."

"Do I know you?"

"Here's a big hint: I used to cry in kindergarten when they made me rub your bald head and said my hair would fall out, too."

I remembered her. "Was your name Lizzie?"

"That was me. Still is, even though I'm dead, too."

"What happened to you?" I asked. It seemed polite to sound interested, although I wasn't so much.

"Suicide. I was fifteen and pissed at the world. Tattooed, pierced, shaved head. Could not get happy, so I just quit. I'm your guide this time because I'm a stellar Rebounder, and you need to go back quick. I couldn't go back—the gift of choice is only allowed once each trip, so, since I chose to die, there were no choices left for me on the dead side. Anyhoo, now I have the lovely job of quick escorts when someone slips through who shouldn't be here yet. That's you, fella. So get going."

"Wait! Please, wait," I stalled. "Am I really in a hurry? Can't I hang around for a while and think and maybe ask some questions?"

She answered carefully, "No, there's no hurry. It's just that you're a special case this time. There's no reason to make any difficult decisions. You're expected to go back. Your matter is waiting and healthy, so back you go. About the other, I don't usually answer questions. Not my specialty. I'm not that kind of guide, like your grampa. I'm more like a traffic cop here on the dead side. Do you understand?"

I did. But I felt good. Peaceful. No hurry. Suspended. And there were so many things to think about. Things I never made time for in my life of studying science and math all day and night.

"I think I'll take my time," I announced. "I won't ask hard questions. Just let me bounce some ideas off you. You can give your opinions on things, can't you?"

"Sometimes."

"All right, let's start with this: if you were still a kid, just fifteen when you died, do you know as much about the universe and life and all the big questions as someone who lived, say, to be eighty?"

"Sure. When you die, your antimatter becomes part of the fabric of the universe. You know everything. Maybe not all at once. That would probably hurt. But gradually, as you think of things, you realize there are no mysteries that you can't fathom. It's cool. Makes me wonder why I spent so much time studying from those books in school while I lived."

"Then, right now, all I have to do is think of something that I want to understand and it will come to me?"

"Pretty much, that's how it seems to me. But since you're going back soon, and I mean very soon—I have other people to help, you know—it's possible you might not be able to get to the big and deep questions."

The big and deep. That sounded incredible. There was so much to the big and deep. I didn't even know where to start. It seemed to me that I could ponder the universe at my leisure forever and maybe never cover all of the big and deep. For the curious geek in me, this was an enticing feature of death.

"And that's exactly why I had to get to you so fast—to intercept and point you back—because we all knew you'd like the dead side a bit more than a normal guy." Apparently Lizzie could hear me thinking. "So, how about it? Ready to get back into the ol' body?"

"Not yet. I can't stop thinking of more big and deep questions. Let's start with this one. I want to understand what happened when I died and came back when I was six. Grampa helped me, but he didn't call himself a Rebounder. What kind of guide was he?"

"No guide, no matter what kind they are, may *ever* make the decision for a newly dead soul when there is a choice to be made. In your case, right now, there is no decision: you slipped through unexpectedly and accidentally, so you must go back. No question. No discussion. No decision. No choices. Just get back in there. But when you were six, your grampa made the decision for you."

"That doesn't seem so bad to me. I was little, and I needed his help. He was the perfect guide for me."

"Of course he was the right guide for you," Lizzie said. "He loved you and made you feel safe. The right guide is always chosen. When the newly dead begin to agonize over their decision, multiple guides can be sent it. But a guide isn't supposed to do more than help the newly dead realize that they have to make decisions, and help them travel to where and when they want to go. Your grampa made your decision for you and then helped you carry it out."

"I guess it makes sense that there are some restrictions for guides. But just like rules and laws in life, are there reasons for the rules out here, or are they just there to keep things uniform?"

"Please!" she boomed. "Do not belittle the universe by comparing it to your little home planet and rules crafted by humans!"

"Sorry." I had a vivid flashback of her temper when she was five and her subsequent screeching back in kindergarten. Lizzie hadn't changed.

Finally, she continued more calmly. "Of course there are reasons for guide rules. In this case, the rule of no help with decisions is because guides know so much. We've had the opportunity to travel at light speed, forward and backward in time, watching over our people on the living side and checking out the coolest and farthest corners of the universe. Don't you see that knowledge of these things is too big and deep for a mere living human on our tiny rock of a planet in our little Milky Way galaxy in our remote corner of all of space?"

"Yeah! Put it that way and it makes me feel so small."

"So small. Yes. And so vital. All matter and antimatter exist in a frantic dance. Together, the most miniscule pieces of matter and antimatter combine to make our beautiful wondrous universe. With all this knowledge, a guide could think she had godlike powers when she helped the newly dead. No small hunk of antimatter, no single soul, may act in a manner to try to control either space or time. Once your grampa decided he was making you go back, he used the power of his antimatter to influence yours. This well-meant mistake resulted in the ultimate sacrifice."

"What happened to him?" I asked, almost afraid to hear the answer.

"He's not in pain of any kind. What he lost was his freedom to roam and explore the universe. He gave up part of his death for you."

"Is he alive then?"

"Not alive like a single human or a flower is alive. He sort of got redistributed."

That sounded bad. "Where is he now?"

"Actually, I have said all I can on this big and deep point. You have the ability to reason the details out on your own. But, really, you shouldn't waste your energy on this. You should concentrate on the task at hand here. You must return to your healthy twenty-year-old atoms. I won't go into the details, but I personally know that there is a lot more living for you to get to. Ready now?"

"No!" I yelled back like a petulant kindergartener. I was so far from ready. I was intoxicated from all that she told me. "Why do I remember dying and coming back when I was six?"

"Eddie, give it up and just go back!"

I didn't respond. She clearly couldn't make me, so I was staying dead until I was ready to live. Eventually, Lizzie caved.

"You're right. You are not supposed to remember any of that. The human mind gets messed up when it understands too much of death. All of this should remain a mystery on the living side. Have you shared any of your experiences with anyone?"

"Nobody. Ever. It seemed that no one knew or remembered I had died, so I sort of sensed that I should keep it to myself. Now, let's get back to my questions. I have two on the table that you are dancing around. What happened to Grampa, and why do I remember so much about being dead?"

"These two things are related. If you figure out one, you'll get the other. Kind of like a puzzle."

"Aren't you going to tell me?"

"I've already gone too far from of my job description with you. Didn't I tell you first thing that my job was to just turn you around and give you a push? I can't make you go back, but I don't have to tell you everything. I'll only listen and guide your reasoning through this. Like bumper pads on a bowling alley."

"All right, bumper pad, you can keep me in line, but give me that push. How do you navigate out here?" I was too young to even try to drive on my other deathdays so I didn't actually know the ropes.

"Try this: think of a question and a person who knows the answer. That'll bring you to a time in your life, or your death, where answers are brewing."

"That's easy. Grampa knew everything. I'm sure he still does."

44
Where Is Grampa?

I THOUGHT HARD ABOUT GRAMPA. He wasn't dead anymore. His antimatter had been redistributed. I started thinking out loud, "Grampa didn't just make the decision for me. He also helped me physically get back through my space-time crack. He used his antimatter to push mine back in. I remember feeling that."

Lizzie answered, "Yes, he did. He guided you back in time to the instant your antimatter and matter separated. He used the force of his antimatter to push you down."

"I remember it was like a big down comforter hugging me and holding me there. How can I figure out what happened to Grampa?"

"Think about what you know about a set of forces acting on an object. In physics class, which I always hated in school, we had to draw those free body diagrams with force vectors all over the place. Matter responds to forces like pushing and pulling, electrostatic and electromagnetic fields, and friction, right? Well, similar force vectors are felt by antimatter and the combination of these forces always results in a net force that is proportional to the mass of the object. F equals M A, right?"

"Right."

"So, think about the forces that were acting on your antimatter when you reentered your body."

"Grampa's antimatter was somehow pushing me, and then my matter started pulling my antimatter in. So both force vectors were in the same direction: toward my body."

Lizzie interrupted, "It wasn't that simple. The pushing force from your grampa wasn't directly toward your body; it was just 'down,' like gravity pulls on matter, toward Earth."

"Right, but then a component of it was pushing to my body."

"Sure. We'll get back to that. Now think about what other force was acting on your antimatter. There must have been something else if your grampa had to push. This would be a force felt before your matter started pulling you in."

"There must have been something pushing or pulling me away from my body. Does the matter repel the antimatter? Or does the universe pull it?"

"It's a little of both. It's not relevant to your analysis here that you understand the exact nature of the force, just know that whatever was keeping your matter and antimatter from recombining at first was overcome by the pushing from your grampa, and eventually the pulling that your matter exerted when your antimatter got close enough to your space-time crack. Are you with me so far?" She was hoping to intimidate me, to make me give up trying to understand and just give in and do what she said. Too bad for her.

"Sure. I loved free body diagrams in physics," I reported.

She groaned.

"All of this is supposed to help me figure out what happened to Grampa, right?"

"Of course."

"Continue then, professor."

She was not amused.

"You were a smart guy on Earth. This one is easy, but I'll help a little more. Imagine you are back in your body, alive, and you act as a single object applying a pushing force. You are pushing a huge boulder to the edge of a cliff in the Grand Canyon. You are pushing with all your strength. It is almost impossible, but you are gradually inching the massive rock to the edge. Can you see this picture? Can you feel it?"

"Yes. Okay, that's what it was like for Grampa's antimatter to push mine down. Almost impossible, but he used all of his strength and got it close to the edge. I suppose the edge here is the space-time crack?"

"Good. Now back to the hunk of rock. Suppose you aren't all alone in your effort to move the rock. Somehow your friends have tied a long, strong rope to it, without your knowledge, and as the rock gets closer to the edge of the cliff, they pull with an instantaneous surprising force. What will the rock do?"

"It'll continue moving but without needing me pushing anymore."

"So what will happen to you?"

"Oh, right. Inertia! I will continue to move with my momentum. Is that what happened to Grampa? He went through my space-time crack, too?"

"Yes, Ed. The force he felt at the last instant was about as strong as a smallish black hole. Even if he wasn't already pushing, he would have been sucked into it just because he was so close to the edge."

"Did he know this would happen? Where is he now?"

"We think he knew. We all know in some part of our consciousness what will happen if space-time cracks are not treated with reverence and distance. Where is he now? You can figure this out."

"Did he come with me? Back into my matter?"

"Yes, but that's not the whole story. Remember where you were when you were six and died?"

"In the hospital. In the pediatric oncology ward."

"There were lots of sick kids there, remember? Many of them were hovering on the edge of life and death. Right on the edges of their own space-time gaps. Some of their antimatter was barely clinging to their bodies. Imagine it like a soul hovering above the body, unsure which force to respond to when, whack! A mess of antimatter comes out of nowhere and smacks them down."

"So Grampa made more kids live besides me?"

"Seven sick kids recovered in a miraculous way, according to their doctors, after that night."

"And Grampa is in all of them, isn't he? He got ripped apart."

"He sacrificed his death for your life."

"Will he ever be whole again?"

"Only after all of those kids, and all of their offspring and grandchildren die. It takes about three generations for the majority of the antimatter to reunite."

Grampa gave up the peace and quiet of the universe to make me keep on living. Why was he being punished for this?

Lizzie responded to my thoughts. "Don't think of it as punishment. He knew what he was doing and what the consequences would be. Your grampa saw the future with you in it and made sure it happened. You might have made the decision on your own, if he gave you time to think about it, but he didn't let you take that path. He intervened, reasoning that a three-generation deficit was mathematically negligible in the scope of the eternity he would eventually enjoy on the dead side. Though small, the ripple of his illicit intervention was significant enough to interrupt the equilibrium."

"Is that why I remember about being dead and coming back? Most people seem to have no idea about any of this."

Lizzie answered kindly, "Don't worry. It isn't possible to remember everything that happens on the dead side when you return. But the pain and isolation in your life, so far and in your future, will most certainly be caused by your unnatural knowledge of death. A much more peaceful existence is experienced by all who live in awe of the mysteries and power of the universe. Your grampa's interference prevented you from reentering naturally, which would have allowed you a memory-free journey."

I thought about all the times when the carefree attitudes of my peers baffled me.

In high school, I was not popular. I was the nerd. The geek. The loser. I enjoyed learning and easily earned high grades. I was envied and ridiculed for my intelligence and curiosity.

Even in my teens, I worried about everything—human population, global warming, greenhouse gases, humanity causing the extinction of so many species. All manner of inconsequential living annoyed me. I always suspected there was some unfinished business I needed to attend to, some higher purpose for my life. I searched and searched through my teens, in high school and college, always confronted with frivolous living, unappreciative use of the atoms of life, and the blatant waste of infinite quantities of staggeringly amazing brain cells. I didn't fit in with normal humans. Now it seemed I might be able to blame my isolation on my blasted, unhinged, swinging door space-time crack.

I wasn't ready to go back. I wanted to sniff around for a while longer on the dead side. Lizzie was hesitant to let me roam, knowing I wouldn't forget all that I learned in death when I returned to life. But Lizzie said it herself: as my guide she was powerless to influence my decision.

I thought hard and decided to investigate my own future for clues. I wanted to find out whether my life would ever get any better.

45
Old Man Eddie's Life

THERE'S A LITTLE BOY eating Oreos under his bed. He has blankets and pillows arranged like a nest. Lying on his back, he pops a whole Oreo into his mouth and closes his eyes while he chews. From far away he hears someone calling, "Joey!" He stays as still as a stone except for his crunching.

Who is this kid? He's not me, and I don't remember him from my life. He pulls an electronic gadget from under his pillow and starts to mash some buttons. I haven't ever seen anything like this thing so I watch for a while. I find I can park on the pillow beside him and look up at the game. It's dark under the bed and the gadget spills a green glow onto his face.

How did I get here?

The kid reaches his hand into his Oreo bag and comes up empty. With a shrug he kicks the bag out from under the bed, spraying brown crumbs onto the rug, and turns back to his game. He plays for a long time and suddenly falls asleep. The game lands with a thud on his chest. After a few minutes it seems to turn itself off. While he sleeps, I'll look around this place and try to understand where it is.

Out in the hallway, there's a girl about my age holding a giant mug of coffee and a pile of books on her lap. She sits in a rocking chair and stares into space. There's some noise from downstairs. I go to investigate.

An old guy with thinning hair is sprawled on a couch. The TV is tuned to a football game. The sounds of the game are familiar to me, but the sports announcers are foreign, and the commercials are insane. One is about something called Viagra, whatever that is. Large text over a miserable guy's head says "Erectile dysfunction?" What the hell! On TV? Are they kidding? The next commercial is about something called identity theft. A small Asian dental assistant is talking, but her voice is coming out like a male country bumpkin's. This is the oddest programming I have ever seen.

There is something very wrong with the dude on the couch. He isn't even watching the game when the crowd goes wild in the last thirty seconds and the wide receiver pulls a Hail Mary catch out of thin air to tie the game. I want to smack him awake to make him watch.

A voice from the kitchen calls out, "Eddie, will you eat a sandwich?"

He doesn't answer. A woman walks in with a glass of water. She tells him to sit up and makes him take two pills. He is complacent. Looks a little in shock.

The chick sits next to him on the couch. She looks at the TV but doesn't seem to see it either. Then she says to him, "Eddie, you have to snap out of this. Joey needs you here with him. He's still hiding under the bed. We might see him soon, when he runs out of snacks. He needs you a lot. I can't stay here forever. You have to start being a dad again."

I take a closer look at this Eddie guy. He has graying, thinning black hair. It curls by his ears. My black hair always curls when I let it grow out. He wears a wedding ring. I am definitely not married. The lady doesn't have on a ring, so maybe she isn't Mrs. Eddie. This is puzzling.

When he finally speaks, I am shocked to hear my voice come out of his mouth.

"I'm still not hungry, Michelle. Thanks, though. It's good that you're here. Anna would have wanted that."

Eddie is me. I will be Eddie. Nobody calls me Eddie now. I haven't been Eddie since I was about six or seven. I am Ed and only Ed. But it appears, somewhere in my future that I will still watch football and I will live in a house with a lady who I'm not married to, a girl my age, and a little kid who eats cookies under his bed. It also appears that I won't give a crap about any of them. I'll just lie around like a slug and not even pay attention to football games on the tube. And who the heck is Anna? If this is my future, maybe I should stay dead.

"No. You should go back!" Lizzie's whiny voice comes out of nowhere.

"What are you doing here?" I ask.

"I can be anywhere I want. I'm your guide, you know, so I can be with you whether you want me here or not."

"Great." I stare at the horrible domestic scene before me and demand, "If you're going to invade my space, at least help me understand what I'm seeing here."

"I don't have to."

She is so annoying. "Then what good are you as a guide?"

"I'm a fantastic guide. I don't mean I don't have to like *I refuse to*, I mean I don't have to because *you don't need me to*. You can figure it out by yourself."

"Oh. Well, how about you listen to me talk about what I see and let me know if I get stuff wrong? Can you at least do that for me—be my bumper pad again?"

"If it'll help you move this agonizing process along, I will. You know, I'm in great demand. The universe has a lot of work lined up for me. We didn't anticipate you taking all my energy for so long."

When I don't answer she says, "Let's get on with it already. Talk, talk, talk!"

"First of all, how is it possible to see my future life when I haven't decided to return?"

"That's easy. Until you decide to go back—and you will very soon, Ed Wixim—when you watch the future, you can see it at least two ways: sometimes with you in it and sometimes without you there. You can even see the same scenes lived out with someone else in your place. In your case, now, your future scenes are clear and strong. You will go back. You know that you are just stalling here, right?"

"Sure. Yeah. I guess so. But if I was wavering, like fifty-fifty, on the fence about the choice, how would the scenes look?"

"More confused. Jagged. Quite like nightmares, so I've heard, but I haven't personal experience from that perspective because there was no future for me. I've just heard of it from other guides. My death had no return gate, and, as a Rebound guide, I most often deal with rapid returners. Ed, you are one bullheaded enigma."

"As are you, Lizzie. But help me puzzle this all out."

I start describing what I've seen. "There's a kid upstairs under the bed. He must be the son of this loser Eddie guy who won't vacate the couch or eat or even watch football correctly. If Eddie is me, then Joey's my kid, right?"

"Of course. Go on."

"I haven't figured out the Michelle chick, but she's nice to Eddie even though he's a loser. Does she love him? Do they live together?"

"Yes to the first, and no to the second question."

"Okay, whatever. And who's the girl upstairs?"

"Here they come. How about shutting up for ten seconds and listening. I bet they virtually spell out who they are."

That Lizzie. She's probably right, but I still want to pop her one on the head.

"Dad," says the girl, "I tried to get Joey to come out. I give up. Will you take a turn? I really need a shower. And Aunt Michelle started packing. I think she's going to leave soon." Boy, did the girl ever need a shower. Her long, greasy hair was a mess, and her crumpled clothes looked like she'd slept in them.

"Sure, Bethany. I'll go up in a minute." Eddie remains a lump on the couch. Bethany refills her coffee and takes it with her to the shower.

I say to Lizzie, "I got a lot out of that one. Michelle is my sister, and Bethany is my daughter. So I have two kids. Who's the wife? I got *married*? Me? I don't even have time to *date*."

"Okay, smart guy. You got most of that right. Do you *remember* having a sister Michelle?"

"No." I think about it. "Is she my wife's sister?"

"Bingo. What else do you need to figure out?"

"Well, I want to see my future wife. Where is she? What's her name? Is she the Anna person that Michelle was talking about?"

"Maybe. Watch some more, and you'll piece it together."

I decide *not* to watch my daughter Bethany take her shower, and figure spending time under Joey's bed while he slept would probably not be enlightening. I resign myself to hanging with my older self. Old Man Eddie. That guy's a thrill a minute.

"Can't we fast-forward this a bit?" I ask Lizzie when I get bored stiff with the Eddie dude.

"Fast-forward, rewind, pause, stop, play? We've got it all. Do what you will, this is your show." She sounds impatient but indulgent. Maybe figuring out the mystery of my future home life would help me decide to live. Not likely; it looked pretty damn bleak so far.

"I'm gonna fast-forward. Can I do it by the hour?"

"However you like. Just think it and I'll get you there," she says.

I think ahead one hour. Eddie is asleep on the couch.

Two hours. He's watching the news.

Another hour. He's still parked, and it's getting dark outside. After a few more hours, the house is dark and silent, and Eddie is missing from the couch.

"Where is he?" I ask Lizzie.

She groans. "Find him yourself."

I search room by room and find him in a bedroom, pawing through a chest of drawers. Women's underwear. The man is odd, and he is crying.

"How about rewind a day or so?" I suggest.

Lizzie grunts assent.

I see Eddie in a car driving alone. It is early evening. He pulls off the road into a school parking lot and gets out of the car. He walks to the door as though to a firing squad. What is wrong with this guy?

The school is dark except for one light by the entrance. A woman is standing just inside the door with a little boy. It's that Joey kid from under the bed. He has on his coat and backpack, and he's making a mess of the window by drawing on fog clouds that he blows on the glass door. There's a light haze of sweat forming on his forehead. Eddie walks quickly to Joey as the lady pushes him out the door.

Eddie lifts Joey up, apologizes to the lady, and carries him away to the car.

While old Eddie wrestles with the kid's seatbelt, Joey asks, "Where's Mommy?"

Eddie is crying when he says, "Mommy died."

The mother died? He's telling the kid in the car?

"Can we go see her? Is she coming home?" the poor kid asks.

Then Eddie blatantly lies to his son. "When somebody dies, they don't come home anymore."

Joey's mommy. That would be Eddie's wife. That would be *my* wife! I'm going to have a wife, and she's going to die?

Lizzie's voice, "Come on, you schmuck. It's not so surprising that you'll end up married. Most people do it."

"But, Lizzie, she's going to die. Look what it does to Eddie! I mean to me! I'm a mess!"

"No kidding." This is my guide's idea of support.

I look back and hear Joey ask, "Did she die like Grammy?"

"Yes, Joe. She's with Grammy now." Eddie loses it. He's sobbing while he drives.

"Lizzie! My wife is with Grammy? Is that her mom? And she's with her now?"

"Her guide is most likely a close relative who died before her. But I can't answer whether she's with her 'now' because time is a pretty loose term here on the dead side."

"'Time is a pretty loose term here on the dead side.' Did you really just say that?"

"Yeah. Relax, you'll get used to it."

I focus back on the car and the little kid in the back seat. "Is it possible his mom will come back?"

"I guess she could if she explores enough to find out that she has the option."

"You don't tell everyone that they can go back?"

"Not everyone can," Lizzie explains. "I couldn't, and I would've in an instant. You can, and you're hanging around here stalling. It all depends on the individual situation."

This is too awful to watch, so I zip us away without any notion of where I'm going. We end up in deep space light years away from my home planet. Much better. Very serene.

"What now?" Lizzie demands.

"How about some peace? Can't I be alone to think?"

"Peace be with you. Alone is dangerous, though. You're not good at determining a path yet. I had to help you get to your future. How did we get here?"

"I have no idea," I admit. "Okay, forget the peace. Tell me how the kid's mom died."

"Nope."

"Thanks a lot. I can find out, though, can't I?"

"Yeah, Einstein. But you have to figure out how by yourself."

She is pissing me off. Too bad I can't pull her hair and make her cry or something.

Instead, I say, "I'll travel back a couple days or weeks from when I just saw them all and watch what's going on. That should help me piece it together."

Her reply: "Lead on." Great, she's coming with me again.

There's that old loser Eddie.

He takes a small roundish thing from his pocket and opens it like a little book. It has hinges and lights up when he pushes the buttons. He's at a hospital. He doesn't look sick though. Oh, right, he's wearing a white coat, not a hospital gown. Well, then, that's cool: seems like he's a doctor. He puts the odd device to his ear like it's a telephone.

Old Eddie says, "Mrs. Wixim?"

It is a telephone!

I wonder if he's calling my mom or his wife, but I can't fathom why he would address either of them as Mrs. Wixim.

He speaks into the phone again. "Mrs. Wixim, you are the lucky winner of a free in-home pest inspection." A pause. The geek grins. "Our highly trained bug engineers will come to your home and look for black and brown and green insects. How about that?"

He listens for a minute and then pulls the phone away from his ear, still smiling.

"Mrs. Wixim? Hello? Are you there?"

He holds the phone away from his ear again, and I can hear a scream come out of it.

He snaps the little device closed and stands there and laughs for five minutes. I get quite strange in my old age.

So Eddie is a doctor of some kind, and he makes prank calls

to his wife or mother whom he addresses as Mrs. Wixim. "Lizzie! Do you find any of this odd in any way?"

"In any way? Dude, it is odd in every way. Nobody can take little glimpses of someone else's life, or even their own future life, and fully comprehend it. Life is made up of all kinds of isolated moments and intertwined experiences. I can tell you that you are very happy, most of the time, with your wife and family. Had enough? Ready to pop back into that twenty-year-old stud body?"

"I don't recall ownership of anything resembling a stud body, and I'm not even close to ready. I need to at least try to understand this old man Eddie. He seems so different from me."

"Whatever." She gives up and is silent again. I'm sure she'll have something snide to say at our next stop.

| | | |

HERE'S OLD EDDIE walking with the Joey kid. They're both wearing strange costumes. It's twilight. Joey is carrying a heavy bag; he's running from door to door and begging for candy.

"You got any chocolate?" I hear him say at one door.

"How about some extra for my dad?" he asks at the next house.

Joey runs back to Eddie. "Dad, can you carry some of this candy? The bag is too heavy for me!" Eddie helps him dump most of it into a trash bag he has slung around his shoulders.

Eddie says, "How about a few more houses and then we'll head back home?"

"Aw, Daddy, come on, it isn't even bedtime yet." At least the kid is spunky.

"Okay, then, how about six more houses?" says old Eddie, the pushover.

"Twenty?" counters Joey, the shyster.

"Ten."

"Fifteen?"

"Twelve." Eddie really drew the line there.

"Deal!" Joey gives old Eddie a high five and then charges off to the next house, thrilled he negotiated for double the original candy offer. He commences a countdown, and when folks open the door he yells, "Trick or Treat! Eleven more! Got any chocolate?"

They return home and dump the huge bag of candy out on the kitchen floor. Joey proceeds to roll around in it, but a lady scoops him up. "All right, Frodo-number-one, pick one piece and then off to bed. School tomorrow."

"Aw, Mom, I'm not tired. I got all this candy, and I'll even share it with ya if I can have more than one piece." He tries to bargain with this woman, his mother. That makes her my wife. I need to pay closer attention.

She isn't too hard on the eyes for an old chick. Not someone I'd look twice at now, but, hey, I'm twenty. She's old—got to be in her forties. I noticed that she didn't give Eddie anything when he came home. No hug, no hello. She didn't even glance at him. Don't they like each other at all? This is horrible. Joey starts whining and arguing with his mom.

"Just one, Joey. Don't argue with me, or one becomes zero. Got that?"

Joey snatches up a peanut butter cup and runs off to his room.

Eddie attempts conversation. "Lots of chocolate, Anna. See?"

"Yeah. Great. Not a Smartie in the pile." She's on her knees sorting through the candy.

"Joey won't miss it if you have some," he suggests awkwardly.

She doesn't look at him. She just barks at him. "I'm bringing it all to school. My students will eat it."

"You've been running so much. You shouldn't worry

about a little chocolate."

"Don't be mean to me, Eddie. I am not fat."

Did he call her fat? Was he mean? Wasn't he just offering candy? Old Eddie and I, both, don't understand his wife.

The old guy walks out of the room, dejected and clearly dismissed by our wife. The man is pathetic. This future wife of mine ignores me and fights with my son. Future me is a pushover and a loser. How did I get so lucky?

| | | |

"LIZZIE! I'M DONE watching them. You really expect me to go back for that? My future family life is a mess." I am disturbed by what I would become. "Am I ever happy?"

Lizzie manages to sound like my therapist when she answers, "Ed, you made choices in your life that made you content. Happiness is a fleeting emotion. We know we are happy when we are laughing or hugging someone. Most other times of the day the living spend negative energy on things like road rage and petty arguments. You'll have a good life with Anna. You will love your family. You just keep picking snapshots of that life that don't portray it accurately."

I'm stumped. "Can you pick a good day for me to see?" I need to see something positive.

"I'll try."

| | | |

HERE IS ANNA in line at a bookstore. She's holding a pile of books. When it's her turn, the guy at the register says, "May I see your discount card?"

Anna says, "I forgot to bring it."

He says, "What's your last name?"

"Muckenfuss." *Muckenfuss? Does this crazy woman not know her own name?*

"Hmm . . ." He types it into his computer. Cool computer.

At least in the future I might enjoy the technology even if I can't relate to the people.

While he's nose deep in his computer, Anna says, "Never mind. It's probably under my daughter's name."

She starts digging in her purse like a squirrel for a nut and doesn't seem to hear him when he asks, "Emily? Is it Emily?" She ignores him so he raises his voice, "Ma'am, is your daughter Emily?"

I thought the daughter's name was Bethany. Is there another one?

"Yeah, no, it's a bit confusing," Lizzie says. "Just watch, and maybe you'll figure it out."

Anna stops digging through the messiest purse I've ever seen. Her mouth hangs open, which I don't find attractive, and she looks like she's panicking, like she might bolt.

The cashier tells her, "You can use your daughter's card. Is her name Emily Muckenfuss?"

No! That's impossible. Even if we do end up with a daughter named Emily, how could she be called Muckenfuss?

But Anna answers, "Yes. That's her." She is a bit pale. I think she's going to puke.

"Wait, Lizzie! Just hold on a minute. This woman is a freak of nature. Why did you think showing me a glimpse of her in a bookstore was a good idea?"

"Sorry," she says. "See, Anna loves to read. She's extremely bright—certainly your intellectual match, which will be really hard for you to find. I thought you'd like to know that you will find one. Maybe there's a better time in a bookstore I can show you. Hold on a sec."

Then we see Anna in a different bookstore. Again she holds a pile of books. None of them look familiar to me. Looks more like a pile of chick lit. Ugh. Did this woman ever use her brain?

When she gets to the register, the cashier, once again, asks for her membership card. I'm waiting for the "I forgot it" line again, when she surprises me with, "I don't have one."

He asks if she wants one, and she counters with, "Are they free?" Perfect. She is cheap on top of all her other lovely qualities.

She smiles when the guy says, "Not for most people, but it would be essentially free for you today."

This gets frugal Anna's attention.

After he patiently explains about a ten percent discount, she asks, "Do I have to use my real name?" Is she serious?

The guy says, "You can be whomever you want." What is with the future world? Identity theft? Erectile dysfunction? Be whomever you want? I don't get it.

Anna looks gleeful when she announces, "I am Martha Washington, and I would like to buy a free membership card." Muckenfuss? Martha Washington?

She gives her address as the White House. What a fruitcake.

I've had enough of Lizzie as my guide. "Halt! Please, no more! This is not working at all. I don't want to go back to that woman!" I'm the one panicking now.

"Sorry, again. Maybe I should abandon the bookstore theme. How about I show you Anna when she was younger?"

"No," I insist. "I don't want to see more."

"Come on, Eddie, I'll hit on a good one eventually."

"Do not call me Eddie. That's *him*. You just showed me two dumpers in a row. One more and that's your third strike. Then you're out. Got that?"

"Sure. You just reminded me of something. Hold on tight, we're gonna whiz back sorta fast here."

Then Lizzie says, "Here we are. You were a lot younger. This is your first date with Anna. See if this helps at all."

So I watch.

A young Eddie and very pretty Anna are having dinner. The waiter has just delivered the dessert menu when Anna says,

"I decided to come with you to get a free steak dinner. Now I'm ready for chocolate cake. But I don't want to go to Abbott and Costello in the middle of campus where everyone can see us. This is our first and last date, and I don't want people thinking there's something going on here. Got that?"

This girl is a beast! Why does she hate poor Eddie?

By coincidence, my younger self asks, "Anna, what can I do to make you stop hating me?"

So I was right: she did hate me.

"I don't hate you," she says. What? So maybe I was wrong then and now? Will I be wrong again when this happens in my future?

"Well, then, how do you feel about me?" This Eddie guy is asking for some punishment.

Anna looks him square in the eye and says, "I have never been insulted in the first five seconds of a date before."

Eddie insulted her? How? Why?

"That makes you a special, unforgettable date. And I haven't been on many dates."

I could see why!

"That also makes you special and unforgettable. But even if I have to live the rest of my life alone, no dates, *forever*, I will never be so desperate that I have to be with a guy who is mean to me. Got that?" She looks like she's about to cry.

Eddie says, "I'm sorry I was mean. I didn't mean it. Please go to the movie with me?"

Anna smiles a wicked smile—which makes her look pretty hot—and says, "I think you are begging me."

"You bet. I am. Really I am. This cannot be the last time I see you." Eddie, the loser, is a head case.

"Why not?" She is teasing him!

Apparently he'd been mean in some way that gives Anna the upper hand. She thinks she has a right to be furious and to string him along in a nasty way. Eddie better come up with something good if he wants to see this witch again. But why would he want to? He should just cut loose right now and run.

He does look desperate, and he's thinking hard, really working. It's incredible, but I find myself starting to root for him a little. Come on, guy, and give her something good. Make her like you. Argue your case. Stand up for yourself. Be a man!

"Because."

That's it?

But Anna smiles!

Later, they walk hand in hand down a path lined with roses. Sickeningly romantic. Not my style. Eddie wears a stupid little smirk on his face when he suggests they sit down on a bench.

As Anna sits down, she says, "Do you bring all your first dates here?"

"No," answers Eddie, the loser nerd.

"Just the ones with awful hair so you don't have to be seen in public?"

What was this about awful hair? Anna's hair looked pretty good to me.

"Actually, it has nothing to do with their hair," he mutters.

Then Ed-the-*man* says, "I just bring the ones I want to kiss."

Bam!

"Really?" Anna's smile is suspicious. She doesn't buy it. "How many times have you been here?"

I find myself rooting for Eddie again. Don't blow it, man. Think about this one. There is only one correct answer. It'll make or break you.

"Never before tonight."

Bingo!

If he messes this up, I'll kill the guy.

With one awkward arm around her shoulders, he pulls her to him. He lowers his face so close to hers I hope neither of them had onions on their steak. He touches her hair and says,

"I love your hair."

Enough with the hair, Eddie.

She laughs and says, "Just kiss me already."

And he does.

| | | |

"AW, THAT TURNED OUT SWEET, don't you think, Ed?" Lizzie asks me.

"It wasn't as bad as the others," I admit. Maybe there's hope.

Finally, Lizzie, my Rebound guide, leaves me alone.

47

Wonder Wander: The Big and the Deep

I LIKE BEING ALONE in space. It's peaceful.

I take stock of my situation. I'm still dead. Still about to turn twenty. I've experienced some mind and time travels and seen some future details of my life. All of it feels like cheating, like knowing the ending of a good book. I always hated that. I'm going back. I know Lizzie's right. I've seen enough to be certain, but I'm still curious, and though I was keen to get away from her, I'm pursuing Lizzie again because I still have questions.

It seems that just the mention of going back is exerting some strong force on me, on my antimatter—I'm traveling at light speed now, no doubt about that—and on my thought processes. I need Lizzie to help me apply whatever amounts to brakes out here on the dead side so I can slow down.

Then Lizzie's voice says, "You don't need me for that. You have complete control of the speed of your return. Just get back in there. The living are waiting for you."

That didn't feel quite true to me. In the life I left behind, I was not exactly surrounded by crowds of friends and family. I spent most of my time studying. I lived as a loner, but I was good at it. So there were not many people anxiously awaiting my return. I could feasibly stay dead.

Lizzie's annoying voice breaks in with, "That's one of the main reasons you need me. Since you slipped through unexpectedly, and you are one of those souls who would love to be dead—would enjoy the death experience, have no fear of it, even understand it—you require a nudge to remind you to return."

"How is that any different from when Grampa pushed me back when I was six?"

She sighs. "You know, for a smart guy, you really kill me."

"You're already dead."

"Ha. Ha."

"And so am I. If you make the decision for me, you're as bad as Grampa," I insist.

"You silly boy. I swear you boys are as dumb grown-up as you were in kindergarten. Listen good, Ed, because I'm only going to explain this simple thing to you one more time. You must go back. You were not supposed to die. It was a mistake. An error. A bug in the plans. It happens all the time with the chaotic design upon which our universe relies, you know, those thermodynamic laws? But in your case, there's no decision to be made. You just go back this time."

"But when I was six?"

"The link between your matter and antimatter was fragile, but you had a choice then—you could have decided to stay dead. But your grampa didn't even let you go through the decision process. Do you not get this yet?" She is annoyed with me, I think.

"Sorry. Yeah, I think I do. But since I have your full attention, now, I have more things I want to talk to you about. I need your help, okay?"

"I'm at your disposal, like it or not." Obviously, she did not like it, but I didn't give a rat's ass.

"Good. How about getting back to some of those big and deep questions?"

"Be my guest."

"Here's the thing. If Grampa's antimatter got sucked into mine when I returned to my body when I was six, and some of him got washed into those other sick kids, too, then if I don't have kids, will that help him to be released when I die?"

"In theory, yes. Most of your grampa does remain within you, so you'd just take him with you. But, Ed, haven't you paid any attention at all? You *will* have kids. Your grampa's antimatter will be further fractioned in them." Lizzie is trying to help, but I have other ideas.

"What if I die for good right now? What if I decide to—what's it called? Depart? Then Grampa's antimatter will be mostly freed, right?"

"Don't even go there, you idiot. You are not going to stay dead! Let's just stop the hypothetical discussions and get on with this, please!" She is close to wailing now. It reminds me of the awful noises she used to make in kindergarten when Jimmy made her rub my baldy-head.

"Help me understand how Grampa's antimatter will be split if I have kids. What makes up the antimatter part of a new person? Is it like genes and DNA? Does it come from both the mother and father?"

"If you'd think for a second, you'd see there is no other way it could be. If a new baby is just matter, it wouldn't survive when it's born." That is the most helpful information so far.

"Of course I'm helpful; I'm your damn guide. What else do you want to know?"

"When does the antimatter of the baby join the baby's matter?"

"First breath. The instant the baby is functioning on its own outside the mother, that's when the antimatter locks on. It's pretty cool."

"It really is." I'm glad I didn't go right back to my life. There's so much to understand that I could never learn while alive.

Lizzie's going to be pissed, but there are even more big and deep areas I want to explore.

"Okay, how about this: It seems to me that humans aren't

evolving anymore. As a group, many are getting dumber. They don't care about learning. As the high intellectual end of human ability develops technology, the great majority of the lower end—who use the technology and depend on it—have no real concept or interest in using their brains from day to day. They watch TV, eat, sleep, and call it a life. It all seems like an incredible waste to me."

"That's just you. You're such a geek! I would have loved fifty or sixty more years of that. You don't understand that at all, do you? Life on our little Earth is so unique, so special. The perfect planet for antimatter and matter to connect and form energy. For life to reproduce itself. It's a beautiful place." To make her point, Lizzie brings into focus a view of our bright marble from deep outer space. It is glorious, all blue and green and white. I'd seen pictures, but it is breathtaking to actually witness.

"I'm sorry. I know I'm not a normal person. In my life I often offended people. I alienated myself and just kept learning. I was driven. Just bear with me, okay? How about this idea of a deathday? Did humans always have a deathday?"

"They must have to ever have died, right?"

"Do most people die more than once and go back?"

"Think about that one. Have you met many people who seem to know about deathdays?"

"No. Nobody but me. Ever."

"Those who return to their lives don't remember anything from the dead side. You're an exception, but even you won't remember all of this. The fact is that most decide to stay dead. They explore a little, find that they understand the entire cosmos with minimal effort, feel the peace of rejoining the fabric of the universe, and don't miss life that much."

"But not all of them?"

"No. There are some who desperately miss life and go back as many times as they can. But they usually make their decision immediately and go back with no memory of the event at all."

When I don't answer with another question, Lizzie suggests hopefully, "How about it? Ready to go back now?"

"Not yet." Under no deadline, no time pressure, I am enthralled by the golden ticket: those who stay dead come to understand everything. Every single mystery is exposed and comprehended. I have the opportunity to do that and then I can still go back to my life. This is irresistible. "I've decided to try a little time travel on my own."

This earns me another groan.

48
Anna's Deathday

SOMEHOW, I DITCH LIZZIE. I'm free and alone in space. It is glorious, amazing, and immense. Yet none of these human terms are adequate to describe it. On the dead side, there should be a new language, a new set of adjectives, to encompass all of the wonders.

Still hesitant to return to the life that will turn me into grumpy old Eddie, I travel, quite well, I think, to revisit the day Anna dies.

There's old Eddie waking up. He leans toward snoring Anna and gets smacked in the face by her elbow as she rolls over. It looks like he's sneaking out of bed.

Anna's sleepy voice pulls him back. "Eddie, what are you doing?" Couldn't this guy even get out of bed without getting into trouble? They almost have a conversation, and Eddie leaves the room, looking guilty, although I don't think he did anything wrong.

I follow him to the kitchen where he finds the boy lying on his belly under the kitchen table. Joey says, "Hi, Daddy. Can I have breakfast right now, right away?"

"Sure," says Eddie. "Whatcha want?"

"Oreos, please." The kid has a definite chocolate addiction. He's grinning like a fool.

He scarfs down the cookies before his mother comes into the kitchen. When Anna sits beside him, Joey says, "Ooh, Mommy. I don't feel too good today." He leans to her for a hug.

"Show me those teeth."

He smiles, reveals the cookies, and gets poor old Eddie in trouble again.

Later, Anna carries her bags to the car. Joey, Old Ed, and I all follow her.

"Honey?" Eddie, the sucker, leans his head in the open window of Anna's car. "How about a day off today? You and me and Joey. Let's all play hooky."

His wife looks at him like he's nuts. He might be. She makes it clear that she has no interest or intention of spending any time with him. Maybe not ever. "Enough with the *honey* crap. You've been a jerk to me for weeks." She doesn't take off her sunglasses but even I can tell she's crying when she says, "I'm going to work. See you tonight. *Honey*," and leaves Old Man Eddie standing there, as pathetic and desperate as ever a man could be.

Damn. Why in the world would Eddie try to get Anna, a woman who is never happy, to stay home and spend a day with him?

That familiar sense creeps up: I'm not alone. I'd rather be alone, because I'd like to watch the rest of this day and find out how Anna ends up dead. An almost comical yet disturbing thought suddenly occurs to me: maybe Old Man Eddie finally lost it and just snuffed her. Is that possible?

A voice, which is not Lizzie's, answers, "No, you fool. Eddie would never hurt me. He wasn't even there when I died."

"How do you know?"

"I *am* his wife, you idiot," the voice says.

"You are the lovely wife of poor Eddie?"

"Poor Eddie? Have you any idea what he put me through the last two months of my life?" She kind of freaks me out when she yells at me. "And what are you doing here? I was time traveling to determine what I should do with my soul, visiting the day I died, trying to understand some things. Can't I ever be alone? What are you doing watching my life?"

"Apparently, that was my life, too."

"Who are you?"

"I'm Ed."

"Ed? Eddie! You're dead, too? Who's with our kids?"

"I'm not dead now. Not in your now, I mean. I've been watching your family after you died, so I know that Old Man Eddie is still alive in your now."

"Then how did you get on the dead side?" she asks.

"It's complicated. See, I died when I was twenty—before we met. According to my guide, I was supposed to just go right back to my body, but I've been looking around first. Kind of checking out my future."

"I was warned not to travel forward in time," she tells me. "My guide, my mother, said that's dangerous and painful."

"I haven't noticed any danger or pain yet, just copious fear. How could my life end up like that?"

"Hold on," Anna demands. "Let me wrap my brain around this. I died when I was in my midforties. I'd been married to you for half of my life. You died when you were twenty? And we just bumped into each other here because we both happened to be watching the same scene in our lives. Don't you find this bizarre?"

"I guess. But see, you also have to understand that I don't know you. At all."

When she doesn't respond, I ask her, "Have you decided? Are you going back?"

"I'm still not sure. According to my parents—my guides—I have a lot of choices. What about you? Why don't you just go back to your body like you're supposed to?"

"I'm just too curious to give up the chance to look around and find things out. Wouldn't you look around?"

"Not if they *told* me to go back. God, I'd love to be told what to do but, in my case, they say I have to make my decision all by myself." Anna sounds confused, so I decide to take a stab at it and act as her guide.

"Well, I don't have to follow those stupid guide rules. I'll tell you what I think. If I were you, I'd stay dead."

"Why?"

"I've been watching your life, and it doesn't look that great. You and Eddie don't talk at all; you fight with your little boy; Eddie is mean to you and has been since you met him, and he has a nasty sense of humor. The guy doesn't even watch football right. And you! You have no memory. You lie at bookstores. You are grumpy all the time. Seriously, all the time, Anna. You are never happy. Why would you go back to that?"

"Ouch. Thanks for the advice." After a while she says, "It's interesting to have my life analyzed by an uninvolved observer. Things have been bad the last few months, but Eddie usually snaps out of his annual funk by now. I was looking forward to it. But in our defense, you obviously haven't seen any of our good times."

"You two have good times? You're telling me the guy has an annual funk? He's like this every year and you stay with him? Why?"

"I love him," she says.

"Does he love you?"

"Can't you answer that for him?"

"No, I'm not him yet."

"I think Eddie loves me."

"Does he say it?"

"Would *you*?" she challenges, a bit defensively, I think.

"I've never loved a girl enough to say it. I mean, I've said it when I needed to, like to get my way—you know what I mean. Everybody, every guy, says it then."

"You ass! If you don't mean it, don't say it. Better yet, you should just avoid the word. You're not qualified to use it. You know, in about five years you're going to be a great guy. I'm glad I didn't meet you when you were twenty."

"Are you advising me to go back?"

"I'm no guide, but yes, absolutely. You should go back, Eddie. Even though I think you're an idiot right now, and my mother will always think you're a talking horse, I know how awesome our life was together. Most of the time. You have to go back. There won't be Bethany or Joey without you there."

"What about you? Are you going back?"

"That's still on the table. But you've given me a lot to think about. If you won't even push me that way, and you are the main reason I'd go back, why should I bother?"

I can feel Anna leaving me, and I don't want her to go yet. I'm compelled by some force to stay with her, and, though she is scary as all hell, it takes almost no effort for me to follow her. I squelch my irrational fear of the woman by convincing myself that she's unaware of my stealth presence.

49
Old Man Running

I WATCH DEAD ANNA spying on Old Man Eddie. She finds him running in the rain. It's dark. He's wearing scrubs and sneakers. His glasses are fogged. He's crying.

I watch them both: my future wife listening to the thoughts of my future self.

I haven't done a single thing right in months. All I do is hurt her. Anna's going to leave me. For good.

Old Man Eddie runs through the downpour, head down, out of the neighborhood and turns left.

I can't talk to her when she's so angry. There's nothing I can say to make her understand what's wrong. She just watches me with those big, sad eyes that accuse me of being mean to her. I just keep hurting her. It's all my fault, I know it, but I can't make it better. She'll be gone soon. What will I tell the kids? How will I tell them that their mother is gone, and I didn't even try to make her stay?

For miles, he runs in the dark with an empty mind and sad heart. Up a hill beside a white church and past some horses. There is nothing to hear. Old Man Eddie just runs and cries in the rain, taking random turns on his path until he loops back to their street and he slows to a walk.

Home. Back to Anna. I made it home without thinking. Maybe it isn't dangerous, her running that loop. There weren't any dogs. He grins, thinking about the pockets in her shorts.

He walks around the house, hidden in the dark, and looks in the window and sees Anna in his blue chair, drinking tea and grading tests. *Right where she should be. Safe.*

Dead Anna murmurs, "Poor Eddie."

"Poor Eddie? Did we just see the same thing?"

She's surprised by my voice. "What are you doing here?"

"Watching, just like you." I'm curious to understand her mindset, so I ask, "What did that look like to you?"

"It looked like Eddie was sad before I died, just like I was. He was thinking about me, about us."

"Well, what I saw was Old Man Eddie acting strange yet again. Who the hell runs in the rain in the dark and then peeps on his wife through the windows of their house?"

"He's hurting, though, just like I was."

"So that makes you feel bad for him? I'll never understand women."

"No. You won't," she says.

"But I think I understand that guy," I insist, "probably better than you do. Do you really think he loves you?"

"I did, but you're confusing me."

"No, you're confusing yourself. Did you listen to him? Even he knew that it was over. Even he knew you were going to leave him. He was ready for it. He accepted it as a done deal. Were you not listening?" She doesn't respond.

Instead, she leaves me. I don't follow this time.

ANNA'S GONE. I should go back, but I'm still not satisfied. I may never have this chance again, and I want to see as much as I can from the dead side. I'd rather do it without Lizzie, so I think strong thoughts: I want to see my future, the distant future. How old might I end up?

On a crowded, noisy street, old Eddie is walking fast with Bethany beside him. She looks to be in her late twenties. They find a hotel room and spend the night. It's filthy, and the door won't lock so they don't sleep much. They carry backpacks loaded with medical supplies, and it seems they are there working on a medical mission. The city is familiar. Definitely in America. Maybe on the East Coast. But everything is dirty, and the people look fierce and foreign as though some military occupation is underway.

The next day we're back on the street. We find an open restaurant and trade my coat for food and then spend the afternoon hiding in the back of the dining room. Three armed men walk in and scan the room, looking for someone. I duck my head. After a few tense moments, they leave. Every face is stressed and worried. Gunshots are fired on the street in the middle of the day.

As it grows dark, we try to leave, but crowds of people block the door from the outside. Who are these armed men that we see everywhere? Military police? I pull on Bethany's wrist, and I try to exit but her hand is pulled from mine. The door closes, and I'm outside in the dark, alone in an angry crowd.

I panic and push my way back into the restaurant.

A man's voice behind me hisses, "What have you stolen, good doctor?"

I turn to face him. I am wild with worry for Bethany. "I have nothing. Where is the girl?"

"We have taken her in the back for a full search. She is a thief."

"No!" I yell. "She's a nurse, and she's under protection for her skills. You cannot harm her."

"No harm, good doctor. Just a search. If she has stolen nothing, we will set her free. Mostly unharmed." He sneers. "She will retain all of her nursing skills, I assure you."

An empty bottle sits on a table nearby. I have no training in self-defense. I have no physical strength. All of my efforts my entire life have been to develop my mind. I am an old man, and I cannot even protect my daughter. He sees me look at the bottle and grabs it. He throws it against the wall with a crash.

"That is not how I saw it! I was there!" I didn't know she was with me, when Anna's voice pulls me from the nightmare. She followed me this time.

"What are you talking about? You weren't there."

"Eddie, I saw that restaurant. I was there with you and Bethany. When I first died, I accidentally traveled alone to the future and saw that. I thought it was just a nightmare. It's different every time I go there. Where was I this time?"

"How the hell do I know? Maybe you stayed dead like I told you to," I suggest.

No reply.

"Anna? Are you still here?"

"Listen, Eddie, I need to rewatch one more thing, and you should see it, too. There was another future scene, a nightmare that I didn't understand. It was Joey all grown up. And there was a baby."

"Whose baby?"

"I don't know. I don't even know whether I can get back to it. Where are all the guides when you need them? I swear, my mother wouldn't leave me alone, and now I can't find her."

"My guide was a pain in the neck, too, and now she's gone."

"She? You had a woman guide?"

"Yeah. So what?"

"Who is she?" she asks, suspicious.

"Anna, I have no idea what your Eddie was up to before you died. From what I've seen, hey, I agree he was an ass."

"So are you," she says. I don't argue.

Awkward silence. The entire universe is silent with us. Then Anna's sad voice says, "This whole time travel thing has been quite disorienting. Then meeting you here and having you be so very different from the man I ended up loving and spending my life with. The whole thing has me very confused."

"Tell me about it. Let's get a guide, huh? Lizzie!"

"Mom! Daddy?" she calls out.

Nothing.

Anna says, "I think my mother is avoiding me. I bet she's enjoying an 'I told you so' moment. Eddie, there's one thing you can do for me that'll help me make a final decision."

"I thought no one could help," I say.

"But you're not my guide. And you're not supposed to be dead. And my decision *will* affect you. So, agree to this: go with me to just one more future place I've seen. It was an awful thing. A baby girl. I tried to help her!"

"Hey, slow down. Just take me there, and we'll watch it together, okay?"

Anna manages to pull us into the future. Early morning light shines on a tiny baby's foot, which is sticking out from beneath a fluffy pink blanket. A hand pats the baby's back, rubs her tiny toes and then rolls her over.

Bethany screams. Joey, all grown up, runs into the room. They are frantic as they try, and fail, to resuscitate the baby girl.

She remains as still as a porcelain doll, beautiful and unresponsive.

"No!" Anna's voice interrupts the scene, "it wasn't Bethany! *I'm* supposed to be there. What the hell is going on? This isn't how I saw it the first time. Don't watch anymore, Eddie. Don't watch it. It's too horrible."

Somehow, Anna pulls us from that place. I am too stunned to speak. We drift together in space.

A long time later, Anna speaks to me. "Ed, I've decided. Living hurts too much. You're right. He doesn't love me, so I can't go back to him."

I reply, "But I do have to go back."

Once decisions are made, there is no hesitation, no pause for reconsideration. I was immediately whisked back to my twenty-year old body, waking up on my birthday in my dorm room, very late for class and feeling hungover.

And Anna? I assume she departed.

Anna or Eddie

51
Dead

Anna

DECIDING TO STAY DEAD—to depart, as my mother called it—turned out to be a simple thing. There was no ceremony or even a pause in the action. On Earth, people were born and people died. The universe went on peacefully. Time continued on its wandering path, fast or slow, forward or backward or stopped.

I could watch events as they occurred in the life I left behind at my leisure. I could watch time as it passed while the world orbited the sun. Living people call this the present. I could fast-forward Earth time to watch the future. Or, of course, I could endlessly torture myself and review the love and pain of my life. At first, I just watched my family in their present time, dealing with life without me. I zeroed in on my memorial service once more.

I nestle down next to Joey, in the spot he saved for me in the front pew, to check him out up close like I used to do each day at breakfast. He looks rumpled in his suit, like he'd been under his bed sleeping in it not ten minutes ago. There's sand in his eyes from a recent snooze, a chocolate mustache above his upper lip, snot wiped on the knee of his pants, and the stubborn cowlick at the back of his head is blooming today. What a mess, my boy. His birthday is coming up. He'll turn six without me to make the cake and wrap the presents. I begin to doubt myself. Maybe I made the wrong choice.

The school chorus launches into an *a capella* rendition of

"River in Judea." It is beautiful and fills the chapel with harmony. It also makes a lot of people cry. This is good. Crying helps. I remember that.

After the song, a pastor who never met me starts to sing my praises. I wonder where he got his information. Most of it sounds rote.

"Today, my brothers and sisters, we celebrate the life of a loving mother, sister, wife, teacher, and friend. Anna Wixim was all of these things to so many of us. She touched our hearts and lives, and she will be missed each and every day. Let us take solace in the knowledge that our beloved Anna is now resting at peace with our Lord."

I check around me. No Lord yet.

He continues reading his script about the dead woman, a stranger to him. "She cared about her community and the environment and was a loving wife and best friend to her husband, Eddie." Best friend, right. I sneak a peek at Eddie to register his reaction. My husband surprises me again. He is weeping, but silent, as he listens.

"As we mourn the loss of our great friend and mentor, we will be comforted by our fond memories of Anna's laughter and sense of humor. Let us pause now and bow our heads and ask for God's grace and blessing of the soul of Anna Wixim as we prepare to return her ashes to the earth."

The church is hushed. My soul feels blessed. What is left of me, my antimatter, is truly eternal. At the instant of the blessing, what remains of me is swooshed into the universe and, with a blinding light, bursts into cosmic energy.

I don't depart. I remain at my memorial service. At the same time, I am everywhere else. I don't mean everywhere like all around the world. I mean everywhere in the entirety of infinity. It is both disorienting and liberating.

Mom was right: dead, I am everywhere and at all time. It is impossible to explain. It can only be imagined until it is experienced.

My husband stands up to speak, and I dread hearing what he'll say. The end of my life with him was so painful. We hurt each other, time after time, every minute of my last months alive. I'm afraid from his actions, and from the perspective and advice his younger self provided to me in death, that the man I loved might be incredibly relieved to be rid of me. How will he manage to talk to this large group without indicating his pleasure in my absence? This is one mystery that I need to have solved.

He walks to the podium slowly, head down. He takes some papers from his pocket and unfolds them, clears his throat, and begins to read.

"As Anna's husband and best friend, I would like to take a moment to talk about how special she was to me. My Anna was a unique and happy person, one whose smile could light up a room. She could always make me laugh . . ."

Boring. He could be talking about a pet turtle. Someone must have put him up to this—told him he had to speak, so he just jotted the first trite lines he could come up with. Perhaps he even Googled "tribute to dead wife." This hurts.

Mom? Are you watching this?

No response. No "I told you so."

Eddie drones for a few more minutes and stops. He looks up at the crowd of people and blinks as though he just realized they were there. Then, with a rough shake of his head, he crumples the paper. There you go, Eddie, tell them the truth about us. I think if I had a heart it would rip in half right now. I was right. Eddie doesn't love me anymore.

He looks out at the hundreds of people crowded into the pews. The sniffling teenagers, the men standing in the back, the chorus sitting on the risers. He looks to Bethany, sitting up so straight, eyes shiny. Our little boy, leaning his head on his Aunt Michelle's shoulder, looking like he might fall asleep. Then

Eddie scans the room and his eyes rest on a teenage boy, about sixteen, in a long black coat in the last row. I follow his gaze, and at first, I don't recognize the kid. Then, with a shock, I know him.

He is Pizza Boy.

52

November 11

Eddie

AFTER ANNA LEFT for work on her final November eleventh, there was nothing left for me to do but worry. She was gone. I knew I was going to lose her. I went to work.

After my morning rotation I needed a status update to find out whether my wife was still alive. I knew Anna had lunch duty on Fridays, but I thought maybe I could catch her at the end of it, before she went to her afternoon classes. I tried her cell phone. No answer. I called the front office and the head secretary answered in a snit.

"Belleview High School," she barked.

"Anna Wixim, please."

"She's in class right now. Care to leave a message?"

"No. No message. Just a question. Is everything all right at the school today?"

"Seems all right to me. What do you mean? Who is this?" she asked.

"This is Anna's husband, Eddie Wixim. I was just a little worried. I wanted to make sure Anna made it to school all right, and there were no emergencies today."

"Well, I know Anna's here, but I didn't actually see her. She called down this morning to tell us she was taking her first class to lab. That's what those science teachers do, you know. They call us all day long telling us where they're going."

"No emergencies?"

"Like what do you mean?"

I tried to explain without sounding like a nutcase. "Like fires or intruders or fights on campus—any of those things?"

"Oh, now, Dr. Wixim, we have some of those things every single day. Today's no different . . ." Her voice trailed off and sounded like she was covering the mouthpiece, talking to someone else. I heard her say, "Yes, sir. No, sir. Of course, I'll call on his walky-talky." Then back to me, "Dr. Wixim, you hit it on the head. We have one of your emergencies right this minute. I have to go help call up all the administrators. I'll tell Anna you called."

"No. Wait!" I yelled into the phone. "What is the emergency now?"

A voice over her walky-talky came through the phone before she could cover the mouthpiece: "Gun in the cafeteria." She hung up.

Gun in the cafeteria. I froze.

Was Anna still in the cafeteria?

I dialed the school again. Busy. I tried again for five minutes, then ran out of the hospital and drove like a mad man to get there. When I arrived fifteen minutes later, I charged into the front office.

"I need to see Anna Wixim right away," I demanded to the secretary at the first desk.

"No sir, we're not allowing visitors right now. Lockdown." She picked up her radio and hissed into it, "Jake? Jake! Get up here and lock these front doors! Now!"

"Why are you in a lockdown?" I asked, as every hair on my body stood at attention.

Her radio beeped. She held up her palm to me while we listened through the static. "Yes, ma'am. I'm on my way."

Back in charge, she turned to me and said, "Dr. Wixim, it's a safety precaution. Everything appears to be okay, and the police are here, but the lockdown helps keep the kids in their places until we know it's safe to change classes again."

"Just tell me where Anna is right now."

"Hold on a sec." She pulled a massive stack of stapled papers from her bottom desk drawer and started flipping through them. She glanced at the clock. "Hmm, 11:27, normally she'd be finished with lunch duty, but I bet she had to stay in the cafeteria until the lockdown ends."

"Isn't that where the gun is?" I was losing control.

"How'd you know about the gun?"

"Heard it over the phone. That's why I came."

"Yes, sir," she admitted, "that's where the gun was spotted, but the administrators are all there, and they haven't confiscated a gun yet."

Somehow, incredibly, I kept breathing. And standing. I didn't pass out, but I was close. I sat down in a chair by her desk, and she said, "Sir, you look a little pale. Are you feeling all right?"

"No. I think I might be sick." Then I was sick into her wastebasket.

Her walky-talky beeped, and a man's voice said, "Front office. All clear. No gun in the cafeteria. Call an all-clear please."

She sighed and said to me, "See? Everything is fine. These things blow over fast around here." She picked up her walky-talky and said, "All clear, I got it. Thanks. And if there's a janitor listening, I need a cleanup in the front office." She gave a weak smile to me and a sick look to the stinking trash can.

I was embarrassed. I got up quickly, nodded good-bye, and got out of there.

53
Pizza Boy

Anna

WHAT IS PIZZA BOY DOING at my memorial service? Why isn't he in jail?

Daddy's voice says, "Calm down, honey. You're not supposed to need a guide anymore after you depart."

"Daddy, that's the kid who killed me! What's he doing here?" I'm shrieking, bordering on hysteria. The peace I felt just a few moments ago has vaporized.

"Anna, that boy did not kill you."

"What? Then why am I dead?"

"Well, consider it. Of course your space-time gap opened up on November eleventh. You left your atoms behind and passed through. That could have happened at any time of the day."

"And it did happen," I say, "right on time. Pizza Boy had a gun in the cafeteria and shot me, and I died at 11:11 on 11/11."

Daddy sighs. "It looks like we need to do a little time traveling to help you clarify your deathday."

So, Daddy takes me to November eleventh. He plops me into lunch duty at eleven o'clock on the final day of my life.

Rewind. Replay.

The cafeteria fills quickly with noisy, hungry, hormonal teenagers. Dreaded Friday Lunch Duty: Four hundred kids, one administrator, four grumpy lunch ladies, twenty-two minutes, not enough ibuprofen, and me. A deadly mix.

At the pizza line, as usual, the skinny mobster is trying to buy pizza with his free tax dollars. After the lunch lady denies him this forbidden pleasure, he has the nerve to argue with her, so I offer my assistance.

He says, "What? Are you the Walmart greeter or something?"

I order him to go to the turkey-and-mashed-potato-entrée line.

"But I don't want no turkey on my tray. I want pizza!" he demands.

"That's your misfortune. Come with me now, or I'll call the resource officer to escort you out of the building."

He takes a stand and blatantly threatens me, warning about gangs and guns in the school.

"I don't care if you have a gun," I reply, aware that my mouth is talking again without consulting my mind. "If you don't have money, you may not have pizza. Even if you have a gun, without money, your only lunch option is the turkey. Now, *move*!"

He drops the tray of pizza on the floor and storms away.

Seventeen minutes to go. Time crawls by.

I block my door to keep kids in or out.

I break up a girl fight.

On my way back across the cafeteria, I hear the growing rumble, the bubbling up of fear, the screaming. The panic on the faces of the children stuns me. Then I hear, "Gun! He's got a gun!" and crowds of kids all run wildly for the door.

I don't see anyone with a gun as I stand in the center of the cafeteria while waves of kids run past me. Then I spot my pizza-not-turkey boy, and he is walking fast. Right toward me.

"This is it, Daddy. It's 11:11. This is when he shoots me!"

"No, Anna. Keep watching." Daddy is calm and certain. I am horrified to watch the details of my death, but I look back.

Pizza Boy walks straight toward me. I stop him and ask, "Hey, the kids saw someone with a gun. Did you?"

He looks right into my eyes and says, "No, ma'am, I didn't see anyone with a gun."

I say, "Well, hurry. Come with me, and we'll get you out before whoever it is gets in here." I take his arm and pull him toward the other door. I lead him and more scared kids into the library and push them under tables. "Code red," I tell them. "Remember? It's the hiding drill. Stay quiet. We'll tell you when to come out." They all huddle together. The nasty, flirty freshmen girls, the two Goths, and my Pizza Boy. They are all just scared kids.

What the hell? "Daddy, he didn't shoot me."

"No, Anna. If you think back, you'll remember the gun kid went out the back door of the school when he was spotted and made a run for it. He drove off campus and was arrested later that day at a gas station."

I do remember now. We closed school early. I got home at around one o'clock. The house was quiet and empty. I was a little freaked out, but antsy. I almost called Eddie to tell him about the excitement at school, but I remembered, just in time, that he was a horse's ass, so I couldn't make myself voluntarily speak to him. Finally, I settled down enough and realized it was a perfect day to run. I figured that would calm me down.

It was a crisp, fall day with an endless deep blue sky. Just like the day when I was a baby and Mom took me for a walk and later Molly chomped my arm. Just like the day I left Bethany's soccer game and got into the car wreck that totaled my van. Just like my other deathdays, a perfect, sunny November day. I see that now. I had no idea of it then.

"Daddy? Did something happen while I was running? Was I hit by a car on the church hill? The road is so narrow there, and the cars whiz by so fast."

"No. You weren't hit by a car. But you did die on that run, Anna. Do you want me to just tell you about it, or do you want to see it?"

"I died running?" That's so ironic that it's almost comical. My entire body and mind churned at high speed when I ran. My thoughts and body were in harmony. My matter and antimatter practically hummed with life. "I don't know if I want to see it. Did I have a heart attack?"

"No."

"Was I alone when I died?"

"No."

"Oh, all right, show me, Daddy."

His ears perk up as he studies me with intense black eyes. I stare back. Then I see the other dogs behind him. My heart beats too fast. I sprint up the hill.

Dogs bark behind me. I run as fast as I can. Fighting gravity. Wanting to live.

Loud barking. Blind fear.

I feel something rip into the back of my leg. I fall hard and my head hits the pavement, and I tumble into a ditch kicking wildly. My foot meets a muzzle with a satisfying crack. The barking stops. I feel pain. And then there's only nothing.

My body lies crumpled in the tall grass in the muddy ditch by the side of the road. Blood is everywhere. Maybe I'm not all the way dead yet. The dogs are gone. I feel blood on my leg, and my head hurts. I go to sleep.

I hear a song. Billy Joel is singing to me. I drift in and out of consciousness, and Billy continues to croon, periodically floating me to the surface, loving me just the way I am. It is so familiar. I know I'm supposed to do something when I hear this song, but I'm so sleepy.

It gets annoying. The song won't stop. Somehow, I realize it's my cell phone. Somehow I pull the bloody phone from the pocket Eddie sewed into my shorts and find the green button.

Eddie's voice in my ear pleads, "Anna?" He sounds scared. Why is he scared?

"Don't be scared, Eddie."

He yells, "Anna! Where are you?"

"Running . . . dogs . . . on the hill . . ." Then I pass out again.

Eddie's truck comes around the corner. He jumps out and finds me in the ditch.

The air is still. So quiet. Eddie is crying and holding me and saying, "Come back, Anna. Come back. Don't listen to that punk. Come back to me! Anna!" He is wailing.

The echo of "come back" rings in my ears. Why didn't I notice it until now?

"There's always so much to listen to and see and consider when you're newly dead. It's difficult, almost impossible, to distinguish a single human voice through all of the turmoil. Especially when you don't want to hear it." Daddy explains this as if he was telling me how to change lanes.

"But, Daddy, this was vital information! I needed to know how I died before I decided to depart! I needed to know that *my* Eddie, not that young Eddie, *wanted* me back. That would've helped so much. It's not fair!"

"Yes, it is. Anna, you saw all you asked to see. You just assumed Pizza Boy killed you. It's over now, honey. Watch the rest of the memorial service, and then you can find some peace."

Eddie

THE HOSPITAL WAS QUIET when I returned from my futile trip
to the high school. I skipped lunch and was making afternoon
rounds when I got that dread feeling again.

I found a phone and called the high school like a paranoid
fool, needing reassurance to calm my fear, to survive this
endless day.

"Yes, Dr. Wixim, everything here is fine. No guns, but we
have closed early because of the commotion. Didn't Anna call
you? The kids were all upset and out of control. Parents started
calling for their kids to go home early. So we just gave up and
cancelled classes for the rest of today." The secretary I almost
puked on was more patient than I deserved. The principal must
be a genius to have found her for the front line.

I asked a colleague to finish my rounds and left early, too.
I got home that afternoon expecting and hoping to find Anna
reading on the swing or napping—her two favorite activities
when she was home alone. But she wasn't there. Like a
detective, I snooped around my own house for clues of where
my wife might be.

Her bag was by the back door, so she had come home from
school.

Her car was in the garage, so she didn't leave by car.

Her cell phone wasn't in the charger and also not in her
purse, which I found in the kitchen. Interesting, where would
she go without her purse?

Then it occurred to me. I didn't need to figure out where she was. I could just call her cell phone. I dialed. No answer. I left a message. "Anna? Call me back." Two minutes later I dialed again. No answer. I was pacing the kitchen while I dialed over and over, when I noticed that Anna's running shoes were missing from the shoe rack.

She was running. Where? I dialed again. It was definitely ringing. Maybe she was ignoring it. Saw it was me and decided to blow me off. I wasn't exactly her favorite person these days. Please, Anna, live through this day. Just a few more hours. Be so very careful.

I dialed again. And then it stopped ringing. Did she answer? No sound.

I yelled, "Anna?" into the phone, helpless and petrified. Where was she?

"Don't be scared, Eddie." Anna's voice. Weak. Far away.

"Anna! Where are you?"

"Running . . . dogs . . . on the hill . . ." And she was gone. On the hill?

Oh. My. God. The dogs. The ones she was afraid of.

I grabbed my keys and leaped into my truck and drove the two miles to the hill where she told me she saw the dogs. I turned the corner and screeched to a stop and jumped out of the truck.

A large German shepherd was pacing on a driveway, looking across the road. I followed his gaze, and there she was.

My Anna.

Lying in a crooked heap.

Blood ran from a gash on her face. Her hands and leg were covered in blood. So much blood. Too much blood for one small woman to lose. Her life dangled by a thread that was snipped by a freak accident. Dog bite meets head injury. Right on the edge of her space-time gap.

I pulled bandages from my medical bag and applied

pressure to the worst bleeding, which was coming from a bone-deep slash in the back of her leg. The gash above her eye streamed blood steadily down her lifeless face. Anna was unconscious. She didn't even know I was there.

I checked her pulse. Weak.

Breathing. Slow.

She was fading fast.

I called 911.

Within minutes, a siren was coming. By then she had stopped breathing, and I was performing CPR on my wife in a ditch by the road. I was sobbing and yelling, over and over, "Come back, Anna. Come back, Anna. Don't listen to him, come back to me." But she was gone. She didn't hear me. That damned twenty-year-old shithead!

The EMT technicians ran to us from the ambulance and assessed her. I moved away and watched. They established what I already knew. My Anna was gone. One of them looked up at me and asked, "We can resuscitate? Intubate her? Try to hold her until we get back to the emergency room and get some blood in her? Is that what you want?"

Is that what I wanted?

"Yes!" I said. A chance. Maybe it would give her time to come back.

Anna, come back!

Then, I yelled, "No!" as he started the tube down her throat. "No!"

If they resuscitated and succeeded in bringing her matter, her body, back to life, it would be without her antimatter. No soul. In a coma, indefinitely. And from what I understood from my deaths, and from what I knew from working with dying children, if my wife came back it would not be in a few days or weeks to a comatose body. If my Anna came back, it would be to her body before she died. When I first arrived, she was still breathing. That was the time she could return to.

I thought hard. Was there a hitch? Did time stutter while I was trying to breathe life back into her? I thought so. The disastrous whirl of dogs barking, me crying, checking her pulse, Anna leaving, performing CPR—it was all in slow motion, then fast-forward, then rewind. Discontinuous time. A hitch for sure. I convinced myself. Yes, there was a glorious, hope-inducing hitch. There was nothing left for me to do but wait.

I remembered watching my parents after I died when I was six. I watched almost the whole next day pass by without me there, and then I came back and they all pulled back to the moment of my death. Indeed, the family never seemed to have any inkling that my death had occurred at all. So I knew Anna could still come back. She could control time and pop back in, and I'd forget any of this ever happened.

For the next three days, I waited in agony. I waited for her to choose me. I waited to go back to November eleventh and get my Anna back.

I remembered that smartass twenty-year-old Ed, that know-it-all punk who watched my life with an air of superiority. He judged my existence and my life with Anna and told her to stay away. To stay dead. I, in some other parallel universe, another layer of time, had convinced my Anna not to come back. I could ache with every atom in my being for her to return to life, to return to me, but my antimatter told her not to.

55
Eddie: Too Late

Anna

MY POOR, SWEET EDDIE stands at the podium, trying to compose himself and continue speaking. He holds his head up and speaks in his calm bedside voice, as though to himself.

"The last time I spoke to my wife, we argued. I tried to keep her from going to work. I knew she should stay home. Safe. With me. She refused." Eddie draws in a deep breath before he confesses, "Later that afternoon, I begged Anna to come back to me, and she refused. Again.

"On our first date, my wife Anna told me we would not be seeing each other again. I had said something stupid about her hair and hurt her feelings, and she milked me for a free steak dinner and intended to get away, to never see me again." He shakes his head and grins. "But, somehow, I convinced her to take a walk with me. I won our first argument and lost our last. On our first date, I even got a kiss. I was in love with Anna before she knew me. I will be in love with her long after I die.

"How is it possible to love someone before they know you? I can't explain it to you. Not because I don't know the answer, but because you wouldn't understand it. But that's okay. You don't need to understand. I'm saying these things, in front of all of you today, but I'm not saying them for you. Not for her friends, or her family, or even for me. No, I'm saying all of this so Anna can hear me. I know she's here with us. I know she's watching. I don't just believe she is, or think she is. I know Anna is here.

"Let me tell you some things about Anna and me. We had a good marriage. She was my favorite person and best friend. Like most married people, we had problems. But unlike normal people, our problems were cyclic, and I knew why they were happening. Cyclic. Every year, at the same time, I would emotionally and physically ache—knowing that Anna might die. Knowing precisely *when* Anna might die. This year I was right, and it happened. But I could never explain to Anna why I was so sad and desperate, so she invented all kinds of possible scenarios to explain what she called my funk. She thought I stopped loving her. We fell apart. She fell apart, and I didn't help her stay together. I didn't love her like I should, not enough or well enough. I didn't take care of her like I should have—like I promised I always would. I know she was hurt by my behavior. But I was so sad and crippled by the thought that she might leave me. I was overwhelmed. Helpless. Hopeless.

"People say, 'Everyone will eventually die.' And 'We can't live in perpetual fear of death.' I would answer that I have no fear of my own death. I know that death is not unpleasant, and the future of our souls, our antimatter, will be incredible. I dreaded how I could live the rest of my life without my Anna, while knowing my greatest mistake was not convincing her that I loved her, not encouraging her to live.

"Anna, I'm sorry. I'm so sorry."

Then, Eddie loses all control. He leans both hands on the podium and, elbows locked, he hangs his head and cries like a baby.

Joey's cleats go click-clack in the weeping church as he walks up the three marble steps to his dad. Eddie hears him and looks up as Joey takes his hand and leads him to his seat. Eddie walks in a trance, and Joey is his guide.

I never realized we had guides in life.

56
Dying, Finally

Eddie

IN THE EARLY MORNING on the second day of April, many decades later, I awoke with a sharp pain in my right arm. Oh, I thought, heart attack. What a cliché way to die. How clever.

I didn't call for help. I remained on my back and let death take me. Take me to Anna, I thought. It was an agonizing process to wait for my heart to stop, for the pain to stop, for my last breath. I was impatient to have it over so I could get on with the death I was sure to enjoy. I'd looked forward to it for too long without Anna. I expected she'd be my guide.

While I waited to die, I flashed onto memories of my life, good times and bad. I'd helped my children survive without their mother, attended their graduations, and helped move them out of our house. I'd walked Bethany down the aisle and delivered my five grandchildren. Those were the best times. I recognized that I'd lived a good long life, yet I hadn't done and accomplished all I'd set out to do. I'd been fearfully anticipating the fall of our country. It never happened. I never walked in fear on a city street beside Bethany. I'd never fought for her life. That future scene, which haunted me from my death, never came to pass. With so many humans making choices every minute of every day, the future I saw from the dead side was a series of what-if scenes. Not to be feared or anticipated. The one thing humans know for certain is that life is not eternal. Only death is.

I looked forward to my final death. I let my body slowly

die. Because it took a long time, the scientist in me agreed with the doctor in me that I was living in my own time hitch. If I wanted to return, I knew my body would take me back. But I knew I wouldn't come back. Once I found her, I would never leave my Anna again.

In the instant that I passed through my space-time gap, I was wrapped in a feeling of peace, so much like coming home. I was annoyed to find my guide was Anna's mother.

Not the best welcoming committee, she greeted me with, "Oh, it's *you*. Hello, Mr. Ed."

"Dr. McElveen, you may call me Dr. Wixim." The woman was always so crotchety to me.

"Right, Ed. Had a good heart attack, did you?"

"So it seems." Could I ditch her? I didn't need a guide anyway.

"Can't go back to that body—no heart, no life. You're stuck on the dead side this time."

"I think you're wrong," I told her. "But I'm staying. No need to hash it out. I understand how things work here, so I'll just say it: I'm ready to depart."

She chuckled. "Know-it-all. I know everything, and you know nothing. There was no hitch, Ed. It just took you a long time to die. No choices for you. When you die with no choices, you're departed as soon as you arrive here."

"I don't want choices. I'm done with my life. Why are you my guide?"

"I was sent to give you the news."

"News?"

"Yes, but I can't give it until you ask The Question."

"I have lots of questions," I insisted, a bit peeved by her unfriendly tone.

"Ask the big one, Ed. We already know what it'll be. The same one Joey asked you in the car after Anna died. Go ahead." The bitch was gloating. Something was wrong.

"Why isn't Anna my guide? Where is she?" Maybe Anna didn't want to see me, even on the dead side.

"Anna isn't here," her mother revealed, somewhat gleefully.

57
To Be

Anna

THE SUN IS COMING UP on a house that I don't recognize.

"Annie!" a woman screams. "Wake up! Oh, my God," she wails. "No!"

When Joey gets to her, she's on her knees holding the tiny infant in her pink blanket.

Every single time I watched this scene in my nightmares it was different. Sometimes, the woman was me and the baby girl was Bethany. Another time, Bethany was the mom. Every time it changed. But every single time, at the end of the dream, the baby died. There was never a thing I could do about it.

"No!" Joe is in a rage. He pushes the woman aside and begins CPR. I watch for endless minutes as he breathes into the baby's tiny face.

Nothing.

Just as expected, we've lost another one.

| | | |

THE LIGHT. The bright whiteness of it. I haven't seen this since I departed.

A tiny soul is with me. My granddaughter. I know it's her, and I want her to go back. Her space-time gap is still wide open. It's a gigantic, gaping hole that delineates the link between her life and her death. I can feel it. I nudge her toward it, and she bounces back to me. She is feeling the pull of the universe to take her away.

I wrap myself around her and give a push.

It takes all of my energy to make her move toward the gap, but together we make some progress. Then there's a perceptible shift, and I don't have to push anymore because she is being pulled back to her life. The attraction of her matter for her antimatter exceeds the pull of the universe once she gets close enough to the passageway.

With a whoosh, she is gone. With another whoosh, as if the edge of a black hole had been formed to add to my momentum, I get pulled in, too.

And then the feeling of earthly love surrounds me. I look up through the eyes of my granddaughter into the loving eyes of her father, my son.

It is, of course, November eleventh.

Acknowledgements

This story was written over many years in multiple layers and would not exist without the love and support of my family and friends. My infinite appreciation goes to all of these people.

My daughters, Lea Lanni Buck and Kate Lanni, were the first souls to whom I fearfully confessed that I'd written a novel. They were my first brave readers so many years ago that they might not remember the story. Linda Klebanow loved the story of Anna and Eddie in its rawest form and never hesitated to point out when revisions veered from the original journey, which she cherished. Meg Murphy and Jim Malone read early versions and encouraged me to revise, seek publication, and share with readers. A special group of writers at the Chapin section of the South Carolina Writers Workshop never tired of listening to chapters, queries, rejections, and offers during my rollercoaster years of submissions.

Judy Arabian, Caryn Karmatz Rudy, and Candace Johnson all worked with me through more revisions than I'd ever imagined, and tirelessly offered insight to tighten the story, reorganize, revise, delete parts, and develop the characters.

And finally, I thank my husband, Mike Lanni, for always supporting and believing in me, forever showing his love, and for never laughing aloud when I marched away from my writing desk and announced dozens of times that my book was finished, again.

About the Author

By day, Laura Lanni teaches organic chemistry and oversees her undergraduate research laboratory. When not teaching or writing, she can be found working with writers in her critique group, running, hugging her grandchildren, riding a jet-ski, blogging, and baking.

Visit Laura's blog at www.lauralanni.com or chat on Twitter @lauralanni.